They came once a month, the boy eager, the mother patient, the two of them a perfect example of why he did this work. And now he'd scared them off. She'd asked the question, hadn't she? How was he supposed to know she didn't want an answer?

He didn't have any reason to feel guilty. "Ma'am?" That sounded all wrong. *Ma'am* didn't suit her.

Their rush out the door slowed, then stopped. She directed the boy to a cutaway view of hibernating insects and rodents before rejoining him.

"If you were going to apologize, it isn't necessary. You were trying to do your job. My son will be fine."

"I wasn't going to apologize."

That ticked her off. "What did you want, then?"

Her phone number, for one thing. The thought came out of nowhere. He had no business wanting her phone number. "The gift shop has a very good book about the mammoth, if you're interested."

"Does it? Thank you."

A dismissive smile and they were on their way. The boy was speaking in an anxious tone, the mother trying to soothe. She was good at conveying a mother's certainty. What she didn't seem to realize was that it wasn't helping.

Dear Reader,

The premise for *A Different Kind of Summer* came to mind after I watched *The Day After Tomorrow*. Leaving the theater, I was surprised to step into a warm, soft spring night instead of a hostile, icy world. If the movie had that effect on me, even for a second, I wondered how a young child would respond to it. What would happen if a single mother got home from work to find that the babysitter had let her five-year-old son watch the video?

I wasn't sure how my editor, Laura Shin, would feel about the idea of a romance novel set against a background of climate change—after all, some of my relatives were asking me how that could be romantic—but to me, love found during troubled times is the most romantic of all. I was so glad when Laura told me to go ahead, because, like my heroine, Gwyn Sinclair, I had always preferred not to think about the problem and simply hoped it didn't exist. This story gave me a chance to read about it as widely as time and my unscientific brain would allow. More happily, it took me back to my early motherhood years, with all their worries and joys.

It also took me back to Winnipeg, Manitoba, my hometown. The area where Gwyn and David Bretton live is a composite of a few real neighborhoods made graceful and welcoming by rivers, aging houses and big, old trees. For a short time the story moves to another of my favorite places, Whiteshell Provincial Park. I've enjoyed so many afternoons and holidays there, hiking, canoeing and reading in the shade.

I hope you enjoy getting to know Gwyn and David, and the people who are important to them. Hearing from readers is always a pleasure. If you'd like to get in touch you can reach me at ctodd@prairie.ca or c/o Harlequin Enterprises, 225 Duncan Mill Road, Don Mills, Ontario M3B 3K9, Canada—or you can often find me chatting with readers and writers on the Superromance thread at eHarlequin.com. We're always happy to see new faces!

Yours,
Caron Todd

A DIFFERENT KIND OF SUMMER

Caron Todd

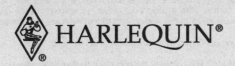

TORONTO • NEW YORK • LONDON
AMSTERDAM • PARIS • SYDNEY • HAMBURG
STOCKHOLM • ATHENS • TOKYO • MILAN • MADRID
PRAGUE • WARSAW • BUDAPEST • AUCKLAND

ISBN 0-373-71355-X

A DIFFERENT KIND OF SUMMER

www.eHarlequin.com

Printed in U.S.A.

Books by Caron Todd

HARLEQUIN SUPERROMANCE
1053–INTO THE BADLANDS
1159–THE HOUSE ON CREEK ROAD
1304–THE WINTER ROAD

To my children, with hopes that you'll like the view in 2050. Thank you for your support—your patience with fast food during deadlines, your insights and, of course, for making me laugh.

Acknowledgment

My thanks to Dr. John Hanesiak of the Centre for Earth Observation Science at the University of Manitoba for taking the time to provide detailed answers to my questions about weather and climate change. Without him, I wouldn't have known about David's remote control plane or rooftop weather station! Of course, any mistakes or misunderstandings that may have found their way into the book are completely due to me.

CHAPTER ONE

"OF COURSE IT COULDN'T HAPPEN, sweetie." Gwyn sat on the bed and stroked her son's cheek. When he didn't lean away from her touch she felt even more annoyed with the babysitter. Then with herself for needing one. "It was just a movie."

Now he did pull away, with an irritated wriggle. "I know it was a movie."

Did he? He so often surprised her, expressing ideas that seemed advanced for his age one minute and showing a complete lack of common sense the next. Maybe all children were like that. Iris had told her about a boy down the street who was convinced Bruce Willis had really saved the planet from an asteroid.

What was Mrs. Henderson thinking? If she wanted to rent a video instead of playing or taking a walk, what about *Shrek* for a five-year-old? Or *Aladdin?* Not a disaster movie, especially one that showed the poor kid's entire country getting flash frozen. Chris knew where Winnipeg was on the map. He knew that according to *The Day After Tomorrow* he and his house were under ice right now. No, from what he'd told her, it was worse than that. He and she and everybody else in the neighborhood *were* ice right now.

He looked so small in his bed, nearly edged out by stuffed animals. The boy-size giant panda from his grandparents had pretty much taken over. It was his favorite. He liked the realistic ones the best, the panda and the tiger and the polar bear. Anything related to nature and science got his attention. Animals and plants, earthquakes and volcanos, rocket ships and the solar system. None of it had scared him before.

"You know," she said, "the hero in the movie wasn't really a scientist. He was an actor saying his lines. The way you did in the play at Christmas."

"Somebody wrote the lines."

"Sure, but not a scientist. A screenwriter, making up a story. Just like somebody made up *Goldilocks and the Three Bears*. Do you think mother and father bears really live with their children in pretty cabins with furniture and porridge?"

He almost smiled. "Maybe."

"An ocean couldn't flood a city so quickly. Could it?"

"Maybe it could."

"All that water, freezing in seconds? It doesn't make sense."

"They said there's a mammoth, a real-life mammoth, frozen solid with grass in its mouth." He emphasized the last words. *Grass in its mouth.* "A real mammoth, Mom. That part wasn't make-believe."

Her feet were aching, and she really wanted to have a cool bath and change her clothes. She knew there was a point she was supposed to be getting about this animal but she just wasn't. "So it died during dinner. These things happen. Maybe it took too big a mouthful and choked."

"Then it froze." He tried to snap his fingers. They rubbed together with hardly a sound.

Now she got it. A real mammoth froze instantly, like the

flood waters and the people in the movie. "An animal that big freezing all at once, right down to the meal it was eating? Do you believe that, Chris?"

"They said."

"People say all kinds of things. I promise, cross my heart, there's no such creature. We'll go to the museum tomorrow and prove it. How's that?"

He nodded, but he still looked worried. He didn't even ask if they could go to the gift shop for astronaut's ice cream.

"Ah, hon. Come here." Gwyn held out her arms and Chris climbed onto her lap without hesitation, the way he used to do. The panda fell behind him, grabbing more space in the bed while it could. She tried to memorize the feeling of small limbs and back curled against her, and the smell of soft hair under her nose. One day soon he wouldn't accept this kind of comfort. Not even on a bad day.

"I wish we'd seen the movie together. We could have had popcorn and laughed whenever it was silly. That's what your dad would have done."

Chris looked at the wall across from them. Enough light came through the window that they could make out the mural they'd painted together during her holidays last summer. Considering she didn't have the slightest spark of artistic ability and he was four at the time she thought it had turned out pretty well. Blue sky and white clouds, smooth green for grass with tufts spiked here and there where they'd tried for realism, trees with bird nests on branches and a small, square house with a triangle roof and white-petaled daisies by the door.

No stick-figure family, though. Instead they'd hung photographs, all of Chris's father. Blowing out three birthday candles, riding his bicycle, draping Bay of Fundy seaweed over his head. By the middle of the wall, he'd grown up. In one picture he wore his high school graduation gown, in another he held a salmon as long as his arm. The last two showed him standing beside a Canadian Forces helicopter, and smiling with Gwyn on their wedding day.

"Your dad knew all about the weather. He had to, to be in a flight crew. What do you think he'd say about huge sheets of ice springing up all over the place?"

"What?"

"He'd say, 'Nonsense. Couldn't happen.'" Not quite. His choice of words would have given the message some added energy.

Chris stared at her with Duncan's eyes—intent, dark blue. They weren't showing any of Duncan's lightheartedness, though. That was something she didn't see in their son very often. Shouldn't a boy named for Christopher Robin be more playful?

"You're not scared of it, Mom?"

"Not for a second."

"I'll check the weather one more time. Okay?"

He climbed off her lap and ran to the living room. Over the droning hum of the air conditioner Gwyn heard the television come on, snippets of music and talking as he rushed through the channels, then a woman's soothing voice mixing the forecast with motherly advice.

"Across the Prairies we'll see above normal temperatures again tomorrow and for the rest of the week. The humidity will make it feel even warmer, so be sensible if you need to be active outside. Drink lots of water and remember to use sunscreen. That's especially important in the middle of the day when UV levels will be at their highest. Firefighters and farmers have been asking for rain, but it looks as if they'll be waiting for a while yet."

Maybe that would reassure him. After an early spring and more April showers than they'd known what to do with there wasn't a drop of moisture in sight, let alone a brand-new wall of ice.

DAVID BRETTON LAY as flat as he could in the bottom of the canoe. His life jacket lumped under him, his knees jammed hard against the canoe's center thwart and the edge of the seat dug into the back of his head.

Drifting downstream without looking where he was going was a dumb thing to do—he could hit a log or other debris—but he didn't think he was creating a hazard for anyone else. He was alone on the river. There were no motorboats, no teams from the canoe club, and there were never any swimmers. No one chose to swim in the Red River. The currents could suck you down, silt clouded the water and he didn't even want to think about the bacteria count.

He shifted his weight, trying to find more room for his legs, but only managed to bang his knees. The view was worth a few bruises. Out of the corners of his eyes he could see trees and the tall, narrow rectangles of downtown buildings. Traffic and crowds and noise receded. Looking up instead of ahead was as good as a holiday. It gave him a different perspective, filled his mind with quiet and a sense of timelessness that he sometimes welcomed. The planetarium captured that: the small band of human activity hugging the ground and the vast sweep of sky above.

A very clear sky right now. No sign of wind or even a breeze, no dusty haze, no cloud, no contrails. Just a pink and violet sunset in the west and a slowly darkening blue everywhere else. Plain sailing from the ground to the thermosphere. The only sign of an upward boundary was the moon. A crescent tonight.

It looked so still up there it gave the impression nothing was going on. Not true. Plenty was going on. Air masses swirled all the time, moving heat from the equator and cold from the poles, deciding—along with the ocean currents—how each day would be. How everything would be.

Even the water he floated in, this warm, dirty liquid, was part of the cycle. It flowed in from Minnesota and North Dakota then up through Lake Winnipeg and eventually found its way into cold, clear Hudson Bay. He told schoolkids who came to the museum to think of human circulation, blood carrying oxygen and nutrients all over the body and helping to regulate its temperature. Most of the time they looked at him with blank, incurious faces—how could the Earth be like a human body?—but sometimes he saw understanding click into place.

The jet stream was invisible, but it was up there, too. Misbehaving lately, curving way up north, drawing warm gulf air into the Hudson Bay lowlands. Thirty-one degrees Celsius in Churchill today. What was that in Fahrenheit? High eighties. The polar bears must have thought they'd been thrown into some southern zoo.

Balancing his weight so the canoe wouldn't rock, David sat up. His plan had been to relax and get some exercise, take his mind off work. Good luck with that. His mind was always on work. It was why Jess had left him. Three years ago now—longer than they'd been together.

"Everything is science with you," she'd said one evening after dinner in the middle of what he'd thought was an enjoyable washing-up conversation.

"Everything *is* science," he'd replied. It was true, but a bad answer under the circumstances.

Her voice had gotten louder. She'd told him he didn't have a drop of romance in him. It must have really bugged her, because she'd underscored the point. "Not a single drop, David." Accusingly. By then he'd been annoyed and he hadn't seen that this discussion was different from the others. So he'd started to explain the science of romance. Next thing he knew he was divorced.

Two sentences—one, really—that summed up the problem. Everything was science. He took an evening on the Red with a setting sun and a faintly glowing ivory moon and riverbanks full of trees and turned it into a satellite image of the weather.

That didn't bother him—in fact, it suited him fine—but he'd never met a woman who was okay with it. Even the weather girl he'd gone out with for a while thought meteorology had its time and place, generally at twenty minutes past the hour on the morning, noon and evening shows. He didn't get that. It wasn't incidental: it was central. The history of humankind was firmly tied to weather and climate. So was its future.

David shifted onto his heels, then dipped the paddle into the water, sweeping it in shallow arcs from back to front and front to back. The canoe began to turn. As it came around he felt the catch of the current. Closer to shore it would be less powerful, but he stayed put.

Right hand on top of the paddle, left on the shaft, he reached ahead and dug the blade into the water. He pulled it through and lifted it out, a quick count, no breaks between or he'd be going north, the way the river wanted. He put the strength of his whole body into each stroke and soon sweat poured off him. His shoulders and upper arms burned.

Just when he was ready for a break he rounded a loop in the river and the current was gone. He took a minute to work the ache out of his muscles, then continued paddling at a leisurely pace.

This was a quiet spot, his childhood playground, behind the backyards of the street where his parents still lived. Through the trees he caught glimpses of the screened porch and a light in an upstairs window. They'd be settling down, feeling dozy, weighing the immediate benefit of tea with lemon versus the annoyance of getting up during the night. He'd be seeing them for breakfast in the morning. A hot breakfast. Something must be up. Nothing bad, though. They hadn't sounded worried when they called.

One more stretch of hard paddling and he was home. Mosquitoes found him as soon as he drew alongside the wooden dock. Swatting with one hand, he lifted the canoe to his shoulder and carried it to the boathouse. He used his building's back entrance and took the service elevator to the twenty-second floor. His door locked behind him as it closed.

He gulped two glasses of water, then drank a third more slowly on his way to the shower. He turned the tap off to soap up, on to rinse. Air drying helped him cool down a little more, then he climbed into a pair of drawstring pajama bottoms and switched on his laptop.

Two rows of charts appeared on the screen. Temperature, humidity, dew point, air pressure, wind speed and direction all measured and graphed by his rooftop weather station. No surprises there. The past twenty-four hours had been hot, humid and still—just as his body told him.

He clicked on a series of radar and satellite maps. There

was a typhoon off the coast of China, monsoons in India, torrential rains in Europe. A tropical storm had developed over the Atlantic—Elton, the fifth named storm of the season even though it had just begun.

The number of severe weather events concerned him, but not as much as what was happening in the North—thunderstorms from Alaska and the Yukon through the Northwest Territories to Nunavut. For the first time in their lives Inuit above the tree line were seeing lightning. And robins—the traditional sign of a southern spring. Only Baffin Island was getting snow instead of rain.

David opened the drapes and went out to the balcony. From this height in the daytime he could see the Red flowing through farmland south of the city and meeting the Assini-boine to the north, at the Forks. At night the water was mostly black, silvery here and there, reflecting city lights.

No point staring at the sky. Whatever happened he wouldn't see it here before the collected data warned him. Still, he came out and looked first thing every morning and last thing at night.

That wasn't scientific at all.

GWYN PULLED the kitchen curtains, closing out the lights from the apartments along the river. Mrs. Henderson had left dishes in the sink. She had a list of things she would and would not do, a list that changed to suit her mood. For the most part meal dishes were fine, but not snack dishes. She didn't mind heating home-cooked food waiting in the fridge, but wouldn't so much as open a tin on her own. If a drink spilled, she'd wipe up the main puddle, but leave a general stickiness behind. She wasn't there to clean, she said.

Tonight Gwyn didn't have the energy to be annoyed. All

she wanted was to ease the burning in her feet. She washed and dried the plates and glasses, put them away behind leaded glass cupboard doors, then shook Mrs. Henderson's dinner crumbs from the newspaper and refolded it. The main headline, two inches tall, stared up at her.

Typhoon Strikes China: Hundreds Dead, Missing.

Underneath that article, in smaller letters: Elton Bears Down on Caribbean.

She turned the paper over so she couldn't see the headlines, then went down the hall to the bathroom. Chris still moved around in bed, talking quietly. His own voice alternated with a very deep one. The panda never spoke and the tiger mostly growled, so she guessed he was having a conversation with the polar bear. Getting advice about life on an ice floe, maybe.

Best not to disturb him. She shut the bathroom door quietly. When the tub was half-full, she stepped into the water and leaned back, gasping when her overheated skin touched cold porcelain. Her eyes closed and her tired muscles began to relax.

It had been a long, difficult evening. They'd had two deaths on the ward. Both were expected. That didn't make anything easier. They were two people she had greeted every shift and tried to make comfortable with back rubs and sheepskin under their heels and fresh ice water to sip, and this evening she'd helped take them to the morgue instead. She never got used to that trip.

When she first started working at the hospital—for the summer between grades eleven and twelve—the head nurse wouldn't let her go. All the staff had been protective, maybe because they knew her mother or because she was only sixteen. "Sweet sixteen," everyone had said and of course one orderly had always added, "and never been kissed."

That wasn't exactly true, but she'd never done any kissing without dwelling on the logistics. A couple of years later she'd met Duncan and all her how-to worries had gone out the window. Her worries and her education. So here she was on a different ward, but still an aide, ten years later.

By the time Gwyn dried off and changed into shorts and a sleeveless blouse, Chris had fallen asleep. In case he called, she left the storm doors to the porch and the living room open and went out to the front steps. The sun had set, but light still glowed in the western sky. People were out on bicycles or walking their dogs, taking advantage of the day's best weather.

"Hey, you." Her neighbor, Iris, appeared carrying a plastic watering can.

"Hey. I don't suppose you watered my lettuce?"

"I did. And your carrots and your beans."

"Thanks! I was joking."

Iris emptied the can into a pot of marigolds, then cut across both lawns to join Gwyn. "That babysitter of yours had all the windows open and the TV going full blast."

"I'm sorry. I'll talk to her."

"I beat you to it. She was on the phone when I came over. Had Chris parked in front of the set."

"You won't believe what movie she rented."

"Sure I would. I heard every line."

Gwyn suppressed an urge to apologize again. "Do you know any responsible, grandmotherly women who would enjoy spending time with Chris?"

"Seriously?"

"Maybe." She'd never fired a babysitter. Usually they left under their own steam because their circumstances changed or because she gave them too few or too many hours.

"I'll ask around. Between us we should be able to find someone who's willing to read stories and play checkers now and then. It sounds like a great job description to me!" Iris held up a hand. "Don't even think it. Unless you're offering a pension and a dental plan."

"How about all the tea and coffee you can drink and some genuine appreciation?"

"Hah." Iris stood up, brushing the back of her shorts and retrieving her watering can. "Back to the lion's den."

"That doesn't sound good. What's the matter?"

"Dear daughter is irritated with me." Molly was older than Chris by several years and growing out of a pleasant, companionable stage. "I interrupted an hour-long phone conversation to tell her to get ready for bed, but I know she'll still be talking when I go in. Tomorrow she'll be in a fog all day and she won't be able to study for exams. There's too much work, she says."

"Summer holidays are nearly here."

"That's what scares me." Iris waved and headed back to her house.

She didn't seem to be joking. Gwyn hoped things weren't getting that tense next door. Molly had a stubborn streak, but she liked to be in her mother's good books.

The last light from the sun had disappeared. Gwyn loved this time of day, the calm and quiet, the big old elms dark against the sky, the air scented by the clove currant she and Duncan had planted when they first moved in. They'd put a pink explorer rose beside it, hosta and bleeding heart in the shade and cranesbill geranium and creamy-white day lilies in the sun. They had liked the same kinds of plants, old-fashioned ones that went with childhood springs and summers.

Even though the neighborhood wasn't far from the

center of the city, it felt like its own small town. That was what they'd liked about it. There was a corner store and a community center and row after row of modest houses built in the 1920s and '30s. The yards were planted with crab apple trees and lilacs, lily-of-the-valley and peonies with blooms so heavy they touched the ground. Closer to the river specialty shops and three-story houses nearly hidden by hedges gave the streets a different character. Her dad had told her that her great-great-grandfather had done the carpentry in some of the houses. She wished she knew which ones.

She slapped a mosquito. If one had found her, more were sure to follow. She took the steps two at a time into the porch, where they could buzz against the screen all they liked but never reach her, and settled into one of the high-backed willow rockers that faced the street.

We'll watch the people go by, Gwyn. That was what Duncan had said when they'd bought the chairs. It was funny because wherever he went he could never keep still. So she'd rocked while he paced to the window and the door, making plans, then back to her side to tell her she was beautiful.

He would have erased Chris's fears in no time. Nothing scared Duncan, and being with him made other people feel as confident as he did. He would have enjoyed the movie and laughed and said it was silly, and Chris would have believed him.

Tomorrow after they went to the museum, he'd believe her, too. Better yet, he'd forget about sheets of ice by morning and get back to his usual worries—the lack of a desk or any homework in kindergarten and his inability to go to Mars anytime soon.

CHAPTER TWO

BUT CHRIS didn't forget. When Gwyn woke up the next morning he was kneeling in front of the television in his pajamas, frowning at the screen. His polar bear sat on his lap.

"There's a hurricane," he said. "First it was a tropical storm but now it's a hurricane. It's got a name. Elton. Did you ever see a hurricane, Mom?"

"We don't have hurricanes on the Prairies." She knelt beside him. "Here's our forecast. What's in store for us today?"

"Sunny."

"That sounds all right."

"They give the weather for the whole world. It's windy where Grandpa and Grandma live." He pointed at the lower end of Nova Scotia.

"We'll have to phone them soon, won't we?" Gwyn got up from the floor and went into the kitchen. "Pancakes?"

When the bowl and spoon clanked together Chris hurried to join her. He reached into the fruit basket for a banana, took a plate from the cupboard, a fork from the drawer and dropped the peel into the garbage before starting to mash. He was organized in the kitchen, just as Duncan had been, cleaning up spills as soon as they happened, putting used dishes straight into the sink. Maybe there was a mop-up, put-away gene. She had a more haphazard approach.

"So, Mom?" He sank the fork through a section of banana, lifted it and pressed again. "The weather's been the same every day, did you notice?"

"Hot."

"Yeah, hot, no rain. For a long time, right?"

"What do you make of that?"

"Dunno." He handed her the plate of banana and watched as she scooped the fruit into the batter. "It doesn't sound very icy."

That was almost a joke. Things were looking up. "It sure doesn't. And it sounds consistent."

"Yeah. Consistent." He nodded appreciatively. As far as he was concerned, the more syllables a word had the better. "That must be good. Do you think so, Mom?"

"I wasn't worried to begin with."

He looked at her doubtfully and she suddenly felt she had failed at something. He let her off the hook. "You didn't see the movie."

"And you didn't wash your hands."

Guiltily, he rubbed them on his pajamas.

"I don't think so. Off you go." She called after him, "Get dressed while you're at it, okay? Nice clothes, because we're going to the museum after breakfast."

She put the first cooked pancakes in the oven to keep warm and spooned more batter into the pan. Eight tiny circles this time, then one pan-size. The contrast would amuse him.

THE SMELL OF FRYING SAUSAGES greeted David when he let himself into his parents' house.

"Is that you, David?"

"That's me." He went down the long hall past the turret

room, the living room and the dining room to the kitchen, where he found his mother in her nightgown, spatula in hand. Her hair, still a natural dark brown with only streaks of gray, was tousled as if she'd just gotten out of bed. In spite of the clear signs that she wasn't ready to be awake and busy there was a bit of a sparkle to her. Again, David wondered what was up. Something good, it looked like.

He handed her a pint basket of strawberries. "See what Johansson's had this morning? They're farm-fresh, no pesticides, grown an hour from the city."

Miranda held the fruit close to her nose and inhaled deeply. "Lovely! Picked by virgins in the moonlight, were they?"

He never knew how to respond when his mother said things like that. "They're early for a local crop. The warm spring must have accelerated the plants' maturation."

Looking amused, she kissed his cheek and put the basket in the fridge. He supposed that meant he wouldn't be having any.

"You find me less prepared than I'd intended. Sausages take such a long time to cook. Why on earth are they considered a breakfast food?"

"Want me to watch them while you get dressed?"

"Would you? Thank you, dear." She handed him the spatula and hurried away. He heard her footsteps light on the stairs, a door closing and then silence.

He stuck his head into the hall. "Dad?" The rooms he'd passed heading to the kitchen had all looked empty, but his father could be burrowed in a corner somewhere with the Saturday *Globe and Mail*.

The house was too big to search while he was responsible for the sausages—it had three stories, including a turret room on every floor. The neighborhood kids used to call it The Castle. Richard might not even be inside. He could be in his workshop, or out for his morning constitutional, or at the end of the yard trying to hook a breakfast catfish. David used to try to catch them, too, he and Sam, while Sarah went on about horrible, awful, cruel boys.

He rolled the sausages over, counting as he went. Even if they could eat six each there'd be leftovers. That definitely suggested an announcement. For his parents, food and announcements went together.

Once—he was in high school at the time, grade ten or eleven—his mother had tried to make Chicken Kiev from scratch. He'd never seen her so exasperated. She'd shaped sticks of garlic butter and wrapped pounded, torn pieces of meat around them. As she'd worked, egg and bread crumbs had encrusted her hands and got dabbed here and there whenever she needed to scratch her nose or push her hair out of her eyes. Finally, a row of breaded lumps had sat ready to cook. She'd said with a kind of desperate cheerfulness, "They're not pretty, but they'll be absolutely delicious!"

As it turned out they came apart in the deep fryer, making a greasy sort of stew. His dad had taken them to A&W instead, and there his parents had announced they were moving to Africa for a year or so, leaving their regular jobs—Miranda was a producer at a local TV station and Richard was a mechanical engineer—to teach in Zambia. The kids could come, too, they said, or move in with neighbors and finish school at home. When they changed their minds about the trip there was no explanation or special meal. Weeks had gone by and no suitcases appeared in the hall, so their children had decided they must be staying.

He heard a knock on the window behind him. There was his father, leaning his forehead on the glass, his mouth moving silently. David banged and pulled the wooden frame until it scraped up a few inches.

"Come on out."

"I'm watching sausages."

"Sausages don't need watching. Come out."

David turned the heat down under the pan and went through the back porch to the stone patio, where his dad waited.

"I want to show you something."

"A catfish?"

"No, no, no. There aren't any catfish in this river. If there were I'd have caught one by now." He strode toward the three-car garage, stopping by the door farthest to the right, the one that led to his workshop. "This is much better than a catfish."

David helped lug the door up. "You and mom are being kind of mysterious."

His father went to a workbench against the rear wall and turned around holding something dull and gray. It was narrow and about four feet long.

"You've started a new model?"

"A helicopter. For you."

"Dad!" It was a remote-control helicopter for collecting upper-level weather data. Richard had already made a plane for the same purpose that David used every week.

"Thought something that went straight up would be useful when you're operating from the top of your building."

"For sure. That's great. It's going to be a beauty!"

Miranda's voice came from behind them. "I knew those sausages would be left to their own devices!"

She didn't seem to mind. The look on her face reminded

David of Christmas morning. She loved secrets, and she loved revealing them.

"What's going on, Mom?"

Her smile widened, and was quickly suppressed. She began to lead the way back to the house but before they reached it the back door opened and a pajama-clad figure came out, yawning.

"Sam!"

He was thin, and his face tight with strain. But home, weeks before expected. David felt himself grinning. He opened his arms for a back-thumping hug.

THE BRETTON FAMILY got together for two weeks every year. The date varied depending on when Sam had leave, but they tried for Christmas at The Castle or summer at the cottage. This year it was supposed to be the cottage, in early August. After the initial pleasure of seeing his brother, David realized having him turn up before his scheduled break was unlikely to be a good thing. Sam didn't offer an explanation, though, so David didn't ask for one.

They had breakfast on the porch with Richard still talking about the remote-control helicopter and Miranda continually touching Sam as if checking that he was really there. When the meal was done she insisted "the boys" go outside rather than help with the dishes. They compromised by clearing the table then strolled down to the river, Sam still in his pajamas, bare feet stuck into a pair of olive green rubber boots left by the door.

"This place never changes," he said. "That's kind of nice and kind of creepy."

"The Yard Time Forgot." It wasn't so much time's fault. It was David and his dad not getting around to mowing and pruning often enough. The whole yard was overgrown, but especially where it met the river. They'd always left it a bit wild there—even before the word *ecosystem* had found its way into everyday conversation. Some people had parklike yards. This one was more of a storybook forest, with unexpected benches and flowers wherever Miranda decided to tuck them.

Sam kicked at the twisted shrubs and mounded grasses. "I'll bet we've got skunks."

"And in case we do, you're trying to annoy them?"

The absentminded kicking stopped. Sam bent over, tugging at the grass purposefully. "Look at this!"

David went closer. Lying upside down under a tangle of grass was their old cedar-and-canvas canoe.

Muttering his annoyance, Sam kept clearing away vegetation. "Out in the weather like this? Didn't we leave it in the garage?"

"Someone must have brought it down to use."

"Sarah!"

"Well—"

"Sarah for sure, and some guy. She'd get excited, oh my, such a romantic outing, and then she'd forget all about it." Sam knocked on the hull. "What do you think?"

"It looks fairly solid, considering. Not past repair."

Sam lifted one side and peered underneath. "The paddles are here." He pulled one out. It had a rounded, beaver-tail design and only reached to his chest, just right for when he was a child. A daddy longlegs ran off the weathered wood and fell into the grass. "I'm going to have to talk to that girl."

"Talking's never been that useful." From birth Sarah had been impervious to her brothers' view of things. The canoe had been a regular source of conflict. Sarah would insist on going with them whenever they took it out on the river, but then she'd free any minnows or crayfish they caught and refuse to do her share of the paddling because it interfered with being the Lady of Shalott.

David thought Sam would want to spend a few days cleaning the canoe, patching it, maybe giving the cedar a fresh coat of marine varnish and the canvas some waterproof paint—or at least stick on some duct tape here and there—but he was already pushing it into the water.

"Are you going to help?"

"You're doing fine, Sam."

"You can pull it in, then."

"The sweaty stuff's up to you. I have to be at work in an hour." But something got to him while he watched his brother struggle with the heavy craft. The squish of river mud or the smell of the water, he didn't know. He kicked off his shoes and tugged off his socks, then stooped to roll up his pant legs. By then the canoe was floating. Sam knelt in the stern, his paddle hard against the riverbed.

"You're going to get wet."

David had already noticed that. He took a giant step from the muddy shore, one foot slipping as he heaved himself into the canoe. It rocked and he nearly tipped them both into the river.

"Idiot!" Half laughing, Sam grabbed David's belt and pulled him down. "Never stand, remember?"

"Oh, right. It's a gondola you stand up in."

They didn't have life jackets. David always used one in his own canoe, but as close as they were to the river, his parents had never owned any. The Bretton kids had grown up with the feeling that danger didn't lurk anywhere. They were never told to be careful, never watched, never scolded for taking risks. Looking back, David thought they must have been just plain lucky.

"Better stay close to shore," he said.

Sam ignored him. With his paddle acting as rudder he was in control of where they went, and he steered them to the middle of the river. David didn't push the point. There was a brittleness about Sam, as if he'd be glad of a chance to push back. It was enough to feel muscles pulling, hear the dip of the paddles and know his brother was safe at home. A kayak passed them and a mother mallard led a line of fluff balls away from them into the reeds, but other than that they were alone.

Here and there dampness seeped through the canvas. "Have we got anything to bail with, Sam? If we need to, I mean?"

"Nope."

"I don't want much of this river in here with us."

Sam didn't answer. Maybe he'd forgotten about the variety of unpleasant things that were dumped into the Red. The water could cause a rash were it touched skin, or cramps in anyone unfortunate enough to ingest it.

"Is this your leave instead of August? We should tell Sarah to come now if she can."

"Don't bother."

"But you'll want to see her."

"Not really."

David wasn't sure what to make of his brother's tone. He didn't sound angry, but he wasn't joking around, either.

"Sam."

"What?"

"Don't be like that."

"Like what?"

"It's just a canoe."

"It's not just a canoe. It's *our* canoe."

They were out of the slow-moving loop. The farther they went the harder the paddle back would be and he'd arrive at work sweaty after all. Unless the steady seeping became leaking and they sank. Swimming to shore through this brown soup would be one way of solving the sweaty problem.

"It's good you came home early, Sam. Mom and Dad missed you."

"They're all right, aren't they? Sarah's not driving them crazy?"

"Sarah's not the problem, not for Mom and Dad, anyway."

"So there is a problem? I thought there was."

"It's nothing serious. Dad's bothered about the big 7-0." It wasn't the age, his father had told him, not the nearly three-quarters of a century behind him. Feeling like a wise old man was fine. The problem was he wanted to keep on being one for another three-quarters of a century.

The canoe had slowed. David looked over his shoulder. Sam wasn't moving. He stared at the riverbank, his face unguarded, exhaustion in every line.

"Sam?"

"I thought it would be…like it usually is. Greener."

"The trees are stressed. One year there's flooding, the next it's dry. We've had thaws in January. It's not what they need." David angled his paddle, pushing away from the current as best he could from the bow. "You all right?"

"Yeah. Yeah, of course." Sam began to turn the canoe around.

To Chris, nice clothes meant matching. He came to breakfast wearing blue jeans and a blue T-shirt, and when it was
time to leave he added a blue baseball cap. Although he
seemed a little wound up about what he might learn at the
museum, Gwyn thought he was happy to be going.

She set the pace, fast enough for them to reach the stop
before the bus, but slow enough to accommodate Chris's
frequent pausing and squatting to watch ants drag dead bugs
across the cement, bumblebees bounce from clover flower
to clover flower and caterpillars invite almost certain death
on the slow crawl from boulevard to nearby lawn.

"Caterpillars are sort of like snakes," he said.

Gwyn took his hand and hurried across the road just
before the light changed. "How are caterpillars like snakes?"

"Same kind of bodies."

"Long and squiggly?"

"Yeah. Why is that?"

"I don't know."

"Then there's larva. Same type of body, too."

He talked about animal bodies all the way to the
museum. Shapes of snouts, lengths of necks, reasons for
tails. When Gwyn stopped to put the change from the admission in her purse he hurried ahead into the galleries. She
caught up with him watching a video about the Earth's
changing tectonic plates. A male voice narrated while colored jigsaw pieces floated around two attached blue ovals,
finally taking the shape of a modern map of the world.
When the video ended Chris pushed a button and watched
the whole thing again.

"So-o," he said. "Things used to be different. All the
land in the world was in one place."

"A supercontinent."

"I kind of thought it was more, you know…"

"Nailed down?"

She was trying to lighten the mood, but he nodded seriously. "I don't really like that idea, Mom. What if it's still doing it?"

"Still moving? I don't think so. Not enough to make a difference to us, anyway. Not enough to make the trip to Australia any shorter."

He gave her a look she would have called world-weary in an older person.

"It *is* a strange idea. You expect the ground under your feet to stay in one place."

"Right." He seemed more satisfied with that response. "All the time, too."

"Because it's not a *boat*. It's a continent."

That got a smile. He led the way around the corner and found what he'd come for: a floor-to-ceiling painting of a woolly mammoth.

Gwyn skimmed the small box of text provided. "It doesn't say anything about your mammoth, Chris. Just about mammoths in general. They lived until around ten thousand years ago, at the time of the last ice age, and then they became extinct. They had long shaggy hair and long curving tusks. Several complete specimens have been found."

"Does it say anything about grass?"

"Not a thing."

Chris frowned with concentration while he tried to sound out the text for himself. He was doing fine at home with Dr. Seuss, but whoever wrote the museum's plaques wasn't into helpful rhyming.

"I'm not sure where to look next, sweetheart. Maybe the library."

"Can I be of any help?"

A man stood a few feet away. Gwyn got the feeling he'd been there for a while. He was tall and dark, with an air of quiet authority. How he pulled that off in casual clothes with his pant legs damp and wrinkled below the knee, she didn't know. A name tag hung from a long string, like a shoelace, around his neck. She got as far as David, then found she didn't want to look at his chest long enough to read the rest. His eyes were dark brown, coffee brown. It was hard to meet them, but hard to look away, too.

He took care of that, turning to smile at Chris. "Did you want to know something about mammoths?"

After all the museum employees Chris had happily questioned on other visits, older fatherly ones and young motherly ones and gangly brotherly ones, he chose this moment to remember not to speak to strangers, not even strangers with name tags. Gwyn looked at the man's collar instead of his warm, dark eyes and explained about the movie and the mammoth.

He nodded, with some enthusiasm. "I know the specimen you mean. A number of surprisingly well-preserved mammoths have been found. I've heard that the scientists who dug up one of them actually cooked themselves a few steaks."

Gwyn's stomach lurched at the thought.

"Eew," Chris said. There was nothing like a disgusting thought to dispel shyness. "But the one in the movie, with grass in its mouth, do you know about that one?"

"Sure. Grass and buttercups in its mouth and stomach. Not digested yet, which led some people to conclude it might have died and frozen very quickly. Is that the part that got your attention?"

"Yeah. Like, in the movie, cold air froze people solid as soon as it touched them."

"That was strange, wasn't it? Pretty unbelievable, too. I don't think that's what happened to the mammoth. One possibility is that it fell into a crack in a glacier."

That was what Gwyn had expected from the museum, a comforting dose of reality. "So it's not a sign that an ice age erupted out of nowhere while the mammoth was eating?" She wanted to make that completely clear to Chris. "It's not suggesting there's going to be a sudden change in our climate?"

"I wouldn't go that far."

Her neck muscles tightened.

"A change in the climate *is* happening." He glanced at Chris then looked back at Gwyn, apparently deciding she was his target audience. "It's complicated and there's still disagreement about the details. Whether or not the Earth could experience another ice age is difficult to say. If it did, it would be a response to excessive warming."

She should have left well enough alone. The mammoth had fallen into a crevasse, end of story.

"Warming?" Chris asked. "You get ice from warming?"

"We have a video that explains how that works. If you like I can take you over to watch it."

"Not today," Gwyn said quickly.

The man glanced at Chris again. "I'd say a true ice age is unlikely. It's speculation at this point. Some changes we can observe and measure, though. The planet's temperature is increasing. So is the level of carbon dioxide in the oceans. The polar ice caps and all the world's glaciers are melting. Permafrost is thawing. We're seeing more extreme weather events—like the hurricane that's pounding the Caribbean today."

How could he talk that way in front of a little boy? Chris had drawn closer to Gwyn's side. She took his hand in hers and smiled, trying to communicate all her confidence and none of her anger. "He's guessing, hon. That's what scientific people do. They make hypotheses and then they disprove them."

She thanked the man for his time and started away from the painting. She would emphasize part of what he'd said and hope Chris wouldn't worry too much about the rest. The message was that weather was a complicated thing to understand, but scientists thought a new ice age was unlikely. That was the main point. Not a very reassuring main point, but it would have to do.

DAVID HAD OFTEN SEEN the woman and child around the museum. They came maybe once a month, the boy eager, the mother patient, the two of them a perfect example of why he did this work.

And now he'd scared them off. She'd asked the question, hadn't she? How was he supposed to know she didn't want an answer? When he'd started to explain her smile had frozen as fast as that mammoth and she'd looked at him as if he'd committed a hit-and-run or something.

He didn't have any reason to feel guilty. "Ma'am?" That sounded all wrong. *Ma'am* didn't suit her.

Their rush out the door slowed, then stopped. She directed the boy to a cutaway view of hibernating insects and rodents before rejoining him.

"If you were going to apologize, it isn't necessary. You were trying to do your job. My son will be fine."

"I wasn't going to apologize."

That ticked her off. "What did you want, then?"

Her phone number, for one thing. The thought came out of nowhere. He had no business wanting her phone number. "The gift shop has a very good book about the mammoth, if you're interested. Pictures. Maps. Discussion."

"Does it? Thank you."

A dismissive smile and she was on her way. She had no intention of going anywhere near the book. Why did she bring the boy to the museum so often if she didn't want him to understand how the world worked?

They trailed out of the room, the boy speaking in an anxious tone that made it impossible for David to continue feeling guiltless. He'd drawn some conclusions from his brief look at the hibernation display.

"Mom, if we got buried in snow I guess we'd be all right. Because bees and mice and gophers are all right deep down in the snow."

"There won't be an ice age, Chris. That's what the man said. We won't be buried in snow. Not ever."

She was good at conveying a mother's certainty. What she didn't seem to realize was that her son had grown beyond being helped by it.

THE BOOK David Whoever had recommended was displayed near the front of the gift shop, all one hundred glossy pages of it, with unnecessarily detailed and colorful photos of the frozen animal and its stomach contents. Hard cover. Forty-eight bucks. Gwyn flipped through it, trying to decide if it would be forty-eight dollars well spent, or just an invitation to sleepless nights for Chris.

"Can we go home, Mom?"

Gwyn looked at him with concern. He liked the gift shop almost as much as the museum itself. Since the store's glow-in-the-dark star charts had first held his attention when he was two she'd found most of his birthday and Christmas presents here. "Sure we can. Don't you want to get lunch in the cafeteria first?"

He shrugged.

"Just home?"

His shoulders came up again. He looked miserable. Gwyn led him out of the gift shop, wishing that David person could see what he'd done. Chris had nothing to say on the ride home, only showing a spark of interest when she whispered in his ear, "How about Johansson's?"

They rode a couple of blocks past their usual stop, and got off near a small brick building on the river side of the street. Johansson's Fine Foods carried gourmet treats, locally grown produce and homemade take-out meals for when people had no time to cook. It had its own small bakery, too, where it made the richest desserts Gwyn had ever tasted. It was a place for special occasions or emergency spirit lifting.

As she'd hoped, the display case of chocolates got Chris's attention. He considered a dark chocolate car, a milk chocolate hammer and a hazelnut hedgehog, then settled on the one she'd suspected he would, a six-inch-high hollow tyrannosaurus that cost as much as a restaurant lunch.

"Do we want anything else? Oysters?" His head shaking and face screwing increased as she went on, "Snails?

Squid?" She looked around the store, hoping to keep going until he laughed. "Parsnips? Fennel bulbs? Oh—"

Strawberries. Tiers of strawberries in pint containers. Picked that morning, the sign said. No pesticides. They were small, lusciously red and smelled sweeter than any berries Gwyn had seen in her entire life. They hardly cost less than the dinosaur chocolate, but she put a pint on the counter anyway, along with two bottles of a fizzy orange drink from Italy that she'd tried before and loved.

"We'd better stop there. My purse is empty."

Chris looked up from his chocolate, his gaze sharp. Gwyn wished she hadn't said anything about money.

"Don't worry. There's more in the bank. And even more waiting for me at work."

Outside, pansies grew in window boxes and there were a few round tables by the sidewalk. Gwyn picked a spot partly shaded by a boulevard tree and put the berries in the middle of the table. With all those seeds and hollows she usually scrubbed berries until they were almost jam, but she put her faith in the no pesticides claim. She picked the one on the very top and popped the whole thing in her mouth. Biting into it was a revelation. It was like taking a drink. She couldn't believe how fresh, how sweet, how juicy the berry was. She looked at Chris, his feet swinging slowly, a faraway expression on his face.

"You've got to have a strawberry, Chris."

Still holding his dinosaur in his right hand, he took a berry with his left. "Mmm." He took another.

"That's the taste of sunshine," she told him.

He frowned. Space was one of his favorite things, and he took it seriously. "The sun is made of gas." He watched her for a moment, looking ready to argue if she had anything else silly to say. She confined herself to eating berries, and his attention drifted.

Hers did, too. Back to the damp-legged man at the museum. He must be new. She didn't remember seeing him before, and she couldn't have seen him and forgotten. It was years since she'd noticed a man, noticed in a way that made looking at his chest to read his name tag uncomfortable. That kind of feeling—the sudden awareness, the catch in the throat—she had thought belonged only to Duncan.

Of course Duncan had noticed her at the same time. He'd given her a slow smile that started small and got bigger until his eyes sparkled. That was it for her, she was a goner. David Whoever, on the other hand, had chosen to talk about mammoth steaks.

Chris was still playing with his dinosaur. He walked it along the table, leaving tiny chocolate footprints on the plastic. It sniffed the berries, and growled, then picked a fight with a paper napkin. Maybe he hadn't found the museum visit as upsetting as it had seemed. He looked like her pre–*Day After Tomorrow* Chris, all about animals and space. Thanks to the strawberries and the filtered sunlight she felt more cheerful herself.

"That dinosaur's headed for extinction," she said when she noticed the footprints getting bigger and stickier. "You'd better eat it while you can."

Chris bit off its head. He chewed and swallowed, then licked his fingers.

"Well," he said slowly, after finishing another mouthful, and from his preoccupied tone she knew he hadn't been thinking about dinosaurs after all, "people live way up north where it's always winter."

She had to remind herself not to mention elves or toy shops. "The Inuit."

"In igloos."

"I don't think they live in igloos anymore."

"But they did. So we could keep warm and get food even if our house was ice."

She'd never seen so much uncertainty in his eyes. "We can do anything we have to do, sweetheart. But our house will never be ice." She put the remaining strawberries and drinks back in the shopping bag and handed Chris a napkin to rub the melted chocolate from his hands.

On the way home he went back to telling her the plot of *The Day After Tomorrow*. She listened more to his voice than to the story. It was higher pitched than usual and every sentence finished with an uncertain upswing, an unasked question. Maybe it would help if they spent the afternoon reading fairy tales. "The Little Mermaid," "Hansel and Gretel." He'd heard those often enough without believing they were true. Or maybe a complete change of pace would be better. They could go to the park and try to skip stones on the river.

"That man was a scientist, right?"

She saw the pitfall immediately. "The one who talked to us at the museum? I don't know what he does there."

"The actor wasn't a scientist and the screenwriter wasn't a scientist but the man we talked to today, he was a scientist."

"We don't know," she repeated. "All kinds of people work there. Even artists, to make the displays. And accountants to work on the budget."

Chris gave her another of those looks. She didn't blame him. David Whoever hadn't sounded like an artist or an accountant. She tried to think of something more convincing. "And tour guides."

"And scientists, I bet."

She had to agree. Scientists definitely worked at the museum. Distracting Chris with stories and outings wasn't going to work.

CHAPTER THREE

TWELVE-THIRTY, and Chris wasn't ready for school. Wearing only Spider-Man briefs, he stood on top of a brand-new shirt in the middle of his bedroom. A narrow line of red trickled down his heel.

He looked at Gwyn guiltily. "I'm bleeding."

It was almost a week since their visit to the museum and Gwyn was still wishing they hadn't gone. She'd tried to keep Chris's days low-key. They'd walked along the river, curled up on the sofa reading and played games like Snakes and Ladders, but nothing had kept his attention from the idea of an impending ice age.

The point he'd fixated on was that the frozen mammoth from the movie was real. If it was real then maybe other parts of the story were, too. Like the field of ice that collapsed under one of the "scientists," like glaciers melting and filling the oceans with too much fresh water. If he wasn't miserable enough trying to get his five-year-old head around those questions, Mrs. Henderson—following Gwyn's instructions—had encouraged him to play outside a couple of evenings ago, but she had ignored the bottle of mosquito repellent kept by the door. Chris was covered with bites.

He had been cantankerous all morning, scratching

fiercely and challenging Gwyn at every opportunity. After falling asleep in the rocker on the porch she wasn't in the best of shape herself. At five-thirty she'd woken to crickets so loud she couldn't believe there wasn't a bylaw against them and a monster kink in her neck that no amount of massaging had fixed.

Holding his foot away from her clothes she carried Chris to the bathroom. "You said you weren't going to scratch those bites."

"They got itchy."

"Why didn't you call me? I could have got the calamine lotion for you."

"I hate that stuff!"

"You sound mad at me. *I* didn't bite you."

He was in no mood to smile. Gwyn sat him on the narrow vanity with his foot in the sink. Cool running water diluted the trail of blood, then washed it away. She dabbed peroxide on the spots of broken skin and stuck on a web of Band-Aids.

"We're going to be late."

Chris was silent. If he missed the second bell he'd have to take a note from the teacher to the principal's office. After a moment he said, "I didn't get blood on the carpet."

It would have been nice if he'd kept it off his new shirt, too. "You did your best, right?" They nodded at each other. "Off you go. Get dressed as fast as you can."

While she waited she kept checking her watch, as if that would help her get to the bus on time. Sooner than she expected Chris came to the door, dragging his backpack behind him. He wore a long-sleeved button-up shirt that looked silly with his shorts.

She hesitated, one hand on the doorknob, the other

holding her keys. "Go back and change into a T-shirt, Chris." He didn't move so she added, "You know, short sleeves, over the head?"

"I like this shirt."

"That one goes with long pants. You might get teased at recess."

"I don't care."

Gwyn put her head to one side and stared at him. He stared back, unblinking. He was younger and smaller than most of the boys in his class, more verbal, and not the least bit interested in sports, unless chess counted. Not that he could play it, yet. He just trotted the knights across the squares and had the bishops confer with the king and queen. The other kindergarteners weren't exactly tough guys, either, but what would happen next year, or a few years from now?

"Chris, do as I say."

He sighed, and trailed back to his room. She heard drawers scraping back and forth, then he returned wearing a T-shirt that looked as if it belonged in the laundry hamper. The mood he was in, maybe he *had* got it from the hamper.

"Let's go. Quick as you can."

That turned out not to be very quick. Every few steps Chris slowed down to scrape his sandaled foot against his ankle, or rub his hand over a swollen bite on his arm. He began to scratch it, absentmindedly at first, then angrily.

"Don't, hon."

"I *have* to." Still scratching, he stopped walking so he could look up at the sky, turning in circles to see all around. "Shouldn't there be some clouds? There's usually clouds."

"We don't have time to talk about the weather, Chris."

"But shouldn't—"

"Chris!"

Minutes after the last bell, they arrived at the school's front entrance. She watched him go through, looking grumpy even from the back. The sight made her ache. Wasn't five supposed to be a happy age?

"IT'S FUNGUS," said the woman in the first bed. "That's what I heard. You slap 'em and you drive this fungus they carry right into your bloodstream. Like a poison dart. And that's it. There's nothing anybody can do for you."

Gwyn stood holding a lunch tray and wishing she hadn't mentioned Chris's discomfort. She'd arrived at the hospital half an hour late, overheated and flustered from hurrying, and found herself explaining why to everyone she saw.

"You don't even need fungus," the woman's roommate added. "Any old infection will do the job. My cousin had a mosquito bite that he would not leave alone. Next thing we know a red line goes snaking up his arm from the bite. And it just keeps going. Up to his elbow. Up to his shoulder. It gets to his heart and—" she slapped her hands together sharply "—that was it. He keeled over right in front of me." She nodded at Gwyn. "But don't you worry about your boy. Things are different now."

"You want to put oatmeal in his bath," the first woman advised. "That'll take care of it."

"Thanks for the tip." Maybe an antibiotic cream would be a good idea, too.

She slid the tray into place on the meal cart and went into the next room. A smiling, fully dressed man sat in the armchair beside an empty bed.

"There you are!" he said. "All the nurses were worried about you."

"You're exaggerating, Mr. Scott."

"Having trouble with your son?"

Gwyn wished she could tell him about Chris's ice age fears. It wasn't that Mr. Scott knew about science. He'd worked in the Grill Room bakery at Eaton's from his high school graduation until the store closed. It wasn't even that he knew about children. He and his wife didn't have a family. Maybe she just wanted to complain to someone about David Whoever. She couldn't use a senior citizen with a heart condition for that.

"We live near the river so we have lots of mosquitoes," she said. "Poor kid's one big bite."

"I remember what that was like." Mr. Scott sounded nostalgic. "You get out with your chums and you don't even notice the darn things until you're home and want to go to sleep. My mother used to soak cloths in baking soda and water and spread them on my skin. Cool water, that's the ticket."

"I'll try it. Thanks." Gwyn picked up her lunch tray. "All ready to go?"

"Yup, they're cutting me loose. I'll miss you."

"I bet you won't." A bowl of pudding sat untouched beside his plate. "Want to keep that for later? You never know how long you'll wait to get signed out."

"They won't let me."

It was true the kitchen liked having all the dishes returned at the same time. Mr. Scott's diet didn't allow many treats, though. Gwyn left the bowl and spoon on his over-bed table, put a finger to her lips and carried his tray out of the room.

In the corridor she almost barreled into the head nurse. Mrs. Byrd always looked stern, whether or not she was feeling that way, so it alarmed anyone with a guilty conscience to find her on their heels. It was just once, Gwyn thought, just half an hour.

"Trouble at home today?"

"I'm sorry. We took too long getting ourselves organized."

"Could you have called?"

It had seemed like one more thing to do, a few more minutes between herself and the bus. "I guess I hoped to get here on time."

Mrs. Byrd still looked stern, but not necessarily disapproving. Gwyn felt a familiar anxiety, an eagerness to please that made her feel eight years old. For years, with the School of Nursing's traditional pleated cap on her head, its gold pin over her breast and the hospital's crest on her sleeve Mrs. Byrd had been the closest thing to her mother Gwyn could see. It gave her feelings of fondness for the woman that made no sense otherwise.

"I'll need you to make up the half hour you missed. There's plenty for you to do after your regular work. You can read to Mrs. Wilton and the shelves in the supply room should be straightened up." Mrs. Byrd walked away without waiting for an answer.

Gwyn rolled her head back and forth and dug her fingertips into the knotted muscle in her neck. She wouldn't be home before Chris and this was Mrs. Henderson's afternoon for aquacize. During her coffee break she'd need to make some calls.

IT WAS ONE OF THOSE rules that everything happened all at once in hospitals. Just as Gwyn was about to leave the ward Mr. Scott was discharged, three patients were admitted and another went into respiratory arrest. In between helping people into gowns and rushing samples to the lab she called the kindergarten mom who had agreed to pick up Chris, found out she was about to leave for a soccer game and, now that Iris was back from work, arranged for him to go there instead.

Almost two hours late she finally got home. There was no fence between her yard and Iris's so as soon as Gwyn walked up her sidewalk she saw Chris and Molly playing. They lay on the grass reaching for each other, right arms outstretched, fingertips barely touching. Chris clutched long cardboard rolls under his left arm. When she got closer she heard them half gasping, half shouting.

"I've got you!" Molly said desperately.

"Take the samples!"

"Throw them here!"

"Ahhh!" Chris rolled away, his voice fading, the cardboard tubes flying into the air.

Iris appeared at the door. "Long day? Come have a cold drink."

"I'm so sorry about this. Thanks for looking out for Chris." Gwyn followed Iris inside. When she looked out the kitchen window the children were on their stomachs again, but their roles were reversed.

Iris handed her a glass of lemonade. "They're playing *The Day After Tomorrow.*"

"Shoot." The mild word didn't feel like enough to say. She repeated it, with feeling.

Iris took a cigarette from a nearly full box. "The ground is cracking apart, they tell me, and they take turns being the guy with the ice core samples who's about to fall to his death."

Maybe acting it out was a good thing. Chris could make

it a game. He seemed happier now than he had trudging into school.

"Don't look so worried. Didn't you ever play *Chitty Chitty Bang Bang?*"

Gwyn smiled, feeling a little sheepish and nostalgic. "*National Velvet.* I trotted everywhere and jumped over things."

"Now that's a picture I'm going to hang on to."

"But our kids are playing The End of the World."

"No, no," Iris said lightly. "Just the end of the world as we know it." She lit her cigarette, smelled the smoke appreciatively, then put it out.

"Think I should quit my job?"

"No, I don't. What brought that on?"

She only worked part-time. Maybe subtracting her small paycheck wouldn't make all that much difference. Then she would be there when Chris needed her, bug spray at the ready. "There's Duncan's pension and life insurance. We'd get by."

"Getting by is all right for a while. You wouldn't like it in the long run. I can tell you for sure from now until he's grown up and settled into his own job you'll always need more cash."

Iris would know. She had longer experience than Gwyn at raising a child alone. There wasn't an ex-husband in the wings, no child support check, no pension. An aunt who lived on a farm not far from the city helped out with fresh produce and a place for free holidays, but that was all.

"How do you do it, Iris?"

"Do what?"

"Work full-time, take care of the house, raise Molly."

Iris shrugged. "Badly?"

Gwyn gave a snort. "You'd better not do it badly. You're my role model."

"Uh-oh." They both smiled, then Iris added, "You can't fix everything for him. It wouldn't be good for him even if you tried."

Gwyn nodded. The urge to make everything better was there, though, along with the terrible feeling of falling short when she saw him struggle. Next year he'd be in school morning and afternoon. That would help, but it brought its own worries. School could be an uncaring place to leave a child for so many hours of the day.

She watched Chris pull Molly back from the imagined precipice again. "He was calming down until he saw the hurricane coverage yesterday. The weather channel should come with an R rating." After churning over the tip of Florida Elton had gathered strength before hitting the coast of Mexico. Their TV screen had been full of shattered houses and drowned livestock.

An idea struck her and she turned back to Iris. "How old is Molly?"

"Twelve, why?"

"I thought she was about ten." Ten forever.

"Ten would be fine. That was a good year. The next one I'm looking forward to is, I don't know, twenty-five?"

It was a spur-of-the-moment idea. She should probably wait and think it through, but it seemed like a perfect solution. A pretty good solution, at least. "Would you mind if I offered her a summer job?"

Iris looked at Gwyn blankly for a second, then started shaking her head. "Oh, no."

"No?"

"You need someone reliable. A grandmother. Remember?"

"This is the happiest Chris has been for days."

"I don't know." Iris's head was still going back and forth. "It's up to you, I guess."

That seemed to be as close as she was going to get to permission. Gwyn hurried outside, Iris right behind her. The kids stopped playing when they saw their parents. Chris lay on his back, cardboard rolls held to his stomach.

"We saved the ice core samples, Mom."

"I noticed, well done. How's the bite?" She meant the one on his forearm. It had been giving him the most trouble.

"Good."

"Let's see." A scab had started to form over the top, so at least she knew he'd stopped scratching. A large area around the bite was pink, swollen and warm to touch. "I bought some ointment that's going to help it feel better."

Chris pulled his arm away. "I hate ointment."

She turned to his fellow scientist. "Your mom told me you're twelve."

Molly dropped her cardboard roll, discarding all appearance of childhood as she rose from the ground. "Nearly thirteen."

"Twelve," Iris said firmly.

"Not for long."

"You're twelve, and you'll be twelve for another four months."

Gwyn sidestepped the brewing squabble. "Are you interested in having a summer job? I need a babysitter who's willing to play with Chris, someone who'll remember bug spray and sunscreen. It would be about twenty hours a week, for July and August. Usually five hours at a time, sometimes more like nine. And if that worked for all of us, in the fall we could talk about evenings."

"I'd love to do it! I can start right now."

"You can start after exams," Iris said.

"Next week, then. How much would I make, Mrs. Sinclair?"

"Molly! She'll do it as a favor, Gwyn. What are neighbors for?"

"I'm paying five dollars an hour now."

"No way, no way." Iris reached into her pocket for her cigarettes again. "She doesn't need five dollars an hour. If you insist on paying her, pay her something reasonable. Two dollars. That's plenty."

"Five times twenty," Molly said softly. She got a faraway look while she did the math. "That's…that's eighty dollars a week! Oh, I'm so going shopping." She gave a little jump. "I can get a new dress for the year-end dance!"

"You see why I want her to study? It's one hundred dollars, Molly. Five times two and move the decimal, for heaven's sake." Iris tapped Gwyn's arm. "Four dollars, and that's final."

Gwyn tried not to listen to Molly and Iris negotiating how much Molly should be paid and whether she should get a bank account and how much she should put away for her education. She hoped this was a good idea. As hard as it was going to be to call Mrs. Henderson with the news, it would be even harder to make the same kind of call to Molly.

AFTER WASHING DIRT from Chris's bites and applying a first dose of antibiotic ointment Gwyn took store-bought salad and a ready-cooked chicken from the fridge and arranged them on the table, moving aside all the cardboard ice core samples he'd brought with him.

"Is Molly instead of Mrs. Henderson?" he asked as he pulled out his chair and climbed onto it. "Or would Mrs. Henderson still come sometimes?"

"Instead of."

"Good."

"Good?"

"I don't like Mrs. Henderson."

"You never told me that before. Why don't you like her?"

He shrugged, lifting far more lettuce onto his plate than he would ever eat. Gwyn watched, thinking about nanny cams and horror stories she'd read in the paper. She repeated, "Why don't you like Mrs. Henderson?"

"She's grumpy."

Gwyn couldn't deny that. "Grumpy, how?"

He started putting some of the lettuce back in the salad bowl.

"You can't do that, Chris. Go ahead for now, but in general you can't. Once you touch food you have to keep it. Grumpy like yelling? Spanking?"

"Like I better stay out of the way. Can I have a drumstick?"

She turned the plate so the drumstick was in easy reach. Grumpy like he'd better stay out of the way? A child in his own home feeling in the way. She should have realized. She had realized. She should have acted sooner.

"Chris, I wish we didn't need a babysitter, but we do for now. So after this will you promise to tell me if there's ever a problem? If the sitter's grumpy—let's say grumpier than I am—or keeps the TV on all the time or makes you feel like you'd better stay out of her way. Will you tell me?"

"Okay. Mom, don't you think there'd be worms in those mammoth steaks?"

"Chris!" Her sharp tone startled both of them. "Not while we're eating. I mean it." He'd been talking about the mammoth all week, now with the added detail about the buttercups and the ten-thousand-year-old steak dinner. She was tired of hearing about the mammoth and she was especially tired of hearing about its meat.

He stared silently at his plate and used a pointy carrot stick to poke at a tomato wedge. "Ms. Gibson says I don't need to know about climate change yet."

"I agree." Scientists could argue about whether or not the climate was changing all they liked, but little children shouldn't have to think about it.

"That's what she calls it. Climate change. Plenty of time for that in high school, she says."

Chris heard that a lot, whenever he wanted to know things like why humans couldn't get to Mars or whether bacteria felt it when you took antibiotics. It was one of the drawbacks of kindergarten.

"And what did you think of that answer?"

"Well, I'm kind of wondering about it now."

"Maybe you weren't doing the lesson she gave you."

Chris jabbed the tomato again.

"Ah-hah."

"It was folk dancing."

"Not your favorite thing."

"Not my *any*thing!" His carrot broke, sending the tomato wedge across his plate. "She wants to see you."

Gwyn stopped eating. "Did she say why?"

"Nope." He stood up and dug around in his pockets, then handed Gwyn a crumpled envelope. She slipped a finger under the flap and tore. The paper had been folded neatly to begin with, but Chris's pocket had added lots of wrinkles.

Dear Mrs. Sinclair,
Do you have time for a quick chat tomorrow?

Before school, during recess in the morning or afternoon, at lunch hour or after school all work for me.
Please call.

Five options. The only way Ms. Gibson could have
made a parent-teacher meeting sound more urgent would
have been to show up on the doorstep. Gwyn was off work
the next day, so any of the times would suit her. She could
walk to school with Chris and meet with the teacher before
afternoon classes.

"Does she say why in there?" Chris asked.

"Not even a hint."

"I didn't do anything wrong. Least I don't think so.
Other than not dancing. Elliott danced but he kept kicking
Drew on purpose. That's worse, isn't it?"

"Maybe she wants to tell me about something you did
right."

Chris looked surprised at the possibility. "I don't think
I did anything right, either."

CHAPTER FOUR

GWYN BACKED INTO the child-size seat her son's teacher offered. Her knees wouldn't fit under the table, so she sat sideways, hands folded on her lap.

Across the table Ms. Gibson arranged a file folder, a piece of paper and a pen. She gave a bright, cool smile. "What a day! And it's only half over."

Gwyn smiled back cautiously. "Busy?"

"It's an energetic group. Don't misunderstand me—we like that! Energy is good. But with end of the year excitement added, and all our special activities, some of the children get a little out of hand."

Gwyn wondered if Chris had got out of hand. It was hard to imagine.

"Of course, we don't need to worry about that with Christopher. He's a very serious little boy." She paused for an unamused smile. "I'm concerned about that swelling on his arm. A mosquito bite, he says."

He says? Didn't she believe him? "It's infected. I've started using an antibacterial ointment. It should clear up quickly."

"That's good to hear." Ms. Gibson moved one corner of the paper an inch to the side, then back again. She looked up with an expression of polite inquiry. "Is everything all right at home?"

The nervous fluttering in Gwyn's stomach, active since she'd arrived at the school, intensified. "I think so."

"Chris seems tightly wound lately. More than usual."

More than usual. He always had something on his mind. Did that mean he was always tightly wound? More than the other kids? Enough that it was a problem? "He's never been a lighthearted child. That's just the way he is. Right now he's worried about the weather."

"Climate change," the teacher said. Her tone reminded Gwyn of a television psychiatrist or detective, skeptical, leaving the door open for the truth. She turned the folder in front of her around so Gwyn could see it upside up, and spread out the papers it held. Drawing after drawing of Earth, seen from space. "This is how he's spending his time. He hasn't even been interested in playing at recess."

Gwyn pulled the file closer. Chris liked drawing planets and rocket ships at home, but there were at least fifty pictures here, all the same. An uneven circle, an approximation of the continents, blue water, green land. "There's no white for ice."

"I don't think this is about ice."

"He didn't tell you he's afraid there's going to be an ice age?" Gwyn explained about the movie again, feeling even guiltier this time. "Then he saw a video at the museum about the continents moving and changing over aeons. He didn't like it—the idea that things haven't always been the same."

"Children need security. Consistency."

Gwyn nodded, but her uneasiness grew. "He told me he was avoiding doing some of the lessons."

"That isn't my main concern. The term is nearly over but we have next year to consider. We want Chris to have a good start in the fall." They both watched Ms. Gibson's pencil tap one of the drawings. "I know you're a single mother."

Gwyn tensed at the teacher's tone. "I'm raising my son alone."

"Yes," Ms. Gibson agreed. She smiled. "It must be very difficult."

"Raising a child can be difficult for anyone."

The teacher nodded. She kept nodding, with a concerned frown, biting her lip thoughtfully. Then she made her point. "I wonder...if you might be relying on Chris a bit too much?"

"Relying?"

"Without another adult in the house to share the responsibility. Maybe you lean on your son. It happens."

Gwyn hadn't realized she'd stood up until the teacher did, too. "It doesn't happen in my house."

"Mrs. Sinclair, I only want to help."

Gwyn tried counting to ten, but she didn't get further than three. "I'll tell Chris to dance when you want him to dance and color when you want him to color. But the next time you want to discuss what's going on with him, don't call me in here and then presume to tell me about us. You don't know anything about us."

"I understand this is tough, but we need to think about Chris's best interests."

"We?" It was all Gwyn could say. The past six years crowded to the front of her mind. Ms. Gibson wasn't anywhere in them. Not when Chris was born, not when he cried with colic, not when he took his first steps or read his first words or suffered through chicken pox or cut his head on the banister and needed stitches. Not when he blew out birthday candles, either, and not when his face lit with wonder at finding a full stocking on Christmas morning.

Her anger began to fade. Ms. Gibson hadn't imagined the problem. Hadn't caused it, either. "I appreciate your concern for Chris. You're right, he is tightly wound." At the moment, so was she. She had to stop and catch her breath. "Other than that, you're completely wrong. You need to learn not to jump to conclusions about people."

"Then let's discuss what you think the—"

"Thank you, Ms. Gibson, but I'll take care of my son."

THOSE LAST ANGRY WORDS followed Gwyn out of the school and down the sidewalk. In the middle of the night with an hours-old baby sleeping in the cot beside her bed she'd whispered that promise. *I'll take care of you, sweetheart.*

She would have been lost without Iris. Iris had known the significance of the car in the driveway and the uniformed officers who'd come to the door. Before that day they'd been polite neighbors; after, firm friends. Iris had helped get the nursery ready and driven her to the hospital when the labor pains began, did the laundry, rocked the baby so Gwyn could get some sleep.

But Gwyn had found her balance. Learned how to get through the days and nights. How to take care of this whole new mysterious human. How to make room for aching, bursting love when she was already full of gnawing grief.

Lean on Chris? On a five-year-old? Rely on him for what?

There was that comment in Johansson's about running out of money. He'd looked worried then. She'd have to be careful about that sort of thing—thinking out loud, especially about ideas a child might not understand.

With a sudden pang, she wished she could speak to her mother. Even after so long that feeling sometimes hit hard. Seven years. That was a big chunk of her life but it still seemed ridiculous that there wasn't a place to go and her mother would be there. "The teacher said what?" she could imagine her saying. "Leaning? How silly!" When her father came in they'd go over the conversation again. He'd give her a hug and tell her what a great mom she was.

It was harder to know how Duncan would react. They'd barely lived together. Never been parents together. What would he think about his son drawing Earth over and over, fifty times, more? All she could picture was him laughing or wrapping his arms around Chris, or both, and the problem going away.

Not like the man they'd run into by the mammoth painting. He'd made it worse.

Without noticing, she'd gone past her house all the way to the corner. A bus was coming. She decided to zip downtown, tell that David person what he'd done with his measured voice and his kind expression, and zip back before school was out.

She fumed all the way to the museum. At the admissions booth she described the man she and Chris had met during their last visit and was directed to his office. She followed the arrows to the administration section, then walked along the hall reading name plates on doors, stopping when she got to D. Bretton, Ph.D. Climatology.

Ph.D. He could still be wrong.

The door opened almost as soon as she knocked. There he stood, taller than she remembered, eyes darker. After a look of surprise, he smiled. It was a very friendly smile and for a moment she wished she was more disposed to like him.

"They said at the front it was all right for me to come through to the offices."

"Of course. My door's always open." He glanced at it, so recently closed, and gave a little shrug. "Figuratively."

"My son and I were here about a week ago—"

"On Saturday, looking at the mammoth painting. What can I do for you today?"

Too many answers all involving Chris, his drawings and his weather watching jumbled together in her mind. One emerged. *Take back what you said.* She waited until something more sensible occurred to her. "It's about our conversation that day."

He stood back from the door. "Come in, sit down. I've made a fresh pot of coffee. Cream or sugar?"

"No, thanks."

"Just black?"

"I mean no, I won't have coffee. But thank you."

It was a small office, crammed with books, papers, boxes and file cabinets. Three computer monitors sat on the desk, all turned on and showing what she thought were radar and satellite images: colored, swirling shapes, one over an outline of North America, another Europe, the third Asia. Behind his desk a map of Canada nearly covered the wall. Red-tipped pins were stuck in from the western border of Alberta to the eastern border of Manitoba. A few were scattered in the north, and in the central parts of the provinces, but they were concentrated heavily in the south.

"Tornadoes," Bretton said.

"We've had that many?" There were hundreds of pins. Maybe thousands.

"Not all lately. Since 1868."

"Still—"

"People are always surprised when they see the map. We've had more but because so much of the country is sparsely populated they're not all reported." He filled his cup, then held the pot in the air. "You're sure?"

"No, thanks." Now that she'd got a whiff of the coffee she wouldn't have minded a cup, but this wasn't meant to be a friendly visit.

"It's shade-grown," he said, as if that might tempt her. "Knowing rain-forest trees haven't been cut down makes me feel good about ingesting caffeine." He smiled. Every time he did that she had to remind herself she didn't want to smile back. "It makes me feel it's my duty to drink a whole lot more."

"I prefer tea."

"Regular or herbal?" He began looking in containers beside the coffeemaker, then in a couple of desk drawers. "I usually have tea bags. My mother must have used them. We should be able to find you something—"

"Dr. Bretton, really, I don't want a drink."

"No? I guess you would have gone to the cafeteria if you were thirsty." He leaned against a filing cabinet, mug in hand. "But you didn't. You came here."

"When we talked before you mentioned a change in the weather."

"In the climate, yes. As I recall, it was unwelcome information."

"Unwelcome?" He didn't need to be so relaxed about it. "How could you scare a little kid like that?"

"I didn't mean to scare him."

"You basically told him the world as we know it is doomed!"

"Is that what I did?"

"Excessive warming, glaciers melting, permafrost thawing…"

"I'm sorry if I upset you and your son." He made a wry face. "Driving people from the museum in a panic isn't part of our mission statement."

"We told you about the movie he saw, didn't we?"

Bretton nodded. "When it first came out it stimulated a lot of questions."

"Why would it? It was a fantasy."

"A what-if scenario."

"What if something impossible happened, you mean?"

"There you have the central question. How impossible is it?"

Now he was being silly, or intentionally annoying. She stood straighter and spoke firmly. "Here's the central answer. Completely. It's completely impossible. In spite of that it frightened Chris. We came here to reassure him, to help him separate fact from fiction."

"That dawned on me a bit late. Our goals are different—"

"You like mixing fact and fiction?"

This time his reply didn't come as quickly. "I'm here to give people information regardless of its power to reassure."

He sounded so calm. Scientists sounded like that on TV, too. Even when they were talking about galaxies colliding or the sun fizzling out. What about the children who were walking to school when one of their nifty theories happened?

Angrily she said, "I suppose you're looking at the big picture. The entire biography of planet Earth—"

His face perked up. "That's a great way to put it—"

"The mammoth had its moment in time and we're having ours? To everything there is a season? Do you realize that's not comforting to a five-year-old?"

"Five! I thought he must be a really little eight."

She wasn't getting anywhere. Either she wasn't saying what she meant or he wasn't listening. "Everything you told us on Saturday about the climate…Chris has connected it to this frozen, doomed animal, to the doomed people in the movie."

"I didn't say humans were going the way of the mammoth. Not yet. We don't anticipate that sudden or extreme a change."

A tight knot formed in her stomach. He was doing it again. The kind eyes, the friendly face, the frightening message. "You don't have kids, do you?"

"I work with them every day. Lots of them. All ages and personalities." He smiled. "And I vaguely recall being one."

"Maybe you should try to recall it more clearly."

His smile faded. "I haven't missed the fact that you're angry with me."

"I'm not—well, I am—but this isn't about that. I'm not here to let off steam."

"You're here to change things."

Something about the simple statement, something in his voice nearly brought tears to her eyes. That would be the last straw.

She sat in the chair he'd offered when she first came in, and he sat at his desk. If she put her hand out she could touch him. Unexpectedly, she found the closeness comforting. Talk about a fantasy. She wasn't here to be soothed by dark eyes and a deep voice.

"Don't you remember how big and shapeless problems seem when you're small? How dark the dark is, how mysterious time can be?" She didn't know why it was so important to reach him. "Chris keeps drawing Earth. His teacher showed me a folder full of drawings he's done in the past week. He watches the weather channel so often he knows all the announcers by their first names. He isn't into make-believe. Godzilla doesn't scare him. This scares him."

"We've got ourselves into a scary situation."

Her butterflies swooped back. "What's the answer, then? How do I reassure him?"

"I don't think you do."

"Of course I do!"

"I can understand that might be a parent's first reaction. Say it works. How long will it last? Ten minutes, ten days? What happens the next time he's frightened?"

Gwyn didn't say what she was thinking. *I'd reassure him again.*

"Can his father help? Maybe he could give your son a different perspective."

Even though she'd wished for exactly that, the suggestion annoyed her. "A male-to-male thing. Toughness and courage and sucking it up, stuff I wouldn't understand."

"My mother is more from the sucking-it-up school than my father is, but yes, that's along the lines of what I had in mind."

He put down his mug and pushed books out of his way so he could lean forward, his forearms on his desk, his hands clasped. It made him look like a family doctor about to say something awful for the patient's own good.

"When I'm worried I need to take action. Otherwise I'm stuck brooding and I can't get anywhere brooding. It sounds as if your son might be like that, too. Why not sign him up for our day camp this summer? We're doing a whole week about climate change."

He had to be kidding. What had happened to childhood? What about finger puppets? Maybe they did have
finger puppets, finger puppets that got walloped by tornadoes and swallowed by glaciers.

"He's five, remember. He may be bright for his age, but
he's still a child. I don't want to overwhelm him."

"Facts can be comforting to children, especially when
they're learning about a serious problem. Then it's not a
nameless monster in the closet. It's an identifiable question
with a list of solutions."

Finally he'd said something that didn't give her a stom-
achache. "Solutions?"

"Well…measures that may ameliorate the situation."

That made her smile. "Ameliorate. Chris would love that."

Bretton smiled, too. "Think you'll sign him up?" When
she didn't answer right away, he added, "It's not child
labor. We have a good time. Kids come back summer after
summer. Willingly."

"Maybe in a year or two." Or ten.

He looked at her the way Chris sometimes did. As if
she'd failed. "That's your decision, of course."

Oh, she hated that tone. Her completely wrong decision, he meant.

"There's a book in our gift shop—"

"About the mammoth. You mentioned it on Saturday."

"The one I'm thinking of now explains weather systems.
It's meant for young children. It gives a really clear, easy
to understand overview."

She'd had enough. She stood up, wishing she could tell
him all the ways he annoyed her. "The books I'm thinking
of for my son involve talking spiders and children who play
games on flying broomsticks."

Bretton stood, too. For the first time his voice sounded chilly. "I thought you said he isn't into make-believe."

"Maybe he should be."

"From the little I remember about being a child that isn't something a parent can force. Are you sure you know what you're doing? Books like that have a dark side. You might be happier with the old Dick and Jane readers. Did you have those in school? Dick and Jane are never afraid. They just bounce balls, watch Spot run and say, 'Yes, Mother.'"

Gwyn stared at him until she noticed she wasn't doing anything but blinking.

He reached into one of his desk drawers and brought out a pamphlet. "Why not take that with you? Just in case."

From Dinosaurs to Black Holes: Science for the Summer. Inside was a chart with dates and prices. A hundred and fifty dollars a week. They should call it This Week Give Your Kid Nightmares Instead of Meals. She folded it in two and put it in her purse.

"This is more than a job to you, isn't it, Dr. Bretton? You're a bit of a zealot." She'd never used the word in conversation, only in history essays. It fit the occasion nicely. The surprise on his face was worth the trip downtown. "Thank you for your time."

GWYN'S PLEASURE AT HER EXIT had lasted all of two minutes. Whatever she'd hoped to accomplish by going back to the museum, she hadn't done it. She'd had some foggy idea that Dr. Bretton would recant if he heard about the folder of drawings, that he had a whole different batch of ideas for five-year-olds who were afraid their world was ending. But no, he had more of the same ideas. Books and day camps full of information to add to Chris's fears.

On the way home she'd stopped at the library. The book about the mammoth with grass in its mouth was there. She'd signed it out along with a few about orbiting planets and how caterpillars became butterflies. *Charlotte's Web,* too, to read aloud.

From Iris's kitchen window she saw Chris sitting under the maple tree in their backyard, a book open in front of him. He'd gone off with the whole pile, except for the one Bretton had recommended. She wanted to check it first then look at it with him, if she decided he should look at it at all.

She turned back to Iris, aware she'd gone a long time without finishing the story of the parent-teacher interview. "Anyway," she said, wrapping it up quickly, "I kind of lost my temper. I hate losing my temper."

"Once in a while you need to stand up for yourself."

"Sure. And alienate your son's teacher who already thinks you're failing him."

Iris pulled a pitcher of sangria from the fridge, put two wineglasses on the table, then slipped off her shoes and lit a cigarette. Gwyn sat across from her.

"There's always somebody who thinks they know what we should be doing. You've got to ignore people like that, Gwyn. Leaning on Chris? Give me a break. You're a great mom. You do everything you can for that kid."

"He's in knots about this, about the idea the weather's changing. Obsessed."

Iris shrugged. She tapped the end of her cigarette in the ashtray to put it out, but kept holding it as if she was going to take another puff. "It is different, isn't it? Ice storms and floods, droughts, warm winters."

"Maybe it only seems that way. We've got 24-hour news

and a channel for the weather. They have to talk about something."

"Could be." Iris poured each of them some of the sangria, careful that the fruit in the pitcher didn't plonk into their glasses. "Don't worry about Chris. Kids get scared. Molly was a wreck about strangers after she started kindergarten. Forget the alphabet, the first thing they taught her was 'be afraid, be very afraid.' She didn't want to go trick-or-treating that Hallowe'en. She wouldn't sit on the mall Santa's knee at Christmas."

"What did you do?"

"Not a thing. She got over it."

Molly came in the door just then. "Me? Hi, Mrs. Sinclair." She shrugged when her mother asked how her exam had gone. "It was okay. Jamie says she flunked. We're going for coffee later."

"I don't think so."

"Not coffee, really. Just out."

"On an exam night?"

"For an hour. It's important, we're planning some fundraising. For hurricane relief."

"That's very nice, I'm glad to hear it. You can do it after exams."

"Half an hour, that's all. The break'll do us good. What did I get over, Mom? Besides Jason." She reached for the sangria pitcher and her mother lightly slapped her hand. "And that arrogant dweeb, Luke McKinley."

"Oh, you're over him now?"

"Completely." She took a juice glass out of the cupboard. "That much? It's healthy, Mom. Look at all the fruit." When her mother ignored her, she brought out an egg cup. "That much?"

"All right. No refills."

Gwyn watched Molly fill the egg cup to the brim and sip appreciatively. "How did you ever fall for an arrogant dweeb in the first place?"

"Have you seen Luke McKinley? He's the cutest, hottest guy ever."

"He isn't," Iris interrupted. "He's just cocky."

Molly nodded emphatically, eyebrows up for extra emphasis. "Hot, cute *and* cocky. You feel like he's looking in the mirror the whole time he's talking to you. Imagine kissing him—"

"Hey! I told you, no imagining kissing until you're sixteen." Iris winked at Gwyn.

"Right, Mom."

"We're getting pizza for dinner," Iris went on, "and you and Chris are joining us, Gwyn. Molly can play with him for a while, won't you, Molly? Chris's teacher thinks he doesn't have any fun."

Molly didn't hide her irritation. "Sure. There's no time for fund-raising for a hurricane, but I can play with Chris."

Gwyn said, "That's all right. I've got dinner planned."

"No, no, stay, Mrs. Sinclair. I didn't mean it like that. I want to play with him. We can rescue each other from glaciers again. Personally, at that age I liked Beanie Babies, but hey."

"That's not a helpful tone," Iris told her daughter. "And the pizza will be here in five minutes, Gwyn, so you really should stay. Chris said he was hungry."

Gwyn went to the window to check on him again. Bitten from head to toe, scared and hungry. Maybe she really wasn't taking good care of him. He was still reading, his knees up and his back resting against the tree. He looked relaxed. For him, trying to figure things out *was* fun. At least she'd always thought so. *Are you sure?* Bretton had asked, about something or other. She was never sure, not about anything.

"I went to the museum after I saw Ms. Gibson to talk to the man who frightened Chris last Saturday. Guess what?"

"What?"

"He's got a Ph.D. In climatology."

"Oh, oh. An honest to goodness expert."

"He's really annoying." That wasn't exactly true. It was more that he was too sure of his facts and too willing to share them. Actually, he seemed—she wouldn't go so far as to say caring—but almost, he almost seemed caring.

"What's that sparkle I see?"

"Sparkle?"

"You got sort of a sparkle when you mentioned this guy."

"That's not a sparkle. That's the sun in my eyes. Or it could be anger. David with the Ph.D. is guaranteed to make a person mad within two minutes of contact."

"Is he cute?"

Molly groaned. "You two sound like children."

"I didn't notice what he looked like. He's your garden variety tall, dark, deep-voiced guy with brown eyes."

"Chocolate brown?" Iris asked.

"More like espresso."

"Except you didn't notice."

Gwyn's cheeks felt warm. It had to be the wine. She never blushed, never. "Iris, you sound like a child."

DAVID LOCKED HIS BIKE to a post in the underground parking garage and took the elevator to his apartment. When he opened the door he smelled oregano and garlic.

Sam had let himself in and was simmering spaghetti sauce on top of the stove. He held the pot's lid in one hand and stirred with the other, looking almost content.

"This is nice," David said. "Like one of those old-fashioned marriages with the wife who stays home cooking—"

Sam balled up a tea towel and threw it at his brother's head. "How was your day, dear?"

"Less relaxing than yours, I'll bet. What did you do, sleep until noon then have tea with Mom and Dad?"

"Pretty much."

David was glad to hear it. Some of the tightness around Sam's eyes was gone, but he still looked as if he could use a lot of lazy days. "Have you finished checking the canoe's injuries?"

"There isn't any one injury. More of an allover structural decline. I can fix it. But I'm sure going to give Sarah a piece of my mind when she gets here."

"Thought you didn't want her to come."

"She will, though."

"I haven't been able to get hold of her. Her assistant says she's in Germany, at a book fair."

"Oh, that big one in Frankfurt. She always goes to that." Sam started a pot of water for the pasta, then tasted the sauce. "Hmm. Perfect." He glanced back at David. "Something bugging you? I hope you don't mind me helping myself to your kitchen."

"No, of course not. Sorry. I keep thinking about a woman who came to see me today."

"A female got under your skin?" Sam leaned against the stove, giving his brother his full attention. "Tell me more."

"There's nothing more." He got two bottles of Fort Garry Ale from the fridge, opened them and handed one to Sam. "She's married, for one thing, and I've been pissing her off, for another."

"It's not like you to be distracted by a married woman."

David had trouble thinking of her as married, but she did wear a ring, and she hadn't contradicted him when he'd suggested her husband could steer her son's thinking in a different direction.

He took a long drink of the cold beer. "I've noticed her before. Don't ask me why. I mean she's pretty, but that isn't why. Pale and sort of delicate. You know when they say someone has alabaster skin? That's what her face makes me think of. And you know when they say someone's an English Rose? That's what she makes me think of, too."

"Alabaster and rose. But that isn't why you noticed her."

"No," David agreed. "I mean it's why I *noticed* her, but it's not why I kept looking."

"Okay. I'll pretend to believe you."

"Sam."

"I believe you."

"Then I finally get a chance to talk to her and next thing I know she goes into that mother bear protecting her cub mode."

"There's a cub?"

"And it turns out she's not so delicate. She's got a glare that could wither a sumo wrestler. Anyway, she's not my type."

"Even if she wasn't married, you mean."

"We talked for quite a while today. We don't have anything in common, that's for sure." He smiled. "She's got a really expressive face. Too expressive, sometimes. Interesting to watch, though."

"David."

"The thing is, her mind is closed. Really, Sam. You wouldn't believe it." The more he thought about it, the more frustrated David felt. "She's got her nice little world and I'd better not shake it up by mentioning reality. I don't understand how people can do that. They've got the facts in front of them but they somehow get through their days while completely ignoring them. You know? If the facts were obstacles, locked gates and hard wooden chairs and patches of quicksand you'd have trouble maneuvering, wouldn't you? You'd have bruises on your legs and sand in your lungs—"

"It's hard to see why she'd get annoyed with you, you being so charming and all."

David stared at his brother. "I didn't say any of this to her. I was completely—"

"Chatting up a married woman with a child who came to you in your capacity as one of the museum's curators."

That sounded bad. "Yes. Exactly." And it was worse. He wanted to talk to her again. Not just talk. He wanted to touch that rosy skin. He even wanted to have another argument with her. Encourage her to look at the world more clearly.

Right, because she'd shown him how much she liked it when he did that. It was a pity, though, to go through life without paying attention to it. Worse than a pity. People could do damage when they ignored what was going on around them.

To remind himself of the central point he said, "She was wearing a ring."

"So I gathered."

He would have to make himself care about the ring.

CHAPTER FIVE

AND OF COURSE he did care. By the time Sam's spaghetti was consumed David had pushed the woman whose name he still didn't know almost to the back of his mind. Soon he hardly thought about her at all. Except when he passed the mammoth painting—eight or nine times a day—and when he checked the weather maps and the sky every morning and night. He told himself it was her fear that made her hard to forget. It bothered him to see a kid and his mom frightened and know he'd had a hand in it.

The office telephone rang. David picked up the receiver and heard a familiar voice, warm but frazzled, going straight from hello into her reason for calling.

He interrupted. "Sarah. Hi."

She paused midsentence, then carried on. "I got your message. Have you seen him? Is he okay?"

"He's perturbed about the canoe."

"What are you talking about?"

"Our canoe. It was left outside and got damaged."

"Am I supposed to care about some canoe? My brother's home two months early from Afghanistan! I'm beside myself here. Is he hurt?"

"No." David started with the straightforward part of the answer, then got into the shades of gray. "He seems fine physically. I don't know why he's home or how long he's staying. He's…burnt out or something. Think you can come for holidays early?"

"Burnt out?"

"That's all I know, Sarah."

"I'll try to clear my desk." She paused. "The canoe…I think that was me."

"That's what Sam thinks, too."

"Could you tell him I'm sorry?"

"You might have to fix this one yourself."

"Oh." She sounded as contrite as she always did after making someone angry. She repeated that she'd get through her work as quickly as possible. It might take a couple of weeks. Maybe more.

They said goodbye and David sat back, doing his best to shift his attention from family to office. The last tour of the morning had just ended. Thirty students had managed to sound like five times that number. Not a single face had lit up at the human circulation analogy. He suspected not a single brain had noted it, either. June was worse than Hallowe'en, worse than the Christmas season. It should be struck off the calendar. No, that wouldn't work. May would be the new June.

A figure appeared in the doorway.

"What's next, Roberta?"

"A grade three class after lunch." Her voice and posture diffident, Roberta stood with a notepad and pen at the ready, as if he might suddenly give dictation. She was an education student hired to help with summer programming but she treated him like the prime minister or something. She added apologetically, "They want to see dinosaurs."

"We don't have dinosaurs."

"I explained that."

"And?"

"They still want to see dinosaurs."

He gave himself a moment to fantasize about saying no sternly, without explanation or apology, just because occasionally it was good for children to hear the word. He should have tried it with the boy, Chris. Is there going to be an ice age? *No.* Should I be scared? *No.*

That wasn't what he'd asked, though. It was what the mother had expected. The boy wanted to understand all about the frozen mammoth, even if he was told it meant an ice age was coming. David hoped she'd bring him back. Then he could try to redeem himself—to both of them.

At the door Roberta made a polite little noise. "The parents arranging the field trip seemed to feel that if we looked hard enough we might find some dinosaurs in the exhibits."

"Do we have ice cubes?"

She hardly paused at the unexpected question. "In the staff room fridge, I believe. Do you want a cold drink?"

Grade threes in June wouldn't listen to a word anyone said. He'd have to show them why a science museum in Manitoba didn't have displays of dinosaurs.

So…ice cubes on the sand table representing the ice sheet that covered the northern part of the continent ten thousand years ago. A pitcher of water in case they didn't melt fast enough. Retreating glaciers leaving a shallow inland sea filled with huge, scary fish and mosasaurs, the almost-dinosaur as far as most kids were concerned. Then, on the newly formed lake's shore, now Alberta, plastic T-rexes and hadrosaurs from the gift shop.

One of his computer monitors had got Roberta's attention. She came closer to the desk, pointing at a looming cloud formation on the screen. That was more like it. Too much respect made him feel like an old man.

"What's going on there, Dr. Bretton?"

"David." Every day he asked her to call him by his first name. "That's the low pressure cell that caused so much trouble in Alberta yesterday." Fifteen funnel clouds, five tornadoes and hail deep enough to shovel. "It's coming our way." He clicked on another map. "You see? An area of high pressure's coming down from the Arctic. Weather's all about conflict and resolution. Warm fronts tangle with cold fronts, air is forced aloft, energy's released."

He stopped. She wasn't interested in why and how. Just where and how much. "It's a huge system. We can't predict exactly where storms will break out. Could be overhead, could be Dauphin, could be Minot. Could be all three. Wherever it hits, it'll be severe."

"But we won't get tornadoes."

"That I can't promise."

"We never do. Almost never." She gave an embarrassed smile. "I don't even like thunder."

"It's not the thunder that'll hurt you."

She edged back to the doorway. "I guess not. Do you want the ice now?"

"Can you take it to the activity room about ten minutes before the grade threes arrive?" In the meantime he'd go to the cafeteria to pick up some lunch—and belatedly think of all the things he could have said instead of *It's not the thunder that'll hurt you.*

My sister doesn't like thunder, either. Makes you jump, doesn't it? That would have been easy. Almost human.

He paid for a ham-and-cheese sandwich and took it out

to the Tyndall stone courtyard. The air was hot and muggy enough that he worked up a sweat just stepping outside. He sat on a bench in the shade of an ash tree, listening to the traffic and looking at the sky.

Clouds were building. Small cumulus clouds, flat and dark on the bottom, the tops lit bright white by the sun, some of them already swelling, adding to their height. Roberta would hear thunder today.

Was fear starting to go around? The kid and his mother, Roberta. People could sense change. They could sense when things weren't quite right. It was early to come to conclusions about weather trends but in his own mind with only himself as critic he was sure the erratic weather patterns of the past few years were more than a blip on a graph. They were the start of something new, something fierce.

Not necessarily today. This storm cell could dissipate on its way east. A little active weather would be welcome. They needed rain. Now, if it would just fall gently.

CHRIS HAD MADE a chart for the kitchen wall. Each day he listened to the weather then drew clouds or a sun on the chart. There weren't many clouds and no raindrops. Square after square was filled with sun. Not smiling and cheerful. He colored it red and sometimes added a frowning face. It made Gwyn think of David Bretton's comment about a monster in the closet. For Chris the monster was in the summer sky, right where everyone could see it.

"I remember a summer like this when I was your age." She'd filled a small inflatable pool so he could splash and cool off after school but he'd come back into the house complaining that the grass was as sharp as needles.

"With tornadoes?"

"No—"

"There was some place that had a bunch of tornadoes yesterday."

She'd heard about that, too, and thought of Bretton adding more pins to his map. "Alberta. That's far away from here. I've never seen a tornado but I do remember heat like this with the grass dried out and crackly to walk on. The community centers didn't fill the wading pools because they didn't want to waste water."

Chris seemed to be listening, but she had no idea what he was thinking. His face was a blank.

"Then the next year it turned around. We had lots of rain and everything was green again."

"Ed Farley says we're going to get rain today." Ed Farley was the morning weatherman.

"There you are, then."

"He says this is the hottest June on record."

Should she meet with Ms. Gibson again? Listen this time? It couldn't be normal for a little kid to worry so much. Why wasn't he getting excited about the end-of-year field trips, like the other children, or begging for a vacation she couldn't afford? There had to be something wrong. An anxiety disorder. Had she failed him in some invisible way? Maybe he'd felt her grief in the womb and in those first months when they'd lived in such close tandem. Did he see her worrying and think he had to worry, too?

"Chris? Let's do something different for dinner. How about a picnic in the park?" Hoping to get both of them in the general spirit of the event she added, "It'll be fun."

He gave a grim little nod.

"Can you empty your backpack for us to carry the food?" Gwyn began rummaging through the cupboards and fridge, looking for picnic fare. When he brought the backpack, already worn from its one year carrying drawings and crafts home from school, she told him, "This is what we've got. Sardines, peanut butter, puffed wheat and apples. Does that make a picnic?"

"Not sardines." He got the rolling pin from a drawer.

"Roll-ups? Good idea."

She took bread from the bread box, cut off the crusts and gave the slices to Chris to flatten. She spread on peanut butter and he rolled the bread around sections of banana. Sliced, the circles looked like food meant for fun. Apples and a bottle of juice went in the bottom of the pack, and bags of puffed wheat and roll-ups on top.

"We need a blanket to sit on."

Chris ran to his room and returned with the one she'd folded away in his closet at the end of April. They rolled it as tight as they could and added it to the backpack. It stuck out the top so that they couldn't pull the drawstring shut.

The preparations, simple as they were, seemed to distract him but as soon as they started walking to the park his conversation returned to his usual subject.

"In the movie they didn't have it getting hotter. They had it getting colder. But the man at the museum said he didn't know if there would be an ice age. It's kind of confusing. We should rent the video again, Mom."

"I don't think so."

"'Cause they call it global warming. Not global freezing."

"It's all mumbo jumbo, sweetheart."

He took an extra big step to avoid a bug on the sidewalk. "Maybe it'll get so hot everything will burn."

"Chris! Let it go. The things in that movie are not going to happen. Nothing bad is going to happen. Remember the

Snow Queen? She lived in a frozen world, right? And the children who went there could freeze in a moment."

Chris gave her a startled glance, then kept on walking, eyes straight ahead. Maybe the Snow Queen was a bad choice.

"What about King Midas, then. What happened to him?"

"Everything he touched turned to gold."

"Was it a true story?"

"I dunno."

"Of course you know."

Chris sighed. "It was sort of a fairy tale."

"Exactly. So if an ocean jumps on a city and freezes everyone it touches, what's that?"

There was a silence. As if she was dragging the words out of him he said, "Sort of a fairy tale?"

"Right again. It's science fiction."

He started walking on the curb, arms out for balance.

"Not here, Chris. The street's too busy."

He trailed back to her side. "Fiction with some science in it or science with some fiction in it?"

Was he supposed to be so ornery? She'd have to ask Iris if Molly had been like this at five. Of course, Iris said Molly was like this now. Maybe Chris was going to argue with her for the next ten years. Twenty.

"Just plain old fiction, Chris. Take my word for it. There have always been outlandish stories and there's always been weather people think is strange. And that's the last I want to hear about it."

Silence and stiffness between them they went past the corner store, then the Dairy Queen and across the road to the river side of the street. Now and then clouds partly covered the sun and the temperature briefly seemed to cool.

They turned into the park. Chris trudged along behind

her as if the backpack was a terrible weight. "But what do you mean, *always* been? Because Earth used to be different. Like they said at the museum, it was all one continent before. With volcanoes and lava everywhere. And there *was* an ice age."

"You know what, Chris? I don't want you to watch the weather station so much."

He looked at her in disbelief.

"Once a day is plenty. We'll watch it together so we can figure out what everything means. All right?" She decided to take his silence as agreement.

The space she wanted, a patch of grass under a huge elm overlooking the river, was free. Chris glowered at the water while she spread out the blanket and put the containers of food on top. Even after she helped herself to an apple he continued standing to one side, as if he had nothing to do with her. He'd never sulked like that before, and over such a small thing. Was it really a hardship for a five-year-old to be limited to one weather forecast a day? She'd have to remember to tell Molly not to let him turn it on when she was at work.

She held out the bag of roll-ups. This was ridiculous. Like tempting a squirrel. Chris glanced at the bag. He edged closer and his hand slid inside, then reemerged with a circle of bread and banana. When he sat down it was on the border of the blanket, his feet on the grass.

"Are you looking forward to seeing Molly tomorrow evening instead of Mrs. Henderson?"

He ignored her. Okay, she was getting it. There was one topic of conversation and it was that or nothing. Did he think she couldn't take nothing? She certainly could.

Gwyn kept her eyes on the river and tried to enjoy

watching ducks and kayakers. A breeze had picked up and she smelled ozone. It was refreshing, and so welcome. Leaves rustled gently, like chimes tinkling. Maybe the hot spell was ending and the rest of summer would be like this.

"Next time I'll plan ahead and make something better. Cold barbecued ribs, and Rice Krispie cake. How does that sound?"

"Good."

The clouds were building quickly. Pretty white puffs had become tall and billowing, threateningly dark on the bottom.

"Is it going to rain, Mom?"

"Not for a while." She didn't want to rush away before they'd eaten. How could she convince him not to worry if she scuttled off at the first sign of a summer storm? There was no thunder yet, no lightning.

She opened a bag of puffed wheat and took a handful, like peanuts, then stretched out propped on one elbow, and started a game of I Spy. At the beginning Chris was reluctant to take part but the chance to win was too tempting. He guessed her first choice easily—a golden retriever playing fetch nearby—and soon they got down to fine detail. The white curtains in a third-story apartment window, the reflector of a bicycle, a dead branch halfway up the trunk of a maple tree. Sometime during the game Chris's feet found their way onto the blanket.

"Imagine living up there." Gwyn pointed at the apartment building closest to them. "I'll bet the people at the top can sit on their balcony and see farmland out past the city. And the people on the lowest balcony can fish in the river."

She could hardly believe it when Chris smiled at her very small joke. "I bet they dive from their balconies, Mom."

She smiled back, happy.

But she was getting concerned, too. The line of dark clouds was closer. There was something oppressive about it, like a lid drawing shut over their heads. Birds had started to flutter and swoop from branch to branch in that nervous way they had when bad weather was coming. Then thunder rumbled and Chris jumped to his feet.

"You're right. Time to go if we don't want to get wet."

Gwyn began gathering the remains of the picnic. They didn't bother shaking grass from the blanket, but just folded the corners to meet. As soon as it was small enough to fit in the pack Chris took her hand and tried to run, pulling her with him.

"Easy does it, kiddo."

A man with a dog on a leash rushed past them. A gust of wind blew, whipping branches in great swooping arcs. The leaves sounded like waves. It was beautiful, but so sudden and intense it made her heart beat with fear.

"Mom, c'mon!" There was a note of panic in Chris's voice.

Gwyn pulled him to her. "It's all right." She knelt so they were eye to eye. Big drops of rain splashed against their faces. She wanted to get out of the park, too, away from the trees before any lightning started. "We're fine. We don't need to run. We'll get wet, that's all."

He wriggled away. Why didn't he trust her anymore?

They were in the middle of the park when the clouds opened up. Like tubs of water spilling. By the time they reached the sidewalk their hair and clothes were soaked. She smiled, hoping to signal adventure, and felt rain in her mouth.

Then the wind let loose. Branches reached for them, young trees bent to the ground. Gwyn picked Chris up and ran. Out of the park and across the street, splashing along the sidewalk with the wind after them.

A door opened, the Dairy Queen door, and an arm waved. They were through. She could hardly see Chris for water running from her hair. She brushed it away from her face, then from his. He was fine. Wild-eyed, but fine.

"Try not to get close to the glass," a man said, his voice edgy. "In case there's hail."

The shop was full, with large windows on three sides. Avoiding the glass couldn't be done.

"There's ice cream," another man said, more calmly than the first. "Free ice cream. The power's out."

Someone handed Chris an ice cream sandwich. Eyes still big, hair still dripping, he dug in.

Gwyn looked around the room. There were kids in shorts, men and women in suits, a teenager comforting a tiny dog. On the far side of the room, seated at a table, was Molly. She was with some girls Gwyn didn't know and a movie-star-handsome boy. They weren't wet, not at all, and Molly was trying very hard not to see her.

THE WIND AND RAIN EASED, then stopped. Twigs and bits of garbage sailed along the street; a sheet with clothespins visible wrapped itself around a stalled car's bumper.

"Would you look at all that water?" someone said. "Where'd it come from so fast? I don't believe it."

Everyone agreed they'd never seen anything like it, the suddenness, the intensity. It felt sociable, like being at a hockey game with friends, but Gwyn didn't want to stay inside and shake her head at the freak storm. She needed to get away from the crowd and humidity, so she took Chris's hand and they made their way to the sidewalk, stepping into warm water.

He lifted one foot into the air. "My shoes."

"Leave them on, hon. In case there's something sharp we can't see. Branches or broken glass."

"They feel squishy."

"That's all right. Pretend you're making wine."

He frowned and shook his head, about to mutiny as the sidewalk filled with people leaving the shelter of stores. "I don't like it. It's like worms."

Being scared made him angry. She understood because she wasn't far from the same response. She bent down, touching her nose to the top of his head. "Shall I carry you?"

That was the last thing he wanted. He began weaving through milling people, lifting one foot or the other out of the water every few steps and muttering his distaste. Gwyn kept an eye on the ground as they waded, so she didn't notice anything special about one pair of pant legs until Chris stopped walking and tugged her hand.

"Mom," he whispered. "The museum guy."

She was about to tell him she wouldn't discuss anything the museum guy had said until they were home and dry and out of their squishy shoes when she saw that her son wasn't trying to start another argument. He was making an observation. David Bretton was right in front of them.

Almost in front of them. He stood ahead and to the side, among upset commuters and laughing, splashing teenagers. Moisture seeped halfway to his knees, but otherwise he was dry. So was the brown paper grocery bag under his arm. She couldn't imagine what he was doing there and had a sudden feeling that he was going to haunt her, pop up everywhere repeating over and over that he'd told her so.

"This isn't anything new," she said when he met her gaze. "Storms like this have happened before."

"Have they?"

"Flooding in Winnipeg, are you kidding?"

"From spring runoff, sure." He smiled as if their last meeting had been a pleasant one. "You're soaking."

She pulled her blouse away from her skin. Having the cloth stuck to her hadn't bothered her when everyone else was soaking, too. "We were in the park when it started. The sky just opened up—" Again, she couldn't keep eye contact with him. Something about the way he looked at her made her uncomfortable.

He shifted his attention to Chris. "So you had a bit of an adventure. Lucky you! I was in Johansson's when it started. Watched through the window. Not very exciting."

"I thought we should leave the park before Mom thought we should."

"Did you? You're a good observer, then."

Chris seemed pleased by that. Gwyn had to stop herself from saying she was a good observer, too. "We should go."

Bretton nodded. "That's a good idea. We'll be getting another burst of activity." He sounded so sure. "It's been nice seeing you again—whoever you may be."

Had she really burst into his office that day without introducing herself? "I'm sorry—Gwyn Sinclair." She glanced at the dark but quiet sky. "What are you doing in our neck of the woods?"

"It's my neck of the woods."

"Did you just move in?"

"I've lived here all my life."

"You can't have. I would have seen you."

"Want to come down the road with me? I grew up in one of those old houses on the river. My parents will vouch for me."

"I've seen horror movies that start like that."

He smiled, almost laughed, so friendly it gave her a pang, then gestured in the opposite direction. "Now I rent an apartment not far that way. I guess that makes me a bit of a homebody."

"Those apartments?" Chris asked, pointing to the park. "High up or low down?"

"Pretty high up."

"Can you see farms?"

"Sure. I can see most of the city, and farms beyond." Traffic had started moving. A car passed too near the curb, splashing water onto the boulevard. Bretton stepped closer to Gwyn. "But I've never seen either of you."

"We've probably passed each other on the sidewalk or in the park without noticing."

"I would have noticed."

Gwyn wasn't sure what to say to that. She thought she would have noticed him, too.

"You know, I used to think of you as 'that nice woman.' Then as 'Chris's mother.' I'm glad to know your name at last."

At last. This was all very odd. She was standing in ankle-deep water with branches floating by and she couldn't tell whether or not the man in front of her was coming on to her. It should be easy to say goodbye and get going again but she felt glued to the sidewalk. He'd thought of her before, before they met. She wanted to ask when and why. But especially what—besides that she was a nice mother. How did the Dick and Jane comment fit into that? His opinion must have evolved.

She thought about apologizing for not introducing herself earlier or asking which big house his parents lived in or telling him about her carpenter great-great-grandfather— but all that came out of her mouth was, "Why is it still hot?"

Oh, that was scintillating. Better than going on gawking, though. "Doesn't it usually cool down after a rain like this?"

"Thirty-four Celsius. Humidity's making it feel like forty."

Chris gave an intense little nod. "That's what Ed Farley said. And he said there'd be a storm. With a chance of tord—tordid—"

"Tornadic activity," Bretton finished.

Doom and gloom, both of them, all the time. She should be fair. It was only most of the time. "We haven't had any of that."

"Not yet."

"Not yet?" Chris repeated.

Apparently unaware that she wanted to shake him, Bretton smiled at Gwyn. "We should do something." He held up the bag he was carrying. "Have dinner. With your family, too, I mean, of course."

"Chris and I had dinner, a picnic."

He looked disappointed. "Too bad. Another time."

"We're having a party soon," Chris said. Whispering to himself he counted off the days. "In five days. Do you want to come?"

"If we still have it," Gwyn said.

Chris stared at her.

"I mean of course we'll have it. Except if…" She wished she could back up. She could see what Chris was thinking. Except if the house blows away. Except if we all freeze without warning. All roads led back to *The Day After Tomorrow*.

"It's at our neighbors'," she explained to Bretton. "A barbecue for our kids to celebrate the end of school, just the four of us." Now she sounded unwelcoming. "But four is an awfully small party. So if you'd like to come…"

"If it's all right with your neighbor and the kids, I'd love to go."

She'd invited him. Now she'd have to tell him where she lived. "We're at 241 Dafoe. The barbecue will be next door, at 243. Right after school on Friday, around four o'clock."

"Great. I'll book off work early."

She picked Chris up, ignoring his indignant protests. At the corner she looked over her shoulder. Bretton hadn't moved. David, she supposed, if he was coming to her house. She nearly turned right as a precaution instead of left, but that would be silly. He knew her address now. He wasn't dangerous. Just frightening every time he spoke.

ONE BACKWARD GLANCE and she hurried away as fast as a woman carrying a five-year-old could hurry through water. It was beginning to be a familiar view.

"Gwyn?" He sloshed to her side. "Let me help you. I'll take Chris if he doesn't mind." He hadn't held a child since Sarah was a baby. Feeling awkward, he put out his hands to accept transfer if she chose but Chris pushed away from both of them and slid to the ground. His body language made it clear he intended to stay there. Thunder rumbled. "How far's your house?"

"Not far. We'll be fine."

"I'll go with you, make sure there aren't any trees or wires down."

She started walking again without telling him to stay away. She didn't point out what he could see, that there were no wires above ground and that the trees on both sides of the street were obviously standing.

"It started like this, Mom."

"What did?"

"The ice age in the movie."

She shot David a look, daring him to speak. "With heat like this?"

"No…"

"With humidity that makes it feel like 40?"

"No."

"It didn't then, did it?"

He's five, David reminded himself. *Keep it simple.* "This storm doesn't mean an ice age is coming, Chris."

They both looked surprised, Gwyn relieved, as well. Telling a partial truth didn't feel right. David wanted to elaborate, explain all that the storm could mean. He had to make himself keep quiet.

Gwyn stopped in front of a small bungalow with a screened porch in front. "Everything looks fine. A few branches down." She felt under the water with her foot. "Here's the path."

David supposed he should leave. "You probably don't have power."

"We have candles. And peanut butter," she said lightly.

He wanted to invite her to his place where he had coal-oil lamps and a month's worth of emergency supplies. Not only her, of course. All of them. Her child and the man who'd put a ring on her finger. If he was around. David was beginning to doubt it. "Do you have matches? And bread?"

When she smiled she looked younger. How old was she? "We have matches, bread, jam—"

"Bananas," Chris said. "Sardines."

The side door of the house on the right burst open and a woman waded to meet them holding her pant legs like a long skirt. "Oh, you're all right! Thank goodness. Gwyn, I don't know where Molly is! School got out hours ago."

"She's fine, Iris. We saw her at the Dairy Queen."

The woman's voice rose and she forgot to hold her cuffs out of the water. "The Dairy Queen? While I've been waiting and watching and calling everyone she knows?"

Gwyn took keys from her pocket. "Come in. We'll have tea."

"Tea!"

"Iced if there's no power for the kettle...if there's ice."

"Tea?"

"I don't have anything stronger. Juice?" She pushed open the door.

David got ready to say goodbye but a longer, louder rumble of thunder stopped him. "Molly's your daughter?" he asked. "I'll go back and look for her." Before he could ask for a description Iris's face cleared.

"Here she is, she's coming. What am I going to do with her? Molly!"

Chris had started back into the water. He did a couple of experimental jumps, splattering all of them.

"Hey, you." David picked him up and set him on the steps. "No going into the water until the storm's done. Maybe not even then. Did you know manhole covers can be forced up when the streets are flooded? You can be sucked into the sewers."

Chris and his mom both looked at him with wide eyes. Great, he was doing it again. No point holding back now. "And when the storm gets going and we've got lightning, you need to stay away from—"

"I've told him," Gwyn said.

"Windows, the telephone—"

CARON TODD   93

"Faucets, electrical outlets."

"Just to be on the safe side."

For the first time she gave him a truly friendly look. She was a woman who loved the safe side.

GWYN WONDERED if she should have asked David to join them. It didn't seem right to leave him outside. He had plenty of his own shelter, though, not one but two riverside addresses to keep the rain off his head.

There was no power but the basement was dry, the windows were in one piece and no water had leaked through the roof. While Iris and Molly argued about what "Come right home after school" meant, Gwyn helped Chris peel off his wet clothes and sent him to get dressed.

Still to the sound of mother/daughter conflict she went into her room to change, but she didn't think about raised voices and she hardly thought about wind and rain and flooded streets. Instead, she explored the realization that she wanted Dr. Doom and Gloom to come to the party.

At least as odd as that, he seemed to want to come, too. He'd even suggested dinner tonight. *With your family, of course.* That little bag? The thought made her smile.

When she went into the living room the fighting had stopped. Iris and Molly and Chris sat on the floor away from the windows, cross-legged as if they were camping. Thicker cloud cover had made the room as dark as it was at dusk. Thunder rolled on and on and lightning flickered with it. Gwyn made sure the television was unplugged, then lit the candles that were mostly for display.

"That's cozy," Iris said.

A cannon crack of thunder shook the house. Chris leapt at Gwyn and wrapped his arms around her waist. Without any gentle introductory tapping, rain and small hail pounded on the roof.

"Here we go again." Iris looked at her daughter with relief and disapproval. "At least I don't have to worry about you this time."

"I was fine, Mom."

"Information unavailable to me."

Gwyn joined the others on the floor. Chris stuck close to her, flinching with every crash of thunder. "I hope Dr. Bretton—David—I hope he's indoors."

"You mean Ph.D. David? Is that who that was?" Iris sounded intrigued. "He didn't seem awful, Gwyn."

"Nobody said he was awful."

"He isn't awful," Chris said indignantly.

"Nobody said he was, sweetheart."

"He's cool. He knows all kinds of things. Glaciers, mammoths, all that."

Iris kept her eyes on Gwyn. "That's very cool."

"We just ran into him," Gwyn said. "He lives near here, so he offered to make sure we got home safely." She didn't want to talk about David Bretton. "Molly, did you and your friends get free ice cream, too? Chris did."

It was a bad diversion. Iris asked suspiciously, "Which friends?" and the arguing resumed. Molly said she shouldn't have to provide a list, so Iris was determined to hear one. With a heavy sigh, Molly gave the names of three girls who were helping plan hurricane relief. She didn't mention a boy.

"How's the fund-raising going?" Gwyn asked.

Molly turned to her gratefully. "Really good. We decided students going to the year-end dance can bring money or clothes or toys to hand in at the door. The Red

Cross prefers money so they can spend it the way they need to but we figured some kids might not have the cash."

Chris asked, "Can I do it, too, Molly?"

"Sure. You can give me something to take to the dance."

Lightning flashed giving one bright glimpse of the room and the street outside. Water flowed the way it did in a creek in spring, rushing to the river.

"I might as well stay here until tomorrow evening," Molly said. "Instead of getting wet going back and forth."

Her mother disagreed. "Between now and babysitting there's a little thing called school."

"They'll cancel. Anyway, exams are over. It doesn't matter."

"Then I guess the dance doesn't matter."

And they were off again.

THE WATER WAS SHALLOW, but its current was fast enough to knock a small person down. Pea-size hail stung David's skin until he reached the thicker canopy of the old trees closer to the river. His parents' front door opened before he got to it showing three silhouettes and three soft pools of light.

"Here he is!" His father pulled him into the house and shut the door behind him. He and Sam carried flashlights, Miranda a candle under a glass chimney. "Let's have a look at you. Are you hurt?"

"Just wet."

"We called you but there was no answer. Your mother was worried."

"We all were." She sounded a little defensive.

"I wasn't," Sam said. "David can take care of himself." He pointed at the shredded paper bag still clinging to the plastic container holding his dinner. "See? He's been out hunting."

David knew they wouldn't let him dry off until he offered an explanation. "The first burst started while I was in Johansson's so I stayed dry through that one. Headed here after giving a friend a hand. But how are you three? How's the house?"

"All's well. We've been in the tower room, trying to make a single thermos of tea last the evening. The lanterns are lit and we've been watching the storm quite happily."

They didn't seem happy. David had the feeling he'd interrupted a fight, or at least some simmering conflict. His mother took the bag he carried and sent him up to his old bedroom to find dry clothes. Sam went, too, and set his flashlight on a shelf on its end so it lit the room.

"There's no more than ten minutes between here and Johansson's," he said. "What really happened?"

"Like I said, I helped a friend. What really happened here?"

Sam didn't pretend not to understand. "Nothing. They're on me all the time, making worried little noises. Exactly the way you do."

"None of us make worried noises."

"You think them. I can feel you think them."

What did he expect? "I'll tell you something else I'm thinking. She's not married."

Sam took a moment to get on the same wavelength. He looked relieved not to be the center of attention anymore. "The woman from the museum? That's the friend?"

"She invited me to a barbecue, a year-end party." His conscience niggled at him and he supplied more details. "It wasn't completely her idea. I suggested dinner first—I forgot about the possibility of a husband."

"You mean the likelihood of a husband."

"Okay, the likelihood. Anyway, I forgot and invited her to dinner. With the water rushing over our feet and people moving all around as if they hardly knew where they were, I held up a bag containing dinner for one and offered to share it with her entire family. It seemed logical for a minute or two. She said they'd already eaten, but then her son invited me. And she seconded the invitation."

"Because her son put her on the spot."

David finished with the clincher. "It's with her neighbor and their children. Just the four of them."

"Husbands could be on a fishing trip."

"When their kids are celebrating the end of school? No way." The more he thought about it the more certain he was she didn't have a husband on the sidelines. She had the look of a person who had worried alone for a long time. Who would be nuts enough to leave her? He didn't like the thought of her being the one who needed to leave someone, someone who didn't treat her well. "Her name's Gwyn. It's perfect for her. Like Guinevere."

"Oh, save us." Sam looked interested, though. "Those games of Sarah's left their mark on you. What does the fair maiden do?"

"I have no idea."

"You don't know anything about her, do you?"

"Sure I do." He knew he liked her. They looked at the world so differently that being drawn to her didn't make sense. That made him like her even more.

CHAPTER SIX

SHE WAS BRAVE. That was his waking thought.

David lay on his childhood bed, a fan stirring the heat, the same branches shading the window that had shaded it all his life. Sleepily, he looked for evidence to support this new idea.

Pictures and feelings came to mind. There was something about Gwyn's determination to protect her son that was about more than fear or control. If they'd lived hundreds of years ago and she faced an enemy horde instead of frightening news he could see her pushing Chris behind her and brandishing a sword....

Sarah's influence again. It had never shown itself before.

Somewhere out back a chain saw started up. David pulled on his clothes and hurried downstairs, noting Sam's empty room as he went.

His mother stood on the porch with a glass of orange juice in hand. "Good morning, dear. No coffee, I'm afraid. The power's still out."

"Dad and Sam cleaning up?"

"Not your father. He's out searching for a hot drink."

She pulled David closer to the window so he could watch Sam making a pile of fallen branches at the side of the yard. "He still hasn't said a word about why he's here. I don't want to push him."

"But you'd like to know what's up?"

"He didn't even call! The last we heard from him was a letter from Kandahar a month ago and then he was here, at the door that evening, the evening I called you about breakfast. *Hi, Mom.* Simple as that. I said something welcoming like 'What on earth are you doing here?' but he didn't answer." After a moment she added, "He takes pills to sleep. Your father said—"

"What did Dad say?"

"He said Sam seems hollow."

The word fit. "He's worn out, Mom. It's like we're always reading in the paper—the armed forces are underfunded and underequipped and they don't have enough personnel for the missions they're asked to do. They've given him a good long leave. That's all."

"He'll tell you what's wrong. One of these days."

David wasn't expecting any heart-to-hearts. Sam didn't have the kind of job he could discuss. "I talked to Sarah yesterday." It felt like a week ago. "She says she'll come home as soon as she can."

Miranda's face brightened. "Wonderful! Sarah always brings out the best in him."

That was a fond belief of their mother's. Good thing she hadn't heard Sam on the river.

"It's exactly what he needs," she went on. "A bit of normalcy, the five of us together. The three of you." She touched his arm. "David? You'll look out for him, won't you?"

"He's hard to look out for, Mom. He doesn't like it. But I'll do my best."

DAVID LEFT THE HOUSE and began walking in the direction of the museum. During the night the water had receded enough to expose the curb. City cleanup crews were picking up debris, unclogging drains, sawing branches.

When he'd gone half a block a shout came from behind him. "Wait, David!" Carrying two paper coffee cups, his father hurried to join him. He arrived puffing. "Where are you off to?"

"I need to check things at work. Then I'll come back and help with the yard."

Richard handed him one of the cups. "I'll go partway with you."

They went slowly, sipping their drinks. David tried not to show his concern at his father's labored progress. Richard used to walk downtown and back every day.

"I'm not actually supposed to have coffee. Did you hear about that? No bacon, either."

"That's rough, Dad."

"Coffee and bacon. They're what make morning morning! What good's an egg, a pancake or a tomato sandwich without bacon? I quit smoking, drinking, cheeseburgers, ice cream, walking on the tracks…when did we get so fainthearted?"

For a week or two after every checkup, Richard tended to rant. David righted a toppled bus stop bench. He sat down and waited until his father did, too. "When you saw your doctor did he do anything besides tell you to avoid life's pleasures?"

"He did plenty, the sadist, but nothing you need to hear about. It wasn't all bad. He said I could run a marathon any time I liked."

"Did he mention if he thought you'd survive it?"

Richard let out a bark of laughter. "Come to think of it, he didn't." His eyes were bright with amusement, but that didn't last long. "Sam's not looking good, is he? The two of you were upstairs for quite a while last night. Did he tell you what's going on?"

"He made it clear he didn't want to tell me anything."

"I did an Internet search for stories about the Canadian Forces in Afghanistan. Didn't find anything major that seemed related to Sam."

"So he'll keep on keeping quiet and we'll keep on wondering. That sounds about normal."

Richard nodded. "Normal for you, too."

David looked at his father in surprise.

"I'd better go help your mother. We'll see you when you're able, eh?" Richard had got his breath back. He strode off at his usual energetic pace leaving his son sorting out the possibility that his parents thought something was wrong with him, too.

GWYN SPENT THE MORNING throwing out spoiled food and picking up branches wherever the water had receded enough to allow it. Her garden was ruined. It wasn't much to start with, just single rows of carrots, beans, potatoes and corn and two tomato plants, more to give Chris the experience of planting and harvesting than out of any real hope of reducing the grocery bill. Some of the plants had been beaten down by the rain, others had let go of the soil and floated away.

She was surprised Chris didn't stomp around predicting they'd all be frozen by noon. He was quiet and calm when he woke up. The evening must have been good for him. While the storm raged they'd played famous people, then charades, then geography. They'd all gotten as comfortable as they could on the living room floor, taking turns telling stories until, one by one, they'd fallen asleep. Maybe they'd managed to turn the storm into an adventure.

That hope faded late in the afternoon. Gwyn was getting ready for work and preparing a dinner for Molly and Chris when she got a call from Ms. Gibson.

"We had a problem today," the teacher said. "Christopher pushed another boy."

"He what?"

"His explanation was that he was the wind."

"The other boy wasn't hurt?"

"He's fine. The three of us sat down and talked things over. Philip accepted Chris's apology. Chris lost a point for his house, punishment enough I think with so little time to earn more."

He never lost points. He won them for building towers that wouldn't fall, for understanding levers, for discovering that red, yellow and blue mixed together made brown.

"Mrs. Sinclair, given our conversation the other day I know this won't please you. I want to put in a referral to the school psychologist. It's late for this year, but she can get right to work in the fall."

Boys pushed each other all the time, didn't they? Not Chris, though. And this wasn't the boys-will-be-boys kind of pushing. He'd said he was the wind. "I'll talk to him. The storm upset him."

"Many of the children found it exciting. As they did *The Day After Tomorrow*. I don't see Christopher's concern about the weather as the problem, Mrs. Sinclair. I see it as a symptom."

A symptom of inadequate parenting, she meant. Gwyn

couldn't argue. Not if none of the other children were frightened.

Minutes after she hung up Chris arrived home, rumpled, flushed, looking ready to either shout or cry. "I lost a point."

"Ms. Gibson told me." Gwyn followed him into his room. He sat on his bed looking at the mural, eyes bright with tears. "You know not to push other children."

"I didn't push. I blew."

"Philip could have been hurt."

A tear rolled down his cheek. "I didn't try to hurt him."

Gwyn looked at the drawings on his table. Were they symptoms, too? "Why so many drawings all the same?"

He gave a big shrug, shoulders up to his ears.

She should try to be open-ended, the way articles about encouraging creativity suggested. No assumptions, no judgments. She picked up the picture on top of the pile. "Tell me about this one."

He shrugged again, avoiding her eyes. It wasn't that he had nothing to say. He chose not to speak. He was putting up a barrier, closing her out.

The doorbell rang.

Molly stood on the step with a book bag over one shoulder and an armload of games. "We've got fun for the early evening and stories for bedtime." She looked over Gwyn's shoulder. "Hey, Chris! Why don't you get some boots on? We can go to the park first." She smiled at Gwyn. "It's one big wading pool."

"I don't think so—"

"We won't go near the river. Mom already told me."

Chris squeezed past them and out the door. "Ready, Molly?" His eyes were still red.

"Mosquito repellent—"

Molly patted her bag. "Don't worry, Mrs. Sinclair. I've thought of everything."

Her new sitter's confidence wasn't all that reassuring. Gwyn generally made an effort to think of everything, too, but that didn't stop her son from telegraphing his distress every day. No matter how late she stayed up or how many magazine articles she read or how many lists she made, she couldn't avoid all the mistakes that were waiting for her. How was she ever going to help Chris reach eighteen in one piece, strong, healthy, unafraid?

FOR THE NEXT THREE DAYS Gwyn raked branches and swept up deposited dirt each morning, waited for but didn't receive another call from Ms. Gibson each afternoon and handed Chris over to Molly each evening. He slept well at night, worn out from playing in the fresh air with his new sitter.

The day before the party she bought new tomato plants from the grocery store and when Chris got home from school they went out together to plant them. They had already dug over the rain-compacted soil and replanted a few faster-growing vegetables.

They wore hats and slathered on sunscreen. Reminding her of the weather announcers' repeated advice, Chris carried out a pitcher of water and two glasses. Every few minutes he stopped digging and jumped up to guzzle water. He got very insistent if she didn't guzzle, too.

"My tummy's swimming. I can't drink another drop." She patted his protruding belly. "And you've got a drum there."

Chris tapped his stomach. He seemed to be trying for an actual tune but Gwyn hadn't managed to identify it before Iris's side door swung open and the sound of shouting reached them. Iris stalked across her backyard, her body stiff, and threw a bunched-up plastic bag into the garbage. Back into the house with a bang.

Chris said, "They're sure mad."

"They sure are."

"I wonder why they're mad."

Iris reappeared. She hurried to the garbage, retrieved the bag and returned to the house, closing the door. No bang this time, but a very definite click.

"They'll sort it out." Gwyn uncoiled the hose and started watering the new plants. A breeze blew cooling spray back at her.

She flicked the hose at Chris, sprinkling his shirt. His expression went quickly from surprise to determination. He tried to wrestle the hose from her and when she wouldn't let go he picked up his water glass.

"Oh, no!" She backed up, laughing.

His arm swung and water arced out of the glass, splashing onto her knees. He ran to the house, well out of the hose's reach.

"You got me!"

He looked very pleased about it.

"Better go in now and wash for dinner. I'll be right there."

Iris had come outside again. "Can I have the hose? I've got someone to douse, too."

"Everything all right?"

"I guess you heard the excitement. Can you believe this girl? First of all, she blows off school and goes shopping with her friends. She gets home, all furtive with this shopping bag, so I tell her to show me what's in it. And what's in it is a slip. They can call it a dress all they want. It's a slip. The very few parts of her body, her twelve-year-old body, you can't see in this dress you can sure see *through* it."

"Oh, Iris. I'm sorry. I paid her last night."

"It isn't your fault how she uses the money. One of these days that girl is going to hold up a shirt and say, 'See my new shirt?' and I won't see anything. Because there won't be anything. They'll be selling kids shirts that aren't even there. And it'll be forty-five bucks."

"At least you'll know it will fit."

Iris snorted. "One size fits all! She says I want her to look ugly. I think I do."

CHAPTER SEVEN

THE AFTERNOON OF the end-of-school party Iris was on edge. "What's keeping that girl of mine? She knows we're having company." David had arrived right on time and promptly started answering questions from Chris about the storm. "She knows we're having steak. There's no point having steak if you're going to be late."

"School's out. She'll have thrown away her watch with her timetable."

"We can't wait any longer." Iris lifted the lid of the barbecue and a smoky, meaty smell reached Gwyn's nose. There were rib-eye steaks, pieces of chicken and skewers of shrimp with mushrooms and peppers.

They were settled in the shade with their plates full of meats and salads when Molly finally sailed in. She really did sail, Gwyn thought, so full of light and energy.

"What a day!" she called. "I had the best, best day!"

Iris seemed to have trouble staying angry in the face of such happiness. "You're not going to have the best, best dinner. It's cooked, cooked, cooked."

Molly smiled widely. "I don't want the meat anyway, Mom."

"You don't want the meat," Iris repeated, her voice flat.

"I don't think I can support eating meat anymore."

"You don't want the rib-eye steak I bought for you."

Molly didn't seem to notice her mother's tone. "Chris will eat mine, won't you, Chris?"

He had put down his fork and his steak knife. "Why don't you support eating meat, Molly?"

Oh boy, Gwyn thought. Thanks.

Iris said, "We don't need to hear why right now, not while some of us are trying to enjoy our dinner. Molly, you haven't said hello to our guests."

Molly's cheeks colored, but she swung around to smile at everyone, wider at David. "Nice to meet you, Dr. Bretton. Chris sure loves going to your museum. He's always telling me about the displays." Duty over, she gave a little jump of excitement and turned back to her mother. "Everybody's taking off for the lake tomorrow—"

"Everybody?"

"Luke and his friends. To celebrate the start of summer. We're going to Falcon Lake, they've got horse rides—"

"What do you mean, taking off?"

"Luke's brother got his license and he's using their dad's car. It's like for three days, in a tent. I've never done that before—"

"No, Molly, absolutely not."

Molly went still. "Mom."

"Wash your hands, then come and eat your dinner."

"Mom."

"We'll talk about it later."

"Mom." Molly's voice had become more intense with every repetition of the word. She stood, chest heaving. Gwyn didn't know if she was going to shout or cry. All the light she'd brought with her was gone. Iris stared at her plate, grimly cutting into her steak, then chewing as if it was a job to get done.

"Fine." Head up, Molly glided to the picnic table. She was like Audrey Hepburn in *Roman Holiday,* sad but dignified, accepting her role in life. With measured, deliberate motions, she opened the lid of the barbecue and used the tongs to pick up a steak, a chicken thigh and a skewer of shrimp. Down went the lid, with a soft clunk. She piled on potato salad and coleslaw, then sat next to Chris, sighed and began to eat with even less enjoyment than her mother.

After an uncomfortable silence David asked, "School's over, then?"

"Yes, Dr. Bretton."

"So next year is—"

"Grade eight."

"Molly's a very good student," Gwyn said. It seemed as if it might be better to ignore her, let her simmer until she was calm, but ignoring her wasn't possible. Her disappointment was a magnet. "Since she started babysitting Chris, my days have been going so much more smoothly. She's good with kids."

"Maybe you'll come work for us when you're older. That's exactly the kind of person we need."

Gwyn looked at David with pretend indignation. "We've barely met and already you're stealing my babysitter?"

"When she's much, much older." He caught Molly's eye and smiled. "Do you have plans for the summer?"

"Not anymore."

"Molly! That's enough."

"Right." She jumped up and banged her plate onto her chair. "In front of everybody like I'm a little kid. Thanks, Mom." She stomped into the house. Even from the backyard they heard an inside door slam shut.

Iris looked from Gwyn to David, her face red. "I'm so sorry."

"No, that was clumsy of me. Iris, if you spent half an hour with my family you wouldn't give this little ruckus a second thought."

"She's twelve. He's thirteen and he already has a reputation. Obviously she can't go camping with him. And she does have plans. She's babysitting for Gwyn for one thing and she says she's going to read *War and Peace.* I don't think she will, but she claims she is. And she goes to stay with my aunt for a week or two every summer."

Poor Iris, trying to defend both herself and Molly. "Iris's aunt lives on a farm a couple of hours from the city," Gwyn explained. "Every time Molly visits she comes back full of stories about kittens and calves and foals. There always seems to be something newborn."

"Chris should go with her this time," Iris said. "He's old enough."

"He'd love it."

"Go to the farm?" Chris asked. "Me and Molly?"

"Molly and I."

He looked confused for a second until he realized his grammar was being corrected, not the plan. He'd never gone anywhere without Gwyn, and she'd never gone anywhere without him. He could use a few days paying attention to farm animals rather than weather forecasts.

"When's Molly going?" he asked.

"I don't know, hon," Iris said. "As soon as possible."

IRIS HADN'T TAKEN a bite of her dinner since her daughter had slammed into the house. Chris had been watching the action, taking in the tensions and undercurrents, looking doubtfully at his meat, even more at his curled pink shrimp. The tail was still on and had received quite an examination.

"Not sure you want to eat your crustacean?" David asked.

Chris perked up. "It's a crustacean? Like a lobster?"

"You can tell because there's no backbone and the body's in segments."

"Those flat little bugs are crustaceans, too, right? Sowbugs? That's funny, that bugs and shrimps could both be crustaceans."

David glanced at Gwyn, surprised a five-year-old could even pronounce crustacean, let alone know that sowbugs were included in their number. She was watching her child with that quiet warmth he remembered from their museum visits.

Chris had pulled the shrimp off the skewer so he could peer at it more closely. David thought Iris was going to cry any minute. Her meal was more or less in ruins.

"Pull the tail off and pop the whole thing in your mouth," he told Chris. He demonstrated with one of his. It was tough from overcooking, and cold now.

Chris did as suggested, pleased, like a kid pulling a Christmas cracker. He looked into the hollow where the tail had been attached to the body and absentmindedly pushed the shrimp into his mouth. He chewed once, then stopped, teeth clenched over his bottom lip, a deer-in-the-headlights expression on his face. David ate another shrimp, hoping Chris would get the idea. Sometimes you just had to be a man about these get-togethers.

"I'm so sorry," Iris said. "Spit it out, hon. I never cooked shrimp before. They're good in restaurants."

"They're good here, too," Gwyn said.

David took a second skewer to underscore that point. "They're an acquired taste for children."

Chris had succeeded in swallowing. "I thought it would be more like fish and chips. But it was good."

David gave him an approving look. "Did you do anything special for your last day of school?"

"Yup, we had sort of a party."

"Partying from sunup to sundown, eh?"

"The parents came and had juice and we sang to them." In a mumble he added, "And danced."

"It was lovely," Gwyn said.

"So that's it for kindergarten. Next year we have desks."

Iris offered seconds of everything and when she had no takers announced she would clear up from the main course before dessert.

Gwyn got up to help. She touched David's shoulder, a quick, light gesture that seemed to surprise her. He found himself standing, consciously keeping his arms at his sides so he wouldn't put them around her. He was full of a very odd feeling, one that wasn't entirely explained by biological drives. The feeling was that she belonged in his arms, that they'd both be fine once she got there.

"I'll carry in the salads," he said.

"No, no. Why don't you play with Chris? Poor guy, this was supposed to be fun. There are water pistols and balls beside the garage, if you want them."

"Great. We'll play catch."

She leaned close and he had to work harder to keep his arms down. She whispered, "He's terrible at catch."

"Is he? Not for long." David backed away from her. "Hey, Chris! Want to get that football?" He nearly laughed at the look on the boy's face. As if he wanted a football even less than he wanted an ice age.

"Football's all about physics. Trajectory. Inertia." He

didn't expect Chris to understand, but he was pretty sure he'd
be intrigued. And he was. He ran for the ball. Well…strolled
for it, with a few assessing glances in David's direction.

"I'M SO SORRY," Iris whispered in the kitchen. "Molly and
me fighting in front of him. He's *so* nice."

"When he isn't frightening children."

"Oh, stop that. Kindness flows out of him. He'd never
mean to scare anyone."

"He wouldn't, would he?"

"Don't be silly about this, Gwyn. He's nice, he likes you,
you like him. Don't go thinking of excuses to avoid him."

"I don't know. I haven't even looked at a man in all
these years."

"All the more reason."

"He *is* nice, isn't he?"

Iris gave her a little push. "Out! I'll cut the cake. You
go bat your eyelashes."

Gwyn had splurged on a three-layer dense chocolate
cake from Johansson's. She was splurging a lot lately.
She'd have to stop or she'd be all splurged out before
Christmas. "Cut a piece for Molly, too. If anything'll help
her feel better, that cake will."

"Let me worry about Molly. You worry about that
gorgeous man out there."

"Now I've got butterflies, all this talk." Gwyn went out
the door feeling exactly the way she had in grade ten going
alone into the school auditorium for the spring dance.

They weren't throwing the football. David sat in a lawn
chair and Chris stood in front of him, talking earnestly.
She couldn't hear what he was saying until she was a few
feet away.

"Why did the movie have an ice age, then?"

"That was a complicated scenario. Remember what the characters said about fresh water from melting ice diluting the salt water of the ocean?"

Chris nodded.

"That's the first part of the cooling trend in the movie. Because warm ocean currents bring heat north from the equator. Wait." David felt in his pockets and pulled out a small coiled notebook and a pen. He drew a circle, then several squiggles.

"See? The warm currents flow north, then sink and circle back to the equator. If the currents aren't salty enough, they can't sink. They stop flowing. Heat is no longer brought north and the northern hemisphere cools. Now, lots in the movie wasn't realistic, but all of that can actually happen. There's evidence it did happen during the last ice age—"

"Dessert?" Gwyn said. Both faces turned to her. "It's chocolate cake and ice cream. Chris, go wash your hands." He didn't move so she added, "Now."

"Again?"

"Again."

She waited until the kitchen door swung closed behind him. "I suppose this is an example of what you teach at your day camp. Dressed up science fiction."

David stood. "I was explaining how the ocean conveyer belt works—"

"You weren't invited here, to a celebration, to a light-hearted dinner, to scare my son."

"I'm sorry, Gwyn. He asked."

"The answer to any question Chris asks you, if he ever

has the opportunity to ask you a question again, is something along the lines of 'It's okay, Chris. Nothing bad is going to happen.'"

"That's a great answer. It'll be a comfort to him for years to come. He'll thank you for it, Gwyn, when the oceans have submerged the country's coastlines and water's rationed because the glaciers are gone."

"You don't get it, do you? He's having a real problem. He's acting as if the movie he watched was a documentary."

"I do get it. What puzzles me is why you don't."

"You're not listening—"

"I'm listening to both of you. You might as well be speaking different languages. And I'm the interpreter—"

"How did you get in the middle? Just because I asked you a couple of questions? Don't you understand what he's afraid of—"

"I do. Perfectly. And he's not alone."

"He's alone in his class! None of the other kids are afraid. They recognize fantasy when they see it. They recognize a normal summer storm. Once he found out the mammoth was real he was convinced other parts of the movie must be real, too—"

"Right."

"Like an ice shelf in the Antarctic breaking apart and the damn ocean submerging New York—" She stopped, thinking of the floods in China and India, even in Europe where monsoons didn't happen.

"An ice shelf did collapse," David said. "The Larsen B shelf, the same one that fictionally collapsed in the movie, really did collapse shortly after filming."

Gwyn felt her body slow down, the way it did for bad

news. "All right. So there's a real frozen mammoth with grass in its mouth and a real collapsed ice shelf. That doesn't have to add up to a real ice age."

"I agree."

"Good. Then you can make that clear to Chris."

"But they could add up to real climate change."

He wouldn't stop. She couldn't believe she'd invited him—well, she hadn't, Chris had. She couldn't believe she'd spent a minute thinking about his eyes. If stubbornness had a color, it was brown, dark, dark coffee brown.

He kept talking, delivering each sentence in a steady, measured tone. Gwyn's head started to ache.

"Since Larsen B splintered from the main ice sheet the glacier adjacent to it has been melting into the Antarctic Ocean. Glaciers all over the world are melting. There are signs now that the conveyer belt system may be slowing. It's possible that one day it really will stop. Not in a few days the way it did in the movie and not causing an intense and sudden ice age, but certainly dramatically changing the world we know."

"I don't think you want dessert, do you?"

"I sure don't."

Iris's voice came from the direction of the house. "There you are. Visiting instead of helping me, Gwyn?"

She must have heard them. Maybe the whole neighborhood had heard them. Gwyn had no idea if they'd been yelling or shouting in whispers. "I'm sorry, Iris, I'll be right there."

"We were saying goodbye." David walked past her, his voice warming as he reached Iris. "Thanks very much. It was a terrific meal. I hope you and Molly have a good summer."

"Thanks. It's shown real promise so far."

CHAPTER EIGHT

IT WAS NEARLY A MONTH since Mrs. Henderson had let Chris watch the video. He still checked the weather channel every day, with one stuffed animal or another by his side. The mammoth book, renewed twice, was still in Gwyn's top drawer, under pairs of white panty hose. She and Chris were stalled, and she didn't know what to do about it.

"Molly will take you to the fireworks, unless you get too sleepy. Stick close to her. I don't want the two of you to get separated. And don't go near the river."

"Okay, Mom."

She touched his chin to make sure she had his attention. "That's important. The water's high after the storm and the river's full of fast currents."

He nodded, his face serious. When the doorbell rang, the unchildish solemnity vanished and he ran to let Molly in.

"Did you bring the marshmallows?"

"You kidding? Like we'd watch fireworks without marshmallows." Molly let him peek inside her backpack. "What else do you see?"

He nearly put his head right in looking. "What?"

She dug around and pulled a package partway out.

"Sparklers!"

"That's so nice of you," Gwyn said. Molly always

brought something fun, games or books from home, bubble gum, glue and construction paper. "You're sure you're okay with this later shift? It'll be close to one before I'm home."

"No problem."

"You can always call your mom if it bothers you to be alone at that hour."

"Sure. But I was wondering, is it okay if I have some friends over, Mrs. Sinclair? They wouldn't distract me from Chris. I thought we could all play with him and go to the fireworks together. It'd be fun."

It might even be good for him. "If it's not too many and you keep your mind on safety—"

"I promise!" Molly looked so happy Gwyn was glad and worried at the same time.

She bent down to give Chris a goodbye kiss followed by a good-night kiss and hug. "Have fun." She looked at Molly. "And be careful."

"Have a good evening at work, Mrs. Sinclair."

THE EVENING DIDN'T START very happily. Mr. Scott was back. "Already?" Gwyn asked Dr. Li, one of the residents. "He was doing so well."

"There's no air-conditioning at home. His wife's arranging to have a window unit installed. We'd better get a break from the heat soon or our seniors will be dropping like flies. I'm seeing people all over the hospital like this."

Gwyn put her pen and notepad in her pocket and went into the tiny kitchen behind the nursing station. She loaded the top tier of a stainless steel cart with carafes of water and juice, put a fresh tray of glasses on the second tier and rolled the cart into the corridor.

At each door she double-checked to see which patients

had fluid or dietary restrictions, then went in and poured requested drinks, raised or lowered heads of beds and found eyeglasses or magazines or crossword puzzle books. She took extra time chatting, because no one was happy to be in hospital for the July long weekend.

One patient didn't seem to know or care. She'd come in from a nursing home two days before with dehydration after the building's air-conditioning failed. Thin, bent and silent, she sat in bed with the side rails up. No one could tell if the hearing aids on both ears and the thick glasses that magnified her eyes helped her see or hear anything.

There was a push fluids sign over the bed. Gwyn stood with a glass in hand, a straw steadied between two fingers.

"Hi, Bess." They'd been told to use her first name. She'd been diagnosed with dementia and the nurses thought if she remembered anything about herself it would be the name she'd been called all her life. According to the date on her wristband she was ninety-eight. What a place to come to after all those years of work and plans.

There was no response. Gwyn touched her hand. The papery skin was bruised from attempts to start an intravenous. "Here's some juice for you. Apple juice."

She slowly waved the glass in front of Bess, hoping the movement would help her see it, then touched the straw to her lips. They quivered, then formed a circle around it. They pulled and worked, and a small amount of juice traveled up the straw. It was a lot of effort for one sip.

Gwyn continued to offer the glass, talking and smiling in case something did get through the barriers Bess lived behind, until a quarter of the juice was gone. Then the old woman's eyes closed. It was a good start. She left the glass on the over-bed table and went on to the next room.

Two visitors, a man and a woman, blocked the doorway. Muttering apologies they moved aside and she saw a familiar face, puffy and pale now, resting against the pillow. Clear tubing looped from his nostrils around his ears to the oxygen outlet on the wall.

"Mr. Scott!"

"I told you I'd miss you."

"I missed you, too. You're the only person I can beat at rummy."

He chuckled wheezily. "Wait till my meds kick in. We'll see who wins then."

Gwyn rolled the head of the bed up farther and his labored breathing began to ease. While she poured the small amount of water he was allowed to drink over the next hour, the man visiting him gave her a warm glance up and down.

"Now I see why you're always checking in here, Eddie." He smiled at Gwyn. "I'll bet you're hard on my brother's pulse."

That was one she'd heard a time or two. She smiled back. "I don't check it, so I wouldn't know."

"She doesn't care, either," Mr. Scott said. "The weaker I am, the better, as far as she's concerned."

"Anything else I can get you, Mr. Scott?"

His visitor chuckled suggestively and the woman with him made an annoyed sound.

"How about some luck?"

"That I wish you every day." She smiled at all three as she left the room.

THE NEXT TIME she popped in Mr. Scott's visitors were gone. He'd slid into a position that made breathing more difficult so she lowered the head of the bed and stood on one side, an arm hooked under his. He pushed with his feet and she pulled until he was settled again. The exertion left him breathing heavily, as if he'd run up a few flights of stairs. Gwyn wound the head of the bed back up.

She squeezed lotion from the bottle on his table and began rubbing his heels and elbows to help prevent skin breakdown.

"Sorry about my brother. He's nervous in the hospital."

"No need to apologize. He seemed very nice."

"I told him not to talk to you like that next time. It's not right, you a young mother." He handed her his glasses. She folded the arms and tucked them inside their case. "Too young to be alone, in fact. Not that it's my business."

"I'm not alone, Mr. Scott."

"Your son, you mean."

Again, she was struck by an urge to confide in this man. It was supposed to be the other way around.

"I did meet someone I…sort of liked." He looked interested so she went on, "We got quite angry with each other, though. Even if we hadn't I don't think I'm his type."

"You'd be any man's type," Mr. Scott said gallantly, through wheezing. "And they'd be lucky at that." He waved a hand at her denials. "What did the two of you get angry about? If you don't mind me asking."

"Global warming."

His eyebrows shot up. He began to laugh, but it changed to a fit of coughing. When he could he said, "Is that what young people are arguing about these days? I thought maybe he whistled at you—like we used to—and you were offended."

It was hard to picture David Bretton whistling at anyone. "I don't think I would have minded that."

"Here's what you do. You go for a nice walk with him.

Get ice cream. My wife and I liked doing that, back when I was allowed to have it. You can't get angry walking and eating ice cream."

"That's very good advice if I ever see him again. Chris has been mad at me lately. Maybe your strategy would work for him."

Mr. Scott shook his head. "You're a hard case." He was beginning to sound tired. She shouldn't have kept him talking so long. "I'll work on you while I'm here. We'll get you turned around."

She touched his hand. "We'll get *you* turned around."

"Deal." He closed his eyes and all she heard was the quiet flow of oxygen.

THE REST OF THE FAMILY had taken off for the cottage but the museum was open for the holiday and David had agreed to work. He spent part of the day answering visitors' questions and the rest preparing for day camp. He'd decided to vary the activities and experiments every second week to allow for kids who wanted to learn more about what was happening to the climate.

At work and later at his apartment, his conscience kept nagging him. Gwyn wasn't one of those who wanted to learn more about it. That was clear from the first. But he had to keep badgering her, didn't he, as if he had a right to insist on teaching her anything. As if badgering her would put him on her list of favorite people.

After dinner he found G. Sinclair in the phone book and dialed the number. He let it ring long enough that someone running from their backyard would have time to reach it. Then a little longer. There was no answer. Maybe she and Chris had gone to see the fireworks.

He turned on the CD player, starting k.d. lang's version of "After the Gold Rush," and when he heard the whistle of the first rocket going up at the Forks he went onto the balcony to watch the bursts of white and red sparks flare and fan, falling in sparkles to the ground.

BY THE TIME they heard the first whistle and bang of the fireworks Mr. Scott was wide awake again, after a coughing spell that had left him a little blue around the mouth. Gwyn could see him straining to look out the window, so she opened the drapes wide, loosened the bed's brakes and rolled it as close to the sill as the oxygen tubing would allow.

"You're a sweetheart," he whispered.

She moved a chair to the bed and sat beside him. "Chris is watching with the babysitter. Can your wife see from your home?"

"I told her to go to the Forks with our neighbor. Poor girl. She's had a rough time with me lately. Says it's what she signed up for."

"Not just the good times."

"We've had plenty of those."

"And you'll have more. Different, maybe, but still good."

"You don't need to stay with me. I know you're busy."

"It was on the list Mrs. Byrd gave me when I came in this afternoon. Watch fireworks with Mr. Scott."

He smiled and relaxed, every now and then muttering his appreciation at a particularly large and colorful display. In the quiet moments between bursts she could hear wheezing deep in his chest. He was much sicker this time. In spite of the noise he fell asleep before the fireworks ended. A nurse came in and helped her push the bed back in place.

Having his blood pressure checked and his pulse and respirations counted hardly disturbed him.

Two hours later Gwyn took one last walk through the ward checking that no one was too cold from the air-conditioning, that water carafes were full and call buttons were pinned within reach. Mr. Scott still slept but two ladies in 405 were wide awake and visiting.

"You're off, are you, dear? Is that it for a few days now?"

"I'll be back Tuesday."

"Have a good rest of the weekend, then."

AS SHE LEFT the well-lit bus stop Mr. Scott's comments came back to mind. Gwyn wasn't used to being in conflict with anyone and now two people were angry with her, the person dearest to her in the world and someone she hardly knew.

Maybe Mrs. Henderson and Ms. Gibson belonged on the list, too. Should she have tried to work things out with Mrs. Henderson? Negotiate expectations? No. Hours of television and layers of repellent could be negotiated, but not attitude. Chris had felt in the woman's way and that wasn't right. She definitely should have made an effort to carry on a useful discussion with Ms. Gibson. Or should she just invite everyone for ice cream?

Taking a walk wouldn't help her and David Bretton get along. They could argue quite easily no matter how pleasant their surroundings were. They'd managed it at a children's party in her neighbor's yard, after all. But if they added ice cream to the picture, could they still? If they were taking little bites of maple walnut and catching the drips before they ran down the cone, would anger be an option?

She unlocked the side door and went into the kitchen. The house was in darkness except for a flickering light from the television. Molly appeared before Gwyn reached the living room.

"Hi," she whispered. "How was work?"

"Quiet. Did you make it to the park?"

She nodded. "Chris was as good as gold. We got back around eleven-thirty and he fell straight to sleep."

"Your friends went along?"

Molly hesitated. "Yeah."

A deeper voice came from the living room. "Hi, Mrs. Sinclair." A boy emerged. "Thanks for letting me come over tonight."

Gwyn recognized the boy from the Dairy Queen, the one she thought was Luke McKinley. No one else appeared. "Where are the others, Molly?"

"They couldn't come. Only Luke could come." She gave a quick, bright smile. "We'd better go, so you can get to sleep."

"I agree. And then tomorrow you'd better come back and talk to me."

"Oh."

"Good night, Molly."

Neither of the kids moved. Luke rubbed his head, making the hair stand up in short spikes, little-boyish, and looked at her with what she guessed was supposed to be a sheepish grimace. Something about him got under Gwyn's skin. He wasn't rude. He wasn't quite polite, either. He seemed...smooth. Smoothness in a thirteen-year-old went down wrong.

"Your son is a lot of fun," he began, his voice too loud and too friendly.

Gwyn held a finger to her lips. "Good night, Luke. See you tomorrow, Molly."

CHAPTER NINE

AFTER THEIR LATE NIGHT Gwyn and Chris had a slow and groggy start to the day, eating breakfast on the porch in their pajamas, then snuggling with the stuffed animals while they read about the International Space Station. It was the most relaxing morning they'd had for a long time but when Gwyn got ready to tend the garden Chris's tight worried focus snapped back into place and he insisted on staying inside to watch his once daily weather report.

Soon after Gwyn began sprinkling the garden Molly joined her. "I guess you want to talk to me." She sounded apprehensive but defiant.

Gwyn turned the valve that cut off the flow of water. "You weren't honest with me yesterday."

"You said I could have a friend over."

"Is that how it went?"

Molly stared at the ground. "I really did call some other people, too, not just Luke, but everybody was going to a party. Luke was the only one who said he'd come." She looked up, her face vulnerable. "It was so nice of him to pick being with me. I couldn't uninvite him."

"Does your mother know he was here?"

The question startled Molly. Apparently this was a complication she hadn't anticipated.

"You'll have to tell her."

Molly was silent.

"Or I'll have to tell her."

"She doesn't understand."

"She understands perfectly." And had been dreading the summer because of it.

"He's really nice."

"That's not the point, is it?"

Molly fidgeted with the hem of her T-shirt. "You know what happened with my dress for the dance, right? It was the first thing I bought with my babysitting money, it was the first dress I had that she didn't pick. And she made me take it back. She didn't have any right. It was my money. I earned it."

A bit of independence, but not much. Gwyn remembered the frustration.

"She wants me to be ashamed of my body."

"I think she wants you to respect it."

Molly made an impatient, disbelieving sound. She looked at Gwyn uncertainly. "Do you still want me to babysit?"

"I want to know I can trust you."

"You can! I promise. It got complicated. I didn't know what to do."

"You didn't?"

Her shoulders slumped, any remaining defiance gone. "Okay, I knew." She trailed back to her house.

Gwyn rolled up the hose and went in to make lunch. Chris was just hanging up the telephone.

"That was Grandpa. He says Happy Canada Day."

"That's nice. Did you wish it back?"

"Yep. And he wanted to hear all about the storm. He says if *The Day After Tomorrow* really happens him and Grandma'll be some of the first Popsicles."

"He said that, did he? What have I told you?"

"It won't happen. But, Mom, if it does…"

The doorbell chimed. Gwyn went to answer, wondering if she sounded as much like the little bird in a cuckoo clock to Chris as she did to herself. *It won't, it won't,* over and over. If she knew more about it maybe she could tell him *why* it wouldn't.

Iris stood by the door. "My daughter's just confessed. I completely understand if you want to fire her."

"Of course not—"

"She didn't used to be like this!"

Her friend sounded so plaintive Gwyn couldn't help smiling, mostly in sympathy. "You know how it is when you're growing up and you get a little extra room. At first you're not sure what to do with it."

"Did you know she went to the dance with this Luke character, too? I didn't say she could start dating. She was supposed to go with some girlfriends."

The telephone rang.

"Help yourself to lunch, Iris. I'll be right with you."

GWYN DIDN'T HANG UP when she heard his voice. David thought that was a promising start. "I'm calling to apologize," he said.

"Oh." She sounded surprised, maybe pleased. He hoped pleased. "I'm glad you did. I've been feeling bad about blowing up at you. You were our guest and I suppose I've forgotten about guests, but I have a vague memory that you don't usually yell at them."

"You didn't yell." He hadn't thought past the apology. "Would you like to go for coffee sometime? Get to know each other better?" She didn't answer right away so he added, "Since we're nearly neighbors."

Still no answer. Either she'd gone to watch TV or she was weighing the pros and cons and not being very tempted.

Finally she said, "I don't think so."

"Ah. Okay."

"I don't date."

"You don't?" That was an odd way to put it. "You're philosophically opposed?" he joked. "Obeying a rule?"

"Maybe you didn't mean a date. Maybe you meant a cup of coffee because we're neighbors. Sort of neighbors."

She sounded embarrassed. David wondered which answer would make her feel better. He decided to go with the truth. "I did mean a date."

"Oh, I see. Well, I don't date."

At least she felt better.

"My husband died awhile ago. In Bosnia. Thank you for suggesting it, though."

He was an idiot. The ring, the worry, the upset son. Every pedantic piece of information he'd insisted on telling her came back to haunt him. He couldn't have known.

"You don't date?" Iris repeated, after swallowing a bite of tuna sandwich. "What did I tell you, Gwyn?"

"Don't avoid him. I know. I think I wish I'd said yes."

"Call him back."

"I can't do that."

"Yes, you can. You pick up the phone and dial the number and take the gigantic risk of getting a cup of coffee with the guy. And then you take it from there. The way the rest of us do."

"Do I even consider going around with a man who gives me nightmares?"

"Why not? Apparently Molly's going around with a boy who gives me nightmares." Iris made a face. "I really don't like that kid. I can't believe at their age I have to worry about what they might be doing. It's not just spin the bottle anymore—and my mother blew her top if she heard I played that at a party! I can't watch Molly when she's out of the house. I can't be there all the time."

"Of course you can't. And remember what you told me. It wouldn't even be good for her if you could always be there."

"I wish I trusted her." Iris glanced at Chris, then lowered her voice. "But how can I, the way she's been sneaking around? It's not that I don't understand. I do. I snuck around, too. And it's not that I regret Molly, I'm not saying that at all, but I know what can happen."

"Maybe her holiday at the farm will help her forget about Luke."

"I wish I could send her right now, but my aunt's got company. I've told Molly not to see that smarmy little rat again." Iris looked at Gwyn uneasily, as if she expected a bad reaction. "She disagrees."

"Can you stop her?"

"I can try."

"Duncan Sinclair," Sam said Monday morning, hanging up the phone. He'd called someone he knew at the Department of Defence. "He was part of the NATO stabilization force in Bosnia-Herzegovina. He and his crew volunteered to fly in medical supplies to an isolated town on one of their days off. They were brought down by some kind of surface-to-air fire."

"I didn't hear anything about that on the news."

"She's using it as an excuse not to go out with you?"

"Using it?"

"He died six years ago, David."

EVERY DAY Gwyn considered calling David and every day she decided not to do it. There was no point having coffee if she wasn't ready for whatever came next. Dinner she could handle. What about after that, though? He wasn't looking for a buddy. Not that they'd get as far as dinner. They'd argue again before the coffee cooled.

The week settled into a routine—not the routine they might have wanted for the first week school was out but an absence of fights and floods seemed good enough. Iris fretted over what her daughter might be up to while she was at work, Gwyn gardened and played and grocery shopped with Chris during the day and worked four-hour shifts at the hospital each evening.

Mr. Scott wasn't doing well. On Thursday she carried a dinner tray into his room and found him blue around the mouth, each breath an effort. His wife sat beside his bed, her eyes damp. The doctor had been in, she said. They were keeping an eye on him.

"Can I bring you a cup of tea, Mrs. Scott?"

"Oh, yes, thank you. No, maybe not. No. I'll go down to the cafeteria soon." She gave a flustered smile. "You won't need to do his heels, dear. I did them earlier. We may need a little help with turning, but I'll do his back, too."

"As much as you want, but don't tire yourself." Gwyn thought Mrs. Scott was going to laugh at that. "All right, good point. Just don't tire yourself too much!"

She went into Bess's room. The push fluids sign was gone. Gwyn set the dinner tray on the over-bed table.

"Hello, Bess."

The patient in the next bed said, "She can't hear you."

"You never know."

"I know and I just got here this morning."

Gwyn smiled at the woman's tone. She sounded like Chris. Grumpy and worried and determined not to feel better. "There's no point not trying."

"Oh, you're one of those."

"Some days, anyway." She held Bess's glasses to the light to check for smudges then rested them on her nose, careful not to scrape the fine-textured skin, tight over bone. She fit both hearing aids into place. "There! Is that better?"

"Much better," said the woman in the next bed.

"Mrs. Coates, right? I'm Gwyn Sinclair."

"And you'll be looking after me this evening?" Mrs. Coates said it in the tone waiters used in restaurants.

"One of many. I'm your go-to girl for juice and clean slippers." She rolled up the head of Bess's bed and wheeled the table holding the dinner tray closer. She pressed Bess's hand, waved the dish of pureed beef in front of her, touched the spoon to her lips.

"They haven't been giving her anything. She choked at lunch so they took down that sign and they haven't been feeding her. She doesn't say a word. I told my doctor I want a different room."

Poor Bess. She'd never been responsive, so Gwyn couldn't tell if there'd been a change in her condition. She lay still, staring at nothing the way she had since admission. Did she know where she was? Think about what was happening to her? Have dreams or nightmares?

Gwyn put the dish and spoon back on the tray and moved the table to one side, then pulled the curtain between the beds. No wonder Mrs. Coates wanted to move. She was in for tests because of difficulty swallowing. The last thing she'd want was to witness someone choking.

"Mrs. Byrd said this is your first admission to hospital."

"Except for deliveries. Two girls and a boy. But that was thirty years ago and it's not the same at all."

"You don't think much of the ward so far, I guess."

Mrs. Coates smiled, giving Gwyn a glimpse of how she'd look stress free. "I don't know how many times I've nearly got up and gone home."

"Has anyone shown you the sitting room?"

"There's a sitting room?"

"With magazines and a TV. It's always on sports, though. You might have to get ready to fight."

Mrs. Coates smiled wider. "Well, that's familiar!"

Gwyn helped her on with her robe and took her down the hall, through the big double doors and into a bright room where visitors and a few of the less sick patients relaxed. Mrs. Coates picked up a newspaper and settled into an armchair by the window.

"I'll come get you if we need you for anything."

"No, no, just ignore me," Mrs. Coates said from behind the paper.

Gwyn paused to read the headline facing her. Tropical Storm Fleur On the Way.

Another one already? They couldn't have a repeat of last year. People were still recovering and rebuilding. In the fall a news anchor had said it was only the second time forecasters had gone through the whole alphabet naming storms and hurricanes, except for the letters they never used, Q and Z and a few others. It was the first time they'd had to start using the letters of the Greek alphabet.

Mrs. Coates lowered the paper. "I thought I felt someone standing there. Are you guarding me?"

"Reading the front page. Sorry."

"The storms?" She folded one corner of the paper over so she could see, then shook her head. "I never thought I'd be glad to live where the winters can go to forty below, but that's about as bad as it gets here, isn't it? A blizzard or spring flooding or a tornado now and then, nothing of this magnitude. We're lucky."

"That's what I keep telling my son."

"He's one of those weather worriers, is he? Like my son-in-law. He's a science teacher. I never understand what he's saying but he sure makes it sound bad. I've told him he needs an end-is-nigh sign and a reserved spot at the corner of Portage and Main."

Gwyn chuckled, but it was David Bretton she saw holding the sign. She went back to the ward thinking Mrs. Coates was better than a coffee break but her mood didn't stay lightened for long. Dr. Li sat at the nursing station writing a patient history for a new admission. She looked up questioningly when Gwyn stopped in front of the desk.

"Can you tell me what's going on with Mr. Scott? He's not well at all today."

"I think it's emotional strain, Gwyn. He should improve with rest. His wife told him this afternoon she wants to sell their house and move to an apartment. That way they can keep all the rooms cool for him, not just one."

"It's a good idea."

Dr. Li nodded. "Easier for her looking after him, too, and easier for Home Care. The trouble is they bought their place when they were newlyweds. The thought of losing it really upset him."

"And Bess? We've been trying to get her rehydrated, but she seems worse off than when she first came in."

"It's her age, her general condition. She hasn't been able to bounce back from the dehydration. Heat waves are hardest on the very young and the very old."

"What more can we do for her? Keep her cooler, give her something else to drink?"

"Keep her comfortable."

Gwyn's heart sank.

TWO HOURS LATER Dr. Li came out of Bess's room writing new orders. "Nothing by mouth now, Gwyn." She asked the charge nurse, "Do we have a next of kin?"

"A grandson in Vancouver."

"Better give him a call."

It was almost time for Gwyn to go home. The aide coming on with the next shift was efficient, but she had a callous attitude to the end of life. Gwyn understood it probably came from fear, but she didn't want it around Bess. She called Molly to see if she could stay longer with Chris, then settled down with Bess to wait. Mrs. Coates came into the room, got the picture and went right back out.

Ninety-eight. Bess had faded so slowly, cruelly slow. Maybe she had a strong, stubborn heart and no matter how much punishment it took from age and illness it just wouldn't stop. Maybe some spark that had carried her through two world wars and the Great Depression, a marriage and children was determined to keep on going. Ninety-eight years and a heat wave? it was saying. No problem.

But it was letting go now. Soon the sheet over Bess's chest no longer moved and her pulse vibrated more than it beat. There wasn't any wheeze or rattle or gasp. Just a deepening of the silence that had been with her from the start. Gwyn didn't know if it was her imagination or wishful thinking, but in a quiet room around the time of death she often thought she felt some other consciousness nearby.

"You did well," she whispered. She waited, thinking something like goodbye or good luck or godspeed.

A heaviness settled over her. Being with people as they died wasn't what she found most difficult. The part she never got used was the preparation after death, the anonymity of the wrapped white sheet, the indignity of the ID tag. But it was the last thing she could do for a patient. Someone had given the same care to her parents and far away in a place she'd never seen someone had given whatever care they could to Duncan.

AN HOUR LATE, Gwyn let herself into the house. Anxious voices came from Chris's room. She hurried down the hall and stopped in his doorway, staring at the wall.

"Oh, Mrs. Sinclair. I'm sorry—"

Huge, out of proportion with the clouds and the trees, was a newly painted sun, an irregular mass, reaching everywhere with blobs and spikes. Flames engulfed the tree closest to it. Chris was still at work, painting brown lines into the grass.

Gwyn had to stop herself from shouting. *You ruined it, you ruined it!* She had to clamp her teeth shut to make sure she didn't say it out loud. She wanted to hit him. Put him over her knee like people used to, and spank, spank, spank.

Clutching the jar of paint in one hand and the brush in the other he turned, his face set in a frown of concentration.

"Christopher." She nearly said, *What the hell do you think you're doing?* "Christopher." *Bad. This is so bad. How could you?*

"What are we going to do, Mom? Bomb it?"

She sat on the edge of the bed, her anger gone just like that. Fear crept in. "Bomb what?"

"The sun. Can we explode it?"

"We don't want to, sweetheart. We need the sun."

"We need it smaller."

"No, Chris."

He dropped the jar of paint onto the floor. Deliberately. It oozed over the carpet, away from his feet, toward hers.

"You'll have to clean that up."

"You clean it."

She grabbed his hand and dragged him out of the room. Shoved him into the bathroom. Slammed the door.

"Mom!"

"Quiet! You be quiet, Chris, and think about what you've done."

"I won't!"

"You're not getting out of there until you do."

There was a tremor in his voice. "Mothers can't lock children in bathrooms."

Maybe he was right. "You'll stay there, Christopher, until you apologize and tell me you'll clean up the paint. Is that clear?"

"Humph!" It was a very indignant noise, delivered by a very angry child on the verge of tears. Gwyn nearly flung the door open so she could hold him and tell him it was all right. But it wasn't all right. Not by a long shot.

"Mrs. Sinclair?"

She had forgotten about Molly. She whipped around, angry again. "Was Luke here?"

"No."

"Because if you had that kid over here again—"

"I didn't! Mrs. Sinclair, I promise."

"Something besides Chris certainly had your attention." She heard her accusing tone and tried to stop it. "He was in his room for a good long time. Upset. Finding paint. Covering the wall."

"I thought he was reading."

Gwyn rubbed her eyebrow. Her head pounded in that one spot.

"We had a really nice evening," Molly went on. "We stayed outside until the mosquitoes got bad and then we turned on a nature program. I thought that was okay for him. It's educational, right?"

Gwyn nodded. He didn't like seeing lions catch zebras but they could tell if that was the way things were going and then they turned it off.

"He was fine until they got to the part about polar bears and global warming."

Gwyn didn't think she'd made any kind of response but Molly paused, watching her. "Go ahead. Polar bears and global warming?"

"They said the ice floes are melting too soon in the spring and the bears can't get enough food. Chris turned off the TV and went to his room. I figured he wanted some time to himself." She repeated her apology. "I'm sorry, Mrs. Sinclair. I should have kept a closer eye on him."

"Present tense?"

"Pardon?"

"The ice floes *are* melting, or some people think they might one day melt?"

"Are melting, they said."

"And the bears can't get enough food?"

"They said the bears go out on the ice to catch seals and fish. When the ice breaks up they have to stay on land and they don't find much to eat. So if the ice breaks up earlier they go longer without food. And I don't know if I believe this part—"

Her voice was like Chris's, Gwyn noticed, uncertain and full of question marks.

"What part, Molly?"

"They said in another fifty years there might not be any ice left in the Arctic."

"That doesn't sound right." She wanted to tell Molly not to worry. "I'll try to find out what they meant, okay? And I'll get back to you. Molly? I'm sorry, too. I was unfair to you."

Molly looked happier at that. Gwyn walked her to the front door and waited until she saw her disappear into her own house. Then she went slowly back to the bathroom door.

"Chris?"

Silence.

"Do you have anything to say to me?"

Still nothing. She imagined him sitting on the side of the tub frowning at the door. The bathroom was a bad place to choose for a time-out. Too many ways to get hurt. Another look at the mural stiffened her resolve. She got her child-rearing book from her bedroom and reviewed the section on time-outs.

She was doing it wrong. Two minutes was long enough, it said, but don't start counting until after the child stopped arguing. Chris had stopped arguing ten minutes ago. She ran back to the bathroom, knocked and opened the door.

There he was, as she'd pictured him, on the side of the tub frowning. With tear-streaked cheeks.

"Have you thought about what you did?"

He nodded.

"And?"

He stared. No, he glared.

"Chris. Don't you have anything to say for yourself? You ruined the mural!" She remembered and added, "And the rug."

His defiance faded. He looked at the floor, trying to keep his mouth from trembling.

She forgot about the book and rules for effective time-outs and knelt on the floor. "Tell me what's going on, Chris."

His shoulders came up, way up, and when they went down she heard a sob. It made him angry all over again. He stamped one foot on the floor and banged a fist on the side of the tub.

"Is it about the polar bears?"

Tears spilled over. In quick response Gwyn's eyes filled with tears, too. She wanted to tell him polar bears had been around for millions of years and would be around for millions more but she finally saw that David Bretton was right. Chris lived in a larger world now with school and television and movies and he couldn't continue running to his mother for help the way he could before. Reassurance was nothing. Worse than nothing, because of the annoying repetitive emptiness of it. He needed to see the evidence with his own eyes. Then he'd know for himself that things were going to be all right.

CHAPTER TEN

EARLY MONDAY MORNING Gwyn and Chris followed painted dinosaur tracks through the back hallways of the museum to a small amphitheater already full of children. David came to the door to meet them.

"Hey, Chris. Good to see you. I've got a bracelet for you—"

Chris leaned back the way he did for calamine lotion.

David held out a circlet of colored beads, stretching the elastic so Chris could examine it. "Each bead is a sensor that measures ultraviolet radiation. When we're out doing stuff like releasing weather balloons, keep an eye on the intensity of the color. If it brightens it's time to apply more sunscreen. If it gets really bright it's time to come inside."

"Cool." Chris slipped the bracelet on. David handed him an ID badge, his name written on a sticker of planet Earth. He patted it into place on the left shoulder of his T-shirt.

"See the kids standing by the poster of the beluga?" There were two boys and four girls who looked about Chris's age. "That's Tundra section. The seven of you will learn all you can about the North this week. You want to join them? We'll be starting shortly."

Gwyn waited until Chris was out of earshot. "Tundra. You're making him jump right in."

"I think it's the best way."

"Do you have a minute?"

"Of course."

Too many people—children, teachers, other parents—were near them. "Can we…"

He led the way into the corridor and found a spot near the fire exit where no one was coming or going.

"I'm still a little worried about this being the right thing to do." She'd already told David about the mural when she called to see if there were any spaces left at this week's camp. "I wish you could have seen the wall. It was such an angry, threatening sun. He used red paint, and he splattered it on so messily. It looked like blood dripping."

"Scary thing for you to come home to."

"Then he dropped the jar of paint on the floor. Right in front of me, staring at me, daring me." She looked at David uncertainly. "He's never been prone to tantrums. He's never been destructive. His teacher got in touch with me twice last month, because of those drawings I told you about and then because he pushed a boy. He said he was being the wind. Now this. I'm wondering…what you think about it."

"About the acting out? The anger? I don't know, Gwyn."

"His teacher thinks it's a deeper problem, that being afraid about the weather is a symptom. She's put in a referral to the school psychologist for the fall." David looked kind and worried and uncomfortable. She'd probably told him more than he wanted to hear. Or maybe he agreed with Ms. Gibson. "I didn't mean to put you on the spot."

"What I've noticed working with kids is that they have a limited set of choices and tools. He's been trying to get your attention, hasn't he?"

"He's had it, he's always had it." She paused. "Okay,

you're right, he *really* got my attention that night. Gave me a lightning bolt moment. He may be only five, but he's got eyes and a brain and I can't keep on trying to convince him not to use them."

David smiled good-naturedly. "However much you may want to."

Since it was true, Gwyn let that pass. He didn't seem in a hurry to get back to the children so she decided to mention another concern. "You said you watched the same program Chris did."

"About polar bears, yes."

"Molly said something about all the ice in the Arctic being gone in fifty years. She must have misunderstood."

"Have you heard what the Arctic Ocean was called a long time ago?"

She shook her head uneasily. She'd expected a quick denial.

"The Frozen Sea."

"That's evocative."

"But not as accurate as it used to be. It's possible that in fifty or a hundred years all or most of the summer ice could be gone. We'd still have a certain amount of winter ice but we're talking about a very different Arctic."

"I don't believe that." The unchanging North was solidly in her mind, white and still or white and windswept, either way desolate, beautiful, deadly. It was part of Canadian consciousness, identity, even though hardly anyone ever saw it firsthand. "That's a lot of ice. It can't all melt."

"If you put ice cubes in a glass can they melt?"

"There's no comparison."

"All right, if you fill a bathtub with ice, can it melt?"

"It's still not the same thing."

"Sure it is. If ice gets warm, it melts."

If ice gets warm, it melts! They were talking about the Arctic, about miles and miles and miles of ice. Particularly cold ice. Ice as big as a country, as big as a continent.

"Hard to grasp, isn't it?" he said. "Go back to the ice cubes in the glass."

"I don't want to go back to the ice cubes in the glass."

"If they melt, will the water level in the glass change?"

She nearly said yes. "No. There's the same amount of water in the ice cubes whether they're frozen or thawed."

"Right. Now, if the glass sat under a dripping tap would the water level rise?"

"Of course it would."

"The Arctic ice cap floats on the ocean. Whether it's frozen or thawed it has the same volume, so sea levels won't change. But glaciers—built up ice resting on land—are melting, too. They're the dripping tap. An added complication is they're made of fresh water."

They were back to that. The ocean conveyer belt. *The Day After Tomorrow.* "You sound so calm."

"It's required, ever since that whole Mad Scientist thing."

She laughed, in spite of the mural, Bess, Mr. Scott, polar bears, ice caps. Then she smiled at him for making it happen.

"Did you want to stay awhile, Gwyn? We can always use a hand."

She would have loved to stay. She would have liked to hear every word said to Chris so she could tell him which things couldn't possibly be true. "I'd better let him do this on his own. I'll be home all day, though, so you can call if he needs me."

"Four o'clock, then. He's in good hands, Gwyn."

GWYN DECIDED TO WALK home so she could stop at an
Internet café she'd often seen from the bus. Not far from
the museum, a block off the main road, it occupied part of
the ground floor of a renovated warehouse. High ceilings
and low lighting gave it a cool, cavelike comfort. Taking
a leap into the unknown she ordered an iced mocha drink
and after the first sugary sip wished she hadn't.

She put the paper cup beside one of the computers,
thought about what to search for and then typed, *Is all the
ice in the Arctic melting?*

A list of Web sites leapt into view. One after the other she
opened several pages and skimmed what they had to say. In
every article, the same careful wording delivered the same
frightening message. According to some research ice in the
Arctic had thinned by half. Winter ice was breaking up
earlier and freezing later. Inuit hunters were falling through
ice that had been considered permanent, as reliable as solid
ground.

Sipping her coffee, she stared at the screen. Then, nearly
reconsidering after each letter, she typed into the search
box, *Could* The Day After Tomorrow *really happen?*
Again, a list of Web sites appeared in seconds.

Twenty-one million responses? That couldn't be right.
She counted the zeros. Six. Twenty-one million sites asked
that question. Maybe they all answered, "No." Maybe they
weren't all exact matches. She couldn't look at even one
of them to check. She'd had enough.

Carrying the too-sweet, odd-tasting coffee with her, she
left the café. She didn't know what to think.

SHE HAD THE SAME uncertain feeling standing in Chris's
room with Iris at lunchtime.

"It doesn't look bad," Iris said. "The real sky isn't always blue. You could pretend the sun's starting to set."

"It looks more ominous than that. It's supposed to be a cozy picture."

The remnants of the big, angry circle and flames were disturbing enough, but the dripping rays that reached into the tree and the house were worse. Chris had tried his best to wash them off and she'd helped, but ghostly pinkish lines remained. One of Duncan's photos was stained, too.

"I understand that he was upset with me, but he likes the mural. We did it together, talking about Duncan, about how Chris still has a father even if he can't be with us. I don't get it."

"It's their aim to wear us down, make us old before our time. Just accept that, Gwyn. I'm sure they have meetings about it."

"Molly and Chris?"

"Children. A worldwide conspiracy. With Molly as president."

Gwyn laughed. "She's learning, though."

"To run the conspiracy? You bet! She was out of the house before I even woke up this morning. When does she ever get up before she has to, before I pound on her door and threaten to drag her out of bed by her feet?"

"Never?" Gwyn guessed.

"I'm sure it's because I'm on holiday. Won't the next few weeks be fun?"

"If it's any comfort she's a very nice girl when she's away from home."

"So I'm the only lucky recipient of her dark side? Cool. It's all been worth it, then." Iris went out to the hall, then to the kitchen. "At least now that she's working for you there'll be twenty hours a week I know where she is."

She opened the fridge door. "Why do you only have things with vitamin C? I'll run to the store and get us something that's actually good. Chocolate, ice cream, cookies?"

"Sure."

"I meant, choose."

"I'm not having that sort of day."

Iris laughed. "Okay, I'll get it all."

While she waited for Iris to return with the treats Gwyn went out to water the perennials. She was getting used to the heat, to the feeling that she always needed a shower, but between drought and drenching the plants weren't doing well. They were all hardy, meant for a changeable northern climate. They could take hot summers and minus forties winters. It was this particular summer they didn't like.

A group of girls across the road caught her eye. She thought they were the ones from the Dairy Queen the day of the downpour. Molly was with them. They all wore shorts and halter tops and had midsummer tans. Without checking for traffic, they began to cross. They went diagonally, staying in the road longer than necessary, then stopped on the sidewalk, separated from Gwyn by her lawn.

She acknowledged them with a smile and said hello uncomfortably, still embarrassed that she'd lost her temper with Molly. "You all look relaxed and summery."

Everyone but Molly looked away, dismissing her.

"Is Chris all right today, Mrs. Sinclair?"

"I hope so. He's at the museum camp."

"He'll like that."

"When I dropped him off I talked to Dr. Bretton about Arctic ice melting."

Molly's eyes shifted away from hers. Whoops. This wasn't a good time for educational pursuits.

The other girls already showed signs of restlessness. They started moving away, walking backward until Molly joined them, but they didn't get far. Iris's voice came from the corner, carrying easily along the sidewalk.

"Molly! Stay right there." When she was closer she called, "Since when do you disappear all day without a word to me about where you're going?"

"Sorry, Mom. I lost track of the time. I'll just walk everybody—"

Iris pointed to the house. "Now."

Molly muttered something to her friends, then trailed home, slowly enough to make it clear what she thought of this treatment, but not so slowly she'd get into any more trouble.

Gwyn went to meet Iris on the sidewalk. "No junk food lunch after all?"

"Sorry, Gwyn." She held out the bag. "Want to take your share?"

"Why don't you put it all away and we'll have it next time we're both in the mood."

Iris's hand fell back to her side. "Am I supposed to yell at her?"

"You're asking me?"

"I haven't forgotten what it's like to be a kid that age. That's my problem. I know she thinks the world's changed and I don't understand it. I know she's going to break rules behind my back and get herself hurt doing it. And I know mistakes are supposed to be good, people are supposed to learn from them, but from what I can see, mostly they don't. There has to be a better way to grow up." Iris pulled a small container of gourmet ice cream from the bag she carried. "I can't wait. I need this! We'd better hurry, it's melting."

GWYN ARRIVED early to pick up Chris that afternoon. She didn't go right in to the amphitheater. If she got within five feet of David all the things she'd read and avoided reading at the Internet café would tumble out and he, being the big believer in scariness that he was, would insist on telling her more awful news instead of giving her what she really wanted. Reassurance. Whatever he and Chris thought of it, reassurance worked well for her.

Chris hopped on one foot from the museum to the bus. All the way home he didn't stop talking. About the other kids in Tundra group, about what *tundra* meant, about the ice core samples they'd started making. He wanted to go to the second week of day camp, too, because the more days they had to make their ice cores the more realistic they would be. Every day they would freeze a new layer of water, not plain water, but water from an air conditioner, from a puddle, water with dandelion seeds thrown in, whatever they could think of, Dr. Bretton had said, it was up to them, because that's how the layers of a glacier were. Scientists could tell things about the weather by studying what was in the ice. Pollen and carbon dioxide and stuff like that. He was wondering if he could kind of breathe into the water to get carbon dioxide in it. Gwyn wanted to remind him that the was only five, that he shouldn't care about these things, that he shouldn't come anywhere near understanding them.

He gave an excited bounce on the seat. "Do we have balloons?"

"There might be some left from the party."

Another bounce. He held his hands cupped near his mouth, demonstrating. "So I'll blow in one, Mom, then put the little end in my water sample and let the air out. There'll be carbon dioxide in that, because we breathe out carbon dioxide." Bounce. "The smoke that comes out of cars! That would be good." His voice quieted. "I'm not sure how I'll get that in the water…."

The thing was, he told her, getting back to his main point, each layer would represent years and years. That was why he needed to go for the second week.

"We'll see," she said.

When they got home he ran to his room and came back to the kitchen table with paper and crayons, then climbed up on a chair, settled onto his knees and chose a blue crayon. He drew a circle with three lines across it, one at the middle, one near the top and one near the bottom.

"So, here's how it works. This line in the middle is the equator."

She turned down the burner under the frying pan she'd started to heat and went to look over his shoulder.

"That's where the Earth is hottest," he said. "It's where the sun shines most. And these lines, up here and down here? That's the Arctic Circle and the *Ant*arctic Circle. They don't get much sun, so they're cold. You know what happens?"

"What happens?"

He drew arrows pointing north and south from the equator. "It's like Dr. Bretton was trying to tell me at the barbecue. The heat evens out. It travels in the air and in the water to where it's colder. That makes wind and storms. But the Earth spins on its…" a slight hesitation, then

"...axis. So the wind doesn't blow straight from the equator. It turns." As he got further into the explanation his voice lost confidence. He rested his cheek on his arm, bringing his eyes almost to the level of the paper.

Gwyn picked up the pencil and did her best to sketch North America in its place. The result reminded her of Babar the Elephant's head. She drew a dot roughly in the middle. "There's Winnipeg."

Standing on the dot, she drew a stick figure. "There's Christopher, soakin' up the rays, making vitamin D and building strong bones. Wearing his sunscreen, of course." She added wavy lines reaching from the sun. "There's warm air going by. Hmm. Nice."

His face still rested on his arm. His cheek was rounded and soft the way it had always been and his hands still looked ready to hold teddy bears and build block towers, but his expression didn't fit. It was scared, but not the way a child looked scared. Gwyn saw apprehension. Deep down, inconsolable apprehension.

"It's going to be all right, Chris. You know that, don't you?"

He didn't even bother looking at her.

Was she supposed to tell him it wouldn't be all right? She was sure it would be. It had to be. She kissed the top of his head. "Get washed for dinner, sweetheart."

That night there was another downpour. The drumming on the roof kept Chris awake so they sat on the porch together watching the drops hit the ground. They hit so hard they bounced up again. No thunder and lightning this time, no branch-breaking wind. Just rain as hard and loud as hail, beating the leaves of her perennials.

ON THE WAY HOME the next afternoon Chris seemed happier, animated even, curving his arms over his head to illustrate air masses. He hurried into the kitchen as soon as she got the door open.

"Can I do an experiment, Mom?"

"Is it a messy one?" He had an enthusiasm for home-made volcanoes.

He got on his knees to look through the cupboard. "Nope. We only need one thing. Water."

"That's all?"

"And heat."

"Two things."

"Three, 'cause we need ice." He held up two saucepans. "Five things."

Gwyn sat at the kitchen table. "Six if we count the cloth to wipe up the counter. Seven for the mop."

"Can I, though?"

"You may."

He put one saucepan half-full of water on the front burner, then dragged over a chair to stand on. His hand hovered near one of the knobs. "This one?"

"That's right."

He turned it to high, then moved the chair over to the fridge. He took a tray of ice cubes from the freezer compartment, twisted it to loosen the cubes and let them fall into the second saucepan.

"David did this in the lab today. It's really neat, Mom." He watched the water in the first pot simmer.

"Should we put some macaroni in there?"

Chris didn't appreciate the attempt at humor. "No, Mom. It's an experiment. Is that boiling?"

Gwyn joined him at the stove. "A bit. Is that enough or do you want a rolling boil?"

"Does that give more heat?"

"It does."

"We want lots of heat, because it was the hottest June on record and it's heading for the hottest July."

"Now it's rolling."

"Okay, you've got to see this." He held the pan of ice cubes in the steam above the pan of water. Gradually, drops began to form on the bottom, and even more gradually, they began to fall. "See, Mom? It's rain."

It was wonderful that he was excited for a change rather than worried. Gwyn relaxed as she watched him and only half listened as he returned to the subject of colliding air masses.

"It's the same, exactly the same as what happens in the sky. Like last night. The air was really hot and it was full of water even though we couldn't see it. At night it touched cooler air that didn't have as much water. The cool air made the hot air let go of its water. Just like this." He pointed at the pot, still dripping. "That's real rain."

Gwyn smiled. "One day I'm going to see you on the weather channel."

"Nope. I'm going to work at the museum, like David."

"You mean like Dr. Bretton."

"He said to call him David, Mom."

"And I say not to."

ON THE THIRD AFTERNOON Chris was in the middle of a game with the rest of his group when Gwyn arrived. David saw her, and smiled. That was all it took. One smile and she didn't want to avoid him anymore.

He made his way to her side, stopping several times to speak with a child or parent before he got there.

"I'm glad to catch you before you left today. I've been wanting to give you a more informed opinion about your son now that I've spent some time with him. He's terrific!"

Gwyn smiled, pleased. "You might have been right about this."

"About learning instead of hiding?"

She looked at him without answering.

"Sorry. Why do I do that?"

"Try to irritate me?" She shrugged. "I don't know. You're a complete mystery."

"I've been told I'm too blunt. People aren't lab reports. You don't hit them with the facts as concisely and clearly as possible. Friendly conversation allows for gaps in information, leaps of logic." He grimaced, honestly embarrassed as far as she could tell, but very appealing. "All this has been explained to me."

Gwyn wondered who had explained it. His mother, a girlfriend on her way out the door? "Sometimes you don't hit people with facts at all. Sometimes you just go for ice cream."

SHE COULDN'T HAVE surprised him more if she'd decided to take his word for it on climate change.

Since neither of them had used a car that day they rode a bus to his favorite ice cream stand, beside the river on Jubilee. It turned out to be Gwyn and Chris's favorite ice cream stand, too, another place where, with a bit of luck, they all might have crossed paths before.

They strolled across the footbridge with their treats—a dipped cone with sprinkles for Chris and hot fudge sundaes for the grown-ups—and David managed not to say anything about the record high water level or the visibly eroding riverbank or compare melting ice cream to glaciers. *Ice cream that stays in the cup when it melts isn't a problem,* he wanted to say, *but any that runs down the side will cause you some trouble.* Maybe it was just as well he didn't have kids. They might find him really annoying.

As she did. Why had she suggested this? She walked along looking with pleasure at the tree-lined river and even more pleasure at the fudge sauce on her plastic spoon. It was the first time since they'd spoken beside the mammoth painting that she looked relaxed instead of scared or angry or worried.

"Chris is enjoying day camp, David. He already seems calmer. I think he feels there's something he can do."

"I'm glad. That's exactly what we want."

"He's eager to go next week, so his ice core will have ten layers, not just five. I'm thinking of signing him up."

She said it as if it was a big step for her. It probably was. "We'd like to have him. He's a natural-born observer. I'm afraid he's going to want to be a scientist, Gwyn."

"Then I won't understand anything he does."

"Sure you will. And when you don't, you can feel good about it."

"That he's gone further, you mean."

David nodded. "This isn't an easy way for him to be. He won't be able to lie to himself."

"The way I do, you mean."

"The way lots of people do. It can be lonely if everyone around you is pulling the wool over their eyes."

"Does everyone around you do that?"

"No, not at all. I wasn't talking about myself."

They were at the midpoint of the bridge. Chris had stopped to watch downed trees travel on the current.

"You said you grew up in a big house by the river. My great-great-grandfather worked on some of those, you know."

"He was a carpenter?"

"His specialty was curled banisters for staircases. My father told me people would ask for him."

"There's a curled banister at my parents' house. I wonder if he left any kind of signature on the ones he made."

"According to my dad if it's the most beautiful, graceful banister you've seen anywhere then my great-great-grand-dad made it."

This was how David had imagined she'd be, before they got off to cross purposes. Easy to talk to, warm and approachable. "And what kind of work do you do?"

She seemed to hesitate before answering. "I'm a nurse's aide. On a medical ward at Winnipeg General."

He'd never met a nurse's aide. "Is that difficult? It must be, being around sick people."

Chris had started walking again, so they did, too.

"I like it. My mother got me the job for the summer when I was in high school. She was a nurse."

"Long summer job!"

She laughed. "It lasted three summers, after grade twelve and first year university, too. And then—then I kept going with it."

He wanted to ask why, but she sounded as if she'd closed the door on the topic.

Not only on the topic. On the afternoon, too. "Chris and I had better head home. I enjoyed this so much, David."

"So did I. We should do it again."

She nodded, but didn't make any suggestions.

"The university is hosting a really interesting lecture series. It's the same material we're covering at day camp, but for adults. The next talk is on Friday—maybe you'd like to go with me." She wouldn't like it. He knew that. She needed to understand what was happening to the climate, though, for Chris's sake. "We could call it Climate Change: The Scary Version."

Gwyn smiled. "Is that a challenge?"

"Of course not." He returned her smile. "Maybe."

"You're on."

CHAPTER ELEVEN

GWYN COULDN'T BELIEVE she'd said yes. The ice cream had been so good, the view so pretty and David's eyes so velvety brown agreement had come out of her mouth on its own. Chris had looked impressed when she'd told him where she was going, though. That was worth a scary evening. They planned to have coffee and dessert afterward, to take the sting out of it.

The speaker was introduced as Belinda Gerrard, a climate scientist with not one but two Ph.D.s, in geography and chemistry. After expressing surprise that so many people had come to listen to her when they could be enjoying a cold one on a secluded dock somewhere she turned off the lights and projected an image onto a screen behind her.

A tanned and leanly muscled man in swimming trunks stood beside a person of unknown gender in a hooded parka with matching pants, mitts and moccasins. Dr. Gerrard nodded in recognition of a few chuckles. "This is what people are asking me," she said. "Which way is the world's climate going?"

"I know which has my vote," a woman called.

"You like the parka, too? Nothing tops caribou hide. It's insulating, it's water repellent—the fabric of choice if you're ever caught in an ice age." Dr. Gerrard smiled, but Gwyn wasn't sure if she was joking. "Let's start at the beginning, for the benefit of anyone who thought this was *How To Get The Most Out Of Your Digital Camera*."

Gwyn whispered in David's ear, "You said there wouldn't be an ice age."

"I said it's unlikely," he whispered back.

"Earth went through a wild infancy and adolescence," the speaker continued, "oceans and volcanoes, one single continent breaking into parts and moving around the globe, a series of darn chilly ice ages, before settling into its rightful condition, its adulthood, its perfect maturity. That's what most of us think, isn't it?"

As she spoke, she clicked through slide after slide. A diagram of the geological time line, another of Pangaea, a third showing the ice sheet that had covered Canada and parts of the United States during the last ice age.

"Perfect maturity," she repeated. "Some of us thought it would stay in that phase forever—well, just like ourselves." She smiled at the uncomfortable laughter. "Of course, the rightful condition of everything is change."

Gwyn knew that was true, but she didn't like thinking about it. With a sinking feeling, she tried to concentrate as the woman went on in a pleasant, conversational tone that made everything she said sound worse.

"More and more people are asking if the Earth's climate is changing. If so, in what way and how will we be affected? Are we playing a part in the change? Should we be doing something about it? What should we do, and how fast should we do it?"

Dr. Gerrard turned to a new slide, a graph with one red line snaking from left to right. Her pointer followed the line's gentle zigs and zags. "The world's climate has always been variable. Here you'll notice over the centuries some rise and fall in the mean global temperature." On the right side of the graph the line spiked. "With industrialization we see a sudden and dramatic increase."

The next slide showed another graph. "We find a similar pattern in the amount of carbon dioxide in the Earth's atmosphere—a slight increase from the mid-1800s to around 1940, then it takes off. If the amount of carbon dioxide and other greenhouses gases continues to increase in this way we can expect global temperatures to continue going up, as well."

She returned to the image of the man in the swimming trunks. "Let's say this is the way we're going. Not bad, you might think. Longer summers, more time at the lake, a longer growing season. Am I right?"

She changed slides again, then again, clicking every second, not speaking now. Images flashed by. An undernourished polar bear with muddy paws. A failed crop in a dusty field. Smog so thick Toronto's CN Tower was nearly invisible. Cars in an English village swept out to sea by flash floods. Wildfires in Utah, in California, in Australia. Villages in Alaska and Bangladesh teetering on the edge of a newly formed coastline.

"Change of this magnitude and speed doesn't happen naturally. It needs a trigger." Dr. Gerrard looked around the room. "Humans are the trigger."

Climate Change: The Scary Version. David hadn't been joking when he said that. Gwyn stopped listening but she couldn't block out everything. Phrases reached her. *Disappearing boreal forest…spread of malaria…drinking water in short supply.* Her stomach knotted and she tried harder not to hear.

Finally the lights came on, revealing somber faces. Some people stayed behind for questions but Gwyn thought she'd burst if she didn't get out of the building. She and David were quiet until they reached the sidewalk.

"What did you think?" he asked.

"Pretty dramatic stuff."

"You were uncomfortable. I shouldn't have asked you to go."

"Why did you?"

He gave an almost imperceptible shrug. "I don't know."

That was hard to believe. He'd been pushing his climate opinions on her since they met. He must have a reason. Gwyn didn't want to hear about all the terrible things that might or might not happen. Terrible things were always happening somewhere, to someone. She couldn't worry about all of them. Maybe he thought it was selfish, but she had enough to do worrying about Chris and her friends and the people she took care of at work. "Did you agree with the speaker?"

"For the most part."

"She wasn't sure about any of it. She kept saying 'the evidence suggests.' So maybe she's wrong. Maybe you're wrong."

"That would be great."

"Scientists do make mistakes."

"If this is a mistake we'll all be very happy. There'll be parties at NATO and the Pentagon and the UN and all the other places where climate specialists have been studying the problem. But I don't believe we're wrong, Gwyn. You and I grew up during a wonderful time. I think it's over."

Her voice rose. "Is that what you wanted me to get out of this little outing? Is that what you want me to tell Chris? It's over?" The bus stop was half a block away. Gwyn started toward it. If David wanted to go back inside and make friends with Dr. Gerrard that would be fine with her. They could cheer each other up predicting the end of the world.

But he didn't go inside. He walked with her and kept on talking. "The change won't happen the way it did in the movie, one big series of storms and then an ice age. It'll be more complicated than that, more varied. Some parts of the world will be warmer, enough to change farming, forestry, fishing. Others might be cooler. It'll happen over decades, a human life span."

"I've had enough of this, David."

"Chris's life span will take him into it. His children will be in the thick of it. Islands and coastlines will disappear. Rivers and lakes will dry up. Severe weather will strike more often, and harder. People will ask why no one told them." His voice kept getting louder, although he caught it several times. "In a hundred years our great-grandchildren will look at this decade and say, 'That's when we knew it was happening.' What will they say next? 'That's when we knew and really started to do something about it?' Or that's when we knew and didn't care?'"

She faced him. "Would you stop? You're scaring me."

"I'm trying to scare you. Do you want a feel-good story or the truth?"

She wanted a feel-good story to be the truth. "What if you're Chicken Little? What if all that's wrong is that a branch fell on your head and now you're panicking?"

Surprise came into his face, then anger. "Denial may be comfy, Gwyn, but it's also dangerous."

"Right, that's me. Public Enemy Number One."

"I'm not saying that. You know I'm not. But if you deny the problem you can ignore it. We can't just keep sending so much carbon dioxide up there. We've got to find a better way. If we don't, that's it, we're done, we're toast."

"I almost never drive my car! I have a tiny house—"

He started walking again, going faster than was comfortable for Gwyn. Did he think she was going to trot along at his side? She set her own pace. He soon noticed how far apart they were and stopped to wait for her.

"I didn't mean to offend you, David." No man wanted to be compared to Chicken Little.

He swung around. "Did you watch the slides? Were we in the same room? The sky *is* falling."

"Don't yell at me!"

"I'm not yelling."

It was true, he wasn't. It just felt like it.

"Gwyn." He took a deep breath and looked away, controlling some emotion. Anger with her? The same general upset she was feeling? "This was a bad idea."

With her, then. "I agree. We're too different, we'll never get along."

"That isn't what I meant. This lecture as an outing was a bad idea. I guess I wanted you to understand."

"I do understand. You think there's a problem and you think I'm part of it."

"We're all part of it." He sounded tired. "We're like lemmings rushing into the sea, so busy following each other we have no idea where we're going, no idea we're about to drown. Will our great-grandchildren thank us for what we do today, or curse us?"

"It's late. I have to catch my bus."

"I thought we were going for dessert."

He had to be kidding.

"All right. But I'll see you home."

"I don't want you to."

The lower the sun got the darker his eyes looked. Almost black. "I'm sorry, Gwyn. I never lose my cool about this. I don't know what was different tonight. All those pictures maybe. It wasn't you."

"Sure it was."

"I was talking in general."

"You were talking to me."

SHE HURRIED AWAY from him—again—and got to the stop just in time. Up the steps and the door swung closed behind her. She was right. He had been talking to her. Because of Chris? For himself? Why had he been so persistent?

Instead of dessert with Gwyn, David dropped in to visit his parents and Sam. They were in the middle of a game of canasta so he sat in a corner of the living room reviewing his performance that evening. He couldn't quite believe he'd said everything he remembered saying. With any luck, he'd only thought some of it. But if he'd only thought some of it would she have refused his company on the bus ride home?

Maybe he was actually getting scared. Maybe she represented all the doubters. Or maybe he just wanted her to believe in the things that mattered to him. If that was it, he'd handled it really well. She didn't date, she'd said, but for some reason she'd been willing to go out with him. And his first step? To be so overbearing and disapproving she couldn't get away from him fast enough.

This was one evening he couldn't tell Sam about.

"SO, YOU BASICALLY hit her over the head with it," Sam said, after the card game was finished and Miranda had gone to make tea.

"Basically."

"And she took it personally. The way you meant it."

"She looked at me like I was a puppy killer."

"I'd say you're sunk."

Richard shook his head in disbelief. "You took a young woman you wanted to impress to hear a talk about climate change? David. Son. That isn't a date."

"It was a very good presentation."

"Sam, will you take your brother under your wing? Clearly I've failed. Introduce him to the rose, the chocolate, the light of the moon—"

"I've got the moon down pat, Dad."

"I'll bet you do. The idea, unless things have changed beyond reason, is to walk in its light without mentioning how many miles away it is or the fact that astronauts have left garbage on its formerly pristine surface. Then, if you've pleased her and the fates are with you, a kiss or two might come your way."

David looked from his father to his brother. They were enjoying this too much.

"Tell her what you told me, David. Tell her about her rose-petal skin."

"Ah!" said Richard.

"Remind me not to confide in you, Sam. And I can't tell her that. Women find that sort of thing creepy."

"Not as I recall," Richard said. "Not if you mean it. Do you mean it? And if so, when are the rest of us going to meet her?"

"I don't think I'm going to discuss her with you two anymore."

"Well! Then I definitely want to meet her." Richard sounded pleased.

"At this point we don't know if she's going to speak to me again, Dad."

Coming through the door with the tea tray Miranda said, "Who won't speak to you? Jess?" She set the tray on the table in front of the sofa. "Or have you alienated another young woman?"

David sat back, letting the soft old sofa swallow him up while his father and his brother happily recounted the evening's events. The story sounded worse every time he heard it.

IT WAS NEARLY eleven o'clock when Gwyn got home. Chris slept peacefully, tired out by an evening of tag in the park. Molly didn't seem in any hurry to leave, so Gwyn filled two glasses with ice cubes and orange juice and sat down with her at the kitchen table.

"Did you have a good time, Mrs. Sinclair?"

"An interesting one, let's say."

"Do you like him?"

"Dr. Bretton? Not that much."

"Oh." Molly sounded disappointed. Like her mother, she'd been determined the climate talk was a date no matter how often Gwyn told them it was an educational evening. "I like him. So does Chris."

So do I popped into Gwyn's head. "It's more that we don't have much in common. He's very intense about things, very scientific. Spending time with him is like taking an extra class."

Molly smiled and groaned. "At least—" She stopped.

"At least what?"

"Nothing."

"At least he's tall? Good-looking?"

"Ah-hah! Now we know, Mrs. Sinclair. You *do* like him."

Gwyn laughed. An hour ago she wouldn't have believed she'd be laughing by the end of the evening. This was like being in junior high again. "Okay, I kind of like him and he's good-looking. We still don't have anything in common."

The odd thing was that Molly looked less and less happy as the conversation went on. Gwyn went back through the past few minutes, wondering when the girl's mood had changed. It was with *At least,* she thought. Molly had been going to say something else then but she'd decided against it. Something about the trouble with her mother over Luke, maybe?

"Thanks for the drink, Mrs. Sinclair. I'd better get home. Mom's paranoid these days. She has to know where I am every second."

It was a tricky remark for Gwyn to answer. "Parents worry."

"No kidding."

Gwyn walked through the porch with Molly and watched until she went into her house. The mosquito population had responded to puddles left by the storm, so she didn't stay on the step. She went to sit in her willow rocker and tried not to think about the evening with David, only about the air warm on her skin and the crazy crickets chirping as if they'd never stop.

They probably wouldn't, either. Things like crickets didn't mind if it was hot or cold or dry or wet. Knowing crickets, they could spend ten thousand years in a wall of ice and come out alive, never mind perfectly preserved. Alive, and ready to keep some other human awake all night. And everyone would reminisce about the lovely ice age, when crickets and wasps and mosquitoes and ants were gone from the world.

What about roses, though? Even the hardiest ones, bred for the northern prairies, wouldn't be keen on ice all year round. What about the clove currant, her favorite shrub, with flowers in spring and sweet berries in August and the scent of cloves all the time? She breathed it in, the spicy smell and the warm soft air.

Like lemmings, he'd said. Charging into the cold, cold Arctic Ocean, the unfrozen sea. Why did they do it? Maybe they couldn't stand the lack of the clove currant.

Gwyn wrapped her arms around her knees and wished for Duncan.

CHAPTER TWELVE

HER PARENTS HAD LIKED HIM, liked him a lot. They wouldn't have been in favor of an early marriage, though. They would have tried to cool the relationship until Gwyn finished school and Duncan got out of the Air Force. If they hadn't died. Just like that, on an ordinary day on the way home from work at an ordinary intersection. After that all she'd wanted was Duncan, a child, a home.

He'd been so strong for her that year. Bit by bit the world had come back into focus. They'd bought their small, friendly house, planted their sweet-smelling shrubs and flowers and looked out from the porch at the view they planned to have forever. Or six months, whichever came first.

When he was sent overseas she'd promised to be his candle in the window. A silly thing to say, maybe, a young, emotional thing to say, but she'd meant it. She'd stay here in this chair on this porch and he'd find his way back to her. It was her job, her responsibility, all she could do. After they'd come to tell her what had happened to him she'd still waited, but it was getting harder to recall him. Now he was a smile, a big sparkling smile—a grin. A pair of strong arms and a wide warm chest. A man who caught salmon and read *Winnie-the-Pooh*. He should have married someone else, someone with a better memory.

"Mom?"

She turned quickly. "Sweetheart? All right?"

"It's too hot in my room."

"Come sit with me." Chris climbed onto her lap, radiating warmth. "I'll run a cool bath for you."

He shook his head, messing up his hair against her blouse, his eyes already closed. She rocked the chair and for a moment felt as if Duncan was watching them.

I'm falling for someone, she wanted to say. Did he know? The thought made her ache and the ache spread through her body. He was supposed to be here, not in spirit, what good was spirit? Spirit didn't pick up a child. Really here.

That was the promise, that was the picture. Duncan here always. Her mom and dad, too. Snow in time for Christmas. Summers long and warm and lazy. Tadpoles, monarch butterflies, rustling leaves and dappled sunshine filtered through them, mud puddles, umbrellas to twirl in the rain.

The ache turned into a small, hard knot. She wished she'd never met David Bretton.

WHEN A SECOND POT of tea had been emptied and his family had finished evaluating his way with women David carried the tray to the kitchen and began washing cups. In spite of the late hour Sam went past him, out to the workshop. David thought his father had gone up to bed but a few minutes later he heard the piano. "A Bicycle Built for Two."

"Dad's teasing me," he said to his mother.

Miranda picked up a tea towel and a cup. "No wonder! From the sound of it you were half-crazy this evening. Was it half-crazy all for the love of this woman?" She didn't quite sing the phrase from the song, but she quoted it rhythmically.

"I don't know her that well. I'm half-crazy intrigued by her."

"Intrigued," Miranda repeated, pleased. "Is she an artist? A writer? I always thought someone left-brained would be good for you."

"She's a nurse's aide."

"Really."

"She lives in a little house on Dafoe. She says her great-great-grandfather might have made our banister."

"A mix of creativity and practicality, then. That would be good for you, too. My advice, if you're interested, is to take her as you find her. That, or arrange to be intrigued by a climatologist, one who shares your views."

David smiled. "Good point." What was the solution, though, if two people liked everything about each other except one thing, but the one thing was important? "If a woman detested violence could she love a boxer?"

"I don't know. Boxers are outside my experience. I suppose it would depend why he liked to box, what it meant to him and what else he did with his day. Why she detested violence would come into the equation, as well as their ability to understand each other's whys and wherefores."

"Compromise, patience, compassion."

"Definitely."

The cups, the teapot and a few dishes that had been lying around were done. David drained the water from the sink. A Chopin nocturne came from the music room now, perfect with the scented summer air and the glimpses of moonlit river through the trees.

"What's Sam doing out there, do you know?" he asked.

"Babying that canoe."

"Are you still worried about him?"

"Not in the slightest. I'm annoyed with him."

"Why, what happened?"

"With him and with Sarah. Have they forgotten how to communicate? 'Mom, X has happened and I'll be staying Y long.' That would do. 'There are X projects on my desk, which I'll take care of in Y days and see you on Z date.' That's all I ask."

"They're caught up with their own concerns."

"Aren't we all? One's own concerns are a fact of life, not an excuse for bad manners. Do I get caught up in my own concerns and fail to communicate?"

The abandoned move to Africa came to mind but David didn't mention it.

His mother nudged him. "I suppose I do. At times, not often."

"You're worried," he said again.

"I'm not the worrying sort."

"Whatever you want to call it."

"I call it information starved."

David smiled sympathetically. "Then I'll talk to them both, give them a real tongue-lashing about keeping you up nights hungry for news."

"Would you? You're better at tongue-lashings than I am. I tend to lose my train of thought before I'm done."

That was true. It didn't take long for her lectures to wander off into her hours of labor, a lie told in grade two, a lost library book in grade five and the society-decaying effects of pop culture. By then, generally, the object of the lecture had stopped listening and all she'd done was give herself a headache.

"Tell me about this young woman."

"Gwyn?" What else could he tell? "She has a five-year-old son, he'll be six in the fall. I think it's always been just the two of them. Her husband was in the Air Force. He died in Bosnia, after volunteering to deliver medical supplies."

"A hero." Miranda patted David's arm. "I can see it might be difficult to find any elbow room. You've got something going for you, though. You're 3-D."

"I might not be showing her all my dimensions. Just the alarmist science guy."

Miranda's voice cooled. "Only someone very imperceptive would miss seeing the rest of you."

"She's protecting herself. It must be hard to raise a child alone. Overwhelming."

"Oh, dear. You're not planning to try and rescue her, are you? It's not good for young women to be rescued."

It was exactly what he wanted to do. "She wouldn't let me. If I tried to carry her away from an oncoming cyclone she'd kick me until I put her down so she could finish denying it was there."

"Oh, dear," Miranda said again.

AFTER BREAKFAST the next morning David called his sister. She wasn't in, so he left a message on her machine.

"Mom says she needs to know what to expect from you regarding your visit. She's worried about Dad and Sam. Don't make her worry about you, too, okay? I know she'll be disappointed if you have to work for another month but do you really think she won't notice if you don't tell her?"

He hung up feeling dissatisfied. That wasn't much of a tongue-lashing. He hoped it was enough to get results.

The storm had damaged his rooftop weather station but after repairs the instruments were functioning again. He turned on his laptop to check the night's readings. He didn't see anything unexpected. High nighttime temperatures, high pressure, high humidity, next to no wind. Uncomfortable, but quiet.

"You're lying in wait, aren't you?" he muttered. Storms could pop suddenly, like explosions in the atmosphere. The trick was to know when and where.

It was the same tracking hurricanes. They were easy to see on radar and satellite but predicting exactly where they'd go was another matter.

He switched to a global weather map. Fleur had angled away from North America, back out to sea, without making landfall, but a new storm, Garson, had gathered steam overnight. Now it showed up as a dense swirl of cloud with radiating arms stretching wide for maximum reach. The pinhole eye in the center was large and distinct, the damaging eye wall well developed. Farther out in the Atlantic two more storms were already brewing.

Seeing all that power used to excite him. Not anymore. A hurricane was a heat transfer. If oceans continued to warm they'd happen more often and become more intense. It would be the same with typhoons in other parts of the world. The cost to people, property, ecosystems—he didn't even want to think about it.

He'd seen a hurricane firsthand once—went with a storm-chasing professor in third-year science. He wouldn't ever forget it. After winds like a thousand battering rams the eye had floated over them. A circle of light, of blue sky, with clouds swirling around. It made him think of heaven. He had his camera with him but lifting it, aiming it, hadn't occurred to him. He'd watched until the winds picked up and the light disappeared, so mesmerized he nearly didn't get to shelter in time.

His mother—usually a believer in adventures—had been horrified when she heard and made him promise not to go again. He hadn't promised not to chase thunderstorms, though, and he had a whole album of tornado photos he'd never show her.

Maybe she and Gwyn would get along. They drew their safety lines in different places but once they perceived danger both were determined it wouldn't get near the people they loved.

Compromise, patience, compassion. The last one he thought he and Gwyn could handle. The others—he wasn't so sure. His concerns about weather and climate didn't go well with her fear and he couldn't see a compromise between the two. If they found one he doubted they'd have the patience to maintain it.

But he definitely wanted to try.

DAVID DIDN'T USUALLY drop in on people but he'd apologized by phone after the party and the lecture fiasco seemed to warrant more effort. As he walked up Dafoe from the corner he saw Gwyn in her front yard talking to her neighbor. Iris noticed him coming and disappeared into her house. He was pretty sure that meant she knew how he'd behaved.

He stopped a few yards away from Gwyn. "I'm an idiot."

She didn't deny it, but she looked amused. Amused and ambivalent. That was more encouraging than he'd expected.

"How would you feel about a real date?"

Her amusement faded fast. Yes, an idiot.

"Okay, how about if you and Chris come to my place for dinner tonight? You're going to eat anyway, right? That's all it would be."

"Easier to wash one sink full of dishes than two?"

"That's my reasoning."

"We wouldn't talk about the weather?"

"The what?"

She gave a hesitant nod. Hesitant, but still a nod.

GWYN SHOWERED and changed her clothes and put on a little mascara. She wanted to look nice, but not as if she'd tried. Last night she'd wished she hadn't met David. She'd completely, honestly wished it.

A few weeks ago life had been so much simpler. Simpler before Chris saw the movie, simpler when she'd thought a trip to the museum would be all it took to reassure him. A nice, healthy dose of reality. As if reality was easy to identify and made everything better.

So she decided to concentrate on the few things that were clear to her. When David had come up the sidewalk, bearer of bad news or not, she'd felt happy. When she'd heard and seen his uncertainty she'd melted. Dinner seemed like a very good idea.

Chris's first few minutes in the high-rise apartment building disappointed him. Closed in the elevator—one that moved so quietly and smoothly only the floor numbers lighting up one after the other convinced Gwyn they were going anywhere—he looked about as interested as he might standing in his closet.

That changed when the doors opened on the twenty-second floor. They went into a furnished lobby with a wide picture window. The city stretched out before them like an aerial photograph.

"I think that's Johansson's," Gwyn said, pointing.

Chris stared in the other direction, at green squares broken up by a grid of thin, white roads and a winding river. "Look, farms."

"And over here? That big rectangle? That's your school. Our house is somewhere under those treetops."

They found David's apartment down the hall and around the corner. Gwyn felt a lift when the door opened and he stood there showered and changed, too, his hair still damp. They followed him in, Chris telling him all they'd seen from the window until he noticed there was another one here showing the other half of the city.

The living room and galley kitchen were very masculine—tailored, modern, efficient. A charcoal gray sectional sofa sat on a pale hardwood floor, a desk held a laptop computer and on a low console against the wall there was an LCD television with a video game player attached. The cord of one of the controllers was unwound. Gwyn pictured David playing while he waited for them.

"I love your apartment."

"Not too stark for you?"

"It isn't stark. It's restrained."

"My sister says it's evidence of a barren soul."

"Nice sister!"

He laughed. "She is, really. Just not as neutral as I am."

"I wouldn't call you neutral." He cared too much about

his work for the word to apply. "Do you have any more brothers or sisters?"

"A brother. He's older, she's younger."

"Do they try to save the world, too?"

It was a lighthearted question, but after a quick grin he answered seriously. "They do actually, in their different ways. Sam's in the military and Sarah's an editor. Children's books." He smiled. "That counts, doesn't it?"

Gwyn nodded but she had focused on the brother. When she'd told him about Duncan he hadn't mentioned Sam.

David looked at Chris. "How about a little exercise before dinner?"

THE TWENTY-SECOND FLOOR, behind walls and glass, had been adventurous enough for Gwyn. Now they were on the roof. David had lugged a remote-control plane as big as Chris from its hangar—the spare bedroom. He wanted to show them how to launch it to collect data about winds aloft. She supposed that wasn't really talking about the weather.

He set the plane down on the rooftop, checking the wings and the controls while explaining to Chris what he was doing. "It's called a Sabre. My dad made it for me because my uncle used to fly the real thing in the fifties. For a short while the RCAF had the fastest jet in the world."

"And that was the one?" Chris looked at the model with respect.

"Soon I'll have a helicopter, too. It'll be able to rise straight up from the roof. More practical because of the limited space, but this one will always be my favorite."

"My dad used to fly a helicopter."

"I heard about that."

"There's a picture of it on my wall. Helicopters kind of look like dragonflies."

"They do, don't they? Ready to see what the plane can do?"

Chris nodded eagerly. David held it at shoulder level and started the engine, then gave it a gentle push and it began to fly. Straight ahead, then ascending, banking around the top of the building to go higher.

"Whoa!" Chris exclaimed. He ran, following the plane. Gwyn cut in front, heading him off, moving him back to safety. She soon felt like a border collie, constantly moving, keeping one eye on the edge of the building and the other on her son.

Except for a couple of glances at the laptop screen, noting numbers that appeared of their own accord, David and Chris watched the sky for the entire half hour that the plane was out of sight, never tiring of the empty view.

"Here it comes!" David said, and Chris called, "Look! It's back!" as the little Sabre reappeared and began its descent. Gwyn noticed she was smiling and had no idea when she'd started. Her cheeks were getting sore, though.

Before they went back to the apartment something new grabbed Chris's attention, a tall pole with boxes and knobs and a rotating part on top something like a propeller. David said it was a rooftop weather station.

While she absorbed the news he had his own weather station he and Chris talked excitedly about its different shiny parts. Then David jerked up straight and looked at her so guiltily she had to laugh.

"This isn't talking about the weather," he said. "Is it? It's just measuring humidity, things like that."

DAVID HAD SET a small table on the balcony. Gwyn didn't know what she'd expected for dinner, but it wasn't the Ethiopian meal he'd prepared, a spicy meat dish served on a kind of flatbread. Chris was intrigued by the way he was expected to eat—not allowed, but expected. Pieces of flatbread were torn off by hand and used to scoop up the meat. David said he'd toned down the seasonings for their benefit, but Gwyn's eyes watered more with every bite.

"Too hot?" David refilled her water glass.

She sniffed and blinked and swallowed. "No, no, it's fine. Delicious."

After a few mouthfuls Chris jumped up to check the view, hands on the barrier, nose pressed against it. David joined him.

"That's the Forks, where the Red and Assiniboine rivers meet."

"I've been there," Chris said. "Lots of times. Shopping and skating and stuff."

"You know what a person can do? Canoe from here to the Forks, then north to Lake Winnipeg and east along the Winnipeg River all the way to my family's cottage in the Whiteshell."

"Did you ever do it?" Chris asked.

"My brother, Sam, and I did the whole trip the year he graduated from high school."

Gwyn couldn't believe they'd gotten away with doing something so dangerous. "What did your parents say?"

"Something like, 'Meet you there.' We paddled right up to our own beach and had a wiener roast."

"Cool," Chris said.

"It was a rough trip. We'd never seen so many rapids and portages." David looked at Chris as if he'd just had an idea. "Maybe you and I should go out on the river one of these days. Would you like that?"

"I never went on the river."

"In a canoe?" Gwyn asked. "Aren't canoes tippy?"

"Only if you stand up and do somersaults."

"It's a very dirty river."

"I won't go in it," Chris said. "Just in the canoe."

David added, "With a life jacket."

"Right. In case he ends up in the water."

They were both watching her. They couldn't go without her permission. She knew she should give it. People went in boats every day. She saw them when she walked in the park. They looked so relaxed. It was the what-ifs that got her. She had to look out for those. Missing a what-if was one of her nightmares.

Chris really wanted to go. He wasn't a pleader, but the intensity of his waiting told her how much he wanted it. Thinking of David convinced her. David and Duncan. She wanted Chris to develop their confident strength.

"When would you do it?"

"How about tomorrow?"

Reluctantly, Gwyn agreed. "I've watched people float by in their boats for years. I never thought I'd be watching my son."

Chris smiled, his teeth against his lower lip as if it was too soon to show his pleasure. He turned to David expectantly.

"Ten o'clock good for you, Chris? That's late for mosquitoes and early for UV rays. I'll rent a life jacket your size and bring the repellent and sunscreen. You bring the other essentials. A hat, chocolate bars. Got it?"

Chris nodded, all business. "Got it."

AROUND MIDNIGHT David came out of the shower feeling lucky that Gwyn was willing to give him a second and third chance to get things right, and found his brother in the darkened living room staring at the blank television screen.

"You used to call and knock like other people, Sam."

"I thought you didn't mind me letting myself in."

"If you're making dinner I don't mind."

Sam smiled faintly. "I needed a change of air."

"Is beer or a glass of Scotch out of the question? Mom told me you're taking sleeping pills."

"I decided to stop."

"So you've stopped sleeping, too?"

Another fleeting smile. "I must be sleeping. Otherwise where are all the dreams coming from?"

"Bad dreams?"

"You know dreams. You can barely remember them a second after you wake up."

He couldn't keep mincing around like this. "Sam, you know we're all worried about you, right? We just don't want to bug you about it."

"Good call."

"You need to think about Mom."

"What about her?"

Annoyance stirred. "You turn up a couple of months early without a word of explanation, looking like you've got weeks to live, stay four weeks and counting when you were expected for two, and you don't think that bothers her?"

"I'm fine."

"You're not. But that isn't my point right now. Mom's not fine."

Sam didn't say anything. Obviously something had happened over there. Someone Sam knew had died or he'd found evidence of an atrocity he couldn't get out of his mind. Had they sent him home to brood until he felt better, had they told him to get help?

If he wasn't taking sleeping pills there was nothing wrong with having a drink. David went into the kitchen, got two glasses from the cupboard and poured a little more Scotch than usual into each. When he turned to go back to the living room he found that Sam had followed him.

"I'll let Mom know it's okay."

"That should work, the shape you're in." Not mincing around had got some response so he went further. "You're on stress leave, I suppose?"

Sam straightened and his shoulders seemed to get wider. "I'm just home."

"You mean you've been discharged?"

"I'm home for as long I'm home. Can we leave it at that?" David decided he couldn't. "You're not AWOL?"

Sam burst out, "Would you shut the... Would you stop?"

The anger had been there all along on a slow burn but it still caught David off guard. "I'll stop when you give me a reasonable answer."

"I'm home for as long as I'm home. What's not reasonable about that?" Sam paced back to the living room, his voice getting louder. "You're home for as long as you're home, aren't you? Correct me if I'm wrong but it seems to me you're the one who's been home forever. You moved out the house and down the road, all snug near Mommy. So I think it's one hundred percent reasonable, no, a hundred and fifty percent reasonable, for me to spend a month at home without getting suspicious looks from everybody who's supposed to know me and trust me."

"This isn't about knowing you—"

"Great, it's about trusting me."

"Sam." David put the drinks on the table beside the sofa. "Sam."

His angry energy was gone. "I take that back. About being snug."

"It's true."

"No. They need you, it's good one of us stayed. And I've seen the tornado pictures. Idiot. Honestly, who stands in front of a tornado?"

They hovered awkwardly, drinks ignored. David wondered if Sam's outburst was a good thing. If it wasn't, he should back off. If it was, maybe he should keep going. He had no idea what was best.

"I'm not that good a listener," he said, "and I'm worse at giving advice, but in a pinch—"

"Hey." Sam looked embarrassed. "Absolutely."

His offer had been acknowledged, if not accepted. Now what? "Want to watch a video? I've got the *Firefly* DVDs."

"Great." It wasn't exactly interest on Sam's face. More the ghost of interest.

"Popcorn?"

"Sure."

So they got comfortable in front of the TV, feet up, with Scotch instead of root beer, each with a bowl of buttered popcorn on his lap, and it almost felt like the old days.

CHAPTER THIRTEEN

"YOU SHOULDN'T PUT your hands in the water," Gwyn said at breakfast on Sunday morning. "And no matter what, even if you drop your paddle or see some neat insect, don't lean out of the boat reaching for anything."

"Okay."

"Because it'll tip."

"Okay."

She had already warned Chris about everything she could think of, but the need to warn was still strong. She bit her tongue all the time they were getting ready and during the walk to David's apartment building. They arrived a few minutes before ten, going over the grass and toward the river rather than inside.

"Hey!" David waved a paddle from the shore.

Chris ran to join him. Gwyn wished she could feel as happy and eager as they looked.

"How strong is the current?"

David winked at Chris. "Not as strong as we are."

"I'm serious."

"We won't go where there's a current. We'll stay near shore, in this quiet loop. You can trust my judgment, Gwyn."

She thought that was probably true, but she kept a close eye on them while David explained the basics of getting into a canoe and sitting safely. He was patient, speaking in the low warm voice she liked whenever it wasn't talking about disaster. Then they were in and ready to go, Chris straight and proud in the front, concentrating as hard as he could on the simple paddling stroke David had shown him.

At first she paced along the shore trying to stay even with the canoe, but tall grass and fallen branches got in her way so she took the blanket from the backpack and spread it on the ground where she could see the whole loop of the river. She sat stiffly, but eventually the cooler air off the water and the sound of Chris's voice carrying across it relaxed her.

They stayed near the bank as David had promised for almost an hour, practicing strokes that moved the canoe sideways, turned it or made it go backward. She couldn't hear what they said but they talked almost constantly, the deep rumble and the higher-pitched child's tone. She could even hear the ripping of their chocolate bar wrappers.

When the front of the canoe came around and pointed toward her she walked down the bank to meet them. "My voyageurs!"

Chris grinned. They'd read about voyageurs together, the French fur traders who'd traveled North America's rivers long ago. David gave her an interested look that puzzled her until she realized she had included him with the word *my*. My voyageurs. He steered to the dock and steadied the canoe while Chris got out.

"Was it fun?"

Nodding eagerly, he began to tell her all the things they'd seen. Ducks, a bug David had called a skimmer that walked on the surface of the water, minnows that scattered with every dip of the paddles.

Gwyn looked over his head to David. "Thank you." She

loved his smile. As soon as she noticed that, that she loved it, she knew she was sunk. "I brought sandwiches."

Chris said, "It's peanut butter and banana. I helped."

There were chicken sandwiches, too, with resealable bags full of ice packed around them, and tomato with cream cheese and green onion. Lemonade, carrot sticks, orange segments and Rice Krispie cake. A much better picnic than they'd made the day of the storm.

David sat on the grass rather than the blanket, refused the hand sanitizer she offered and picked up half a peanut butter sandwich with one hand and a carrot stick with the other. Chris sat on the grass, too, tried unsuccessfully to resist the sanitizer, crossed his legs the way David did and crunched his carrot as loudly.

When Chris lost interest in eating and went to throw breadcrumbs to the ducks David said, "You look as if you need sleep, Gwyn." He added quickly, "I mean you look beautiful, but tired, as well."

She yawned as soon as she heard the word *sleep*. "Too many nights wide awake on the porch, I guess."

"What keeps you awake? Work, lectures, thunder?"

"The river this time."

"All for nothing. There was no reason to worry, was there?"

"As it turned out. Anyway, I like staying up late. Just me and the crickets."

"You need someone to help you get to bed."

It could be a simple observation, she supposed. If she wasn't going to follow good sleep habits she might need someone to encourage her to do it. That could be what he meant. Her heart beating harder than usual she waited, wondering if he would back up or go ahead.

"People need a routine," he continued, "and you don't seem to have one."

"But I do. It's a routine of staying up until two in the morning."

"That's a very bad routine, Gwyn." He spoke with a mock-serious, intimate tone that made her smile. "Maybe I should come over tonight and get you started on a healthier path. I'd run you a cool tub, say around ten-thirty, with bubbles, of course."

"Bubbles give me a rash."

"We'd have to find better bubbles."

"We?"

"And you'd need someone to wash your back. There's nothing more relaxing than that."

She remembered. Warm water running from her shoulders, a strong hand massaging tension from muscles.

"Then when you're all dry and wearing a very light cotton nightgown, something that lets the air through, you should get between cotton sheets with a really high thread count—my sister tells me it makes a difference. How does it sound so far?"

"Kind of stimulating."

"Oh, oh. Then I've failed."

He hadn't moved, but Gwyn felt as if he had. He felt closer.

"Something wrong?"

She shook her head. She couldn't tell him how much she ached to be touched. "So," she said, "around ten-ish, a bubble bath, followed immediately by ridiculously soft sheets pulled up to my chin. Is that about right?"

"More or less."

"Great advice, thanks a lot. I'll take it under consideration."

"If you need assistance—"

"That's very kind." And very tempting. "I'll be fine on my own."

STICKY WITH SUNSCREEN and sweat but more relaxed than either of them had been in who knew how long, Gwyn and Chris got home to the sound of raised voices next door.

"They're always mad, Mom," Chris said.

"It's beginning to seem like that, isn't it?"

"Don't they like each other anymore?"

"They like each other a lot." She shut the door and the angry voices faded. "They're having disagreements, that's all. Now, I want you to go take a good wash in case any river water got on you."

He dug around in his toy box and found a boat to take in the tub with him. He was still playing when the doorbell rang half an hour later. Molly was there, looking as if she'd got the worst of the argument. She said she'd come to check which days Gwyn would need her in the coming week. They'd already talked about it in detail but Gwyn invited her in and began to go over the schedule again.

"I have three shifts, Monday to Wednesday, all during the day while Chris is at camp."

"So I'll take him to the museum on the bus?"

"And pick him up, too." Gwyn wouldn't see David until Thursday. "I'll leave enough bus tickets on top of the fridge. It doesn't give you many hours, does it?"

"That's okay, I have plans with my friends. Do you need help with anything this afternoon? Laundry, even? Cleaning?"

"You could read to Chris after his bath."

She brightened a little. "We're in the middle of *Charlotte's Web*. We can finish that."

When Molly and Chris disappeared into his room Gwyn went outside to see if the shrubs and flowers needed water. Iris soon joined her.

"She's with you, is she?"

"Reading to Chris."

"We had a fight. Did she tell you?"

"She didn't, but we noticed."

"Sorry." Iris's voice changed. "It's that kid. She's been creeping out to see him."

"Creeping?"

"She'll say she's going to a girlfriend's house—well, she does, but then he's there. I don't know why she told me all of a sudden. They've been e-mailing, too, talking all the time, setting up meetings."

"She told you this?"

Iris nodded grimly. "So why did I explode, right? Maybe she wanted me to tell her off. You think? Like criminals who do something wrong hoping they'll be shot by the police? She wants to be punished."

"I don't know, Iris."

"I'll try again when she comes home." Fingers to her lips, she made a zipping motion. "And this time no shouting."

RICHARD WAVED the Sunday paper at David as soon as he walked into the kitchen. He'd come to check on Sam. "Wind power in southern Manitoba. That's what we need, innovation. Makes you feel better about the whole day, doesn't it?"

On her way to the counter Miranda gave her husband's shoulder a pat. "Since the news hasn't upset you perhaps we can indulge in a cup of coffee."

"Make the dark roast, would you?" In a conspiratorial whisper he said, "So that's how it works. Calmness is the key! I wonder if it'll get me bacon?"

"You can't fool me, dear. I see right through you."

"Sorry to tell you, Dad, but we all do." Sam came into the room and put an arm around Miranda. "I hear you've been worried about me, Mom."

"Certainly not. Whatever gave you that idea?"

He looked at David pointedly over their mother's head. "Just so you know, I'm absolutely fine."

"Of course you are. We knew that, didn't we, David?"

"Did we? I thought we were wondering what he's doing here."

"Lucky thing I did come. If the canoe had been caught in that storm it would have been a goner."

"Is this the day we're taking it out on the river?"

"Not yet, Dad. Soon. It needs more varnish."

"You've got to stop sometime or you'll sink the thing."

Sam didn't answer. He often did that, filtered whatever he didn't want to hear. "David had company yesterday and today, both. Female company. Did he tell you?"

Two sets of curious parental eyes turned to David.

"She's forgiven you for the lecture?" Miranda asked.

"Weren't we talking about Sam?"

Miranda looked at her oldest child. "What's she like?"

"I only saw her from a distance. Didn't want to interrupt. Things were so cozy."

"Things weren't cozy!"

"She's what, about five-eight? Dark hair, ivory complexion with rosy cheeks. Sort of Snow White-ish—"

"She's not Snow White-ish. Her coloring's more subtle than that."

"And the child—" Sam's pleasure in teasing his brother was already waning. "I don't know. Littler. Harder to see."

"Stalked by my brother," David said.

"And didn't know it."

Richard asked, "But why did you stalk your brother?"

"He was practicing," Miranda suggested. Everyone in the family suspected Sam was a spy although he always denied it. "It's like ballet. The skills are lost if they aren't practiced every day."

A minute ago David had wanted to deflect attention to Sam. Now he wanted to deflect it away from him. "Chris is a great kid. Kind of a sweet mix of his actual age, five, and a really bright fifteen-year-old. I've got him at camp again next week." And he hoped to see him after that, too.

Instead of a tired, teasing expression Sam now looked sharply interested. "So, which one actually stole your heart?"

It was clear all three of them wanted to hear David's answer, but Richard said, "Now, now. We all need a bit of privacy from time to time."

Miranda nodded reluctantly. "Although if you ever need a second opinion, a sounding board…"

Sam said, "Yes, anytime. Me, too. Not that I'm a very good listener."

"Oh, and David," Miranda said, "your sister called so you can ignore what I said the other night. She'll be here next week. If not, the week after. She can even justify leaving work early, because one of her authors lives near here. Three Hills, I think, or Three Rivers. Something topographical."

"Creeks," Richard said.

David wasn't sure his mother was any further ahead in the information department. At least now Sarah had com-

municated her indecision. He went to the counter to fill a
mug with coffee. His family's noise made him think of
Gwyn waiting on the riverbank with that quiet, worried
watchfulness. She shouldn't have to be so watchful all the
time. Chris shouldn't have to be so watched, either.

GWYN WAITED until Chris fell asleep, then ran a bath,
shallow, cool, no bubbles. She squeezed water from the
cloth over her skin and tried to imagine David's hand doing
it. Instead she saw Duncan's.

She dried off, pulled a nightgown over her head and
went out to the porch. In nearly seven years she'd never
wanted a sleepover or wondered how to manage one. For
a while someone Iris had liked had come and gone next
door at odd hours. She'd never asked if Molly knew, or how
she'd reacted. It was crazy, anyway. She couldn't even
imagine a man in her bed. Her mind stopped working if
she tried to picture clothes coming off.

She tried again. David in her bedroom, her taking off
her blouse—

No. No way.

How long did it take people to go to bed with each other
these days, anyway? She'd got the impression from movies
and TV that it was very quick. Basically people said, "Nice
to meet you" and got horizontal. Unless they preferred
walls or kitchen counters, both of which looked very uncomfortable, even dangerous, depending where the knives
were kept and whether there was anything breakable on the
drainage board.

A man in his thirties would certainly consider sex part
of dating and it didn't seem likely he'd want to wait a year
or two. Not even six months. First came sushi, then came

a Cinematheque movie with subtitles, then nakedness and incredibly intimate activities with a near stranger.

It was different with Duncan, different at nineteen, with a pre-baby stomach and pre-nursing breasts. How did a person take this step now? Was she supposed to come right out and ask him if he had anything contagious? So far she'd handled the issue with abstinence, monogamy and then more abstinence. Had she really just met Duncan eight years ago? It felt like fifty. She felt like an old lady.

"What do you think, Duncan? Do I keep seeing this guy?"

In a movie one of the stars would stand out from the others, shining brighter, and she would know it was her answer. Approval. Approval from space. Why a sudden gleam should be seen as favorable and not a burst of rage, she didn't know.

But there was nothing, no twinkle, no voice in her head, no calm that could mean only one thing. Wherever Duncan was, he didn't seem to be giving advice to the lovelorn.

CHAPTER FOURTEEN

STRUCTURE AND ROUTINE. It was a relief. A uniform, soft-soled shoes, her day summarized on a list in her pocket. Any tasks that weren't written down came naturally or as an instruction to obey.

So Gwyn took a patient to X-ray, picked up a chart from admitting, found one woman's missing hearing aid and helped another tidy her hair before a visitor's arrival. She played checkers with a patient who felt well enough to be bored, then filled carafes with ice water and distributed glasses of juice, all without thinking about Duncan or David. They lurked at the back of her mind, but she was glad to keep them there.

Before she and the cart reached Mr. Scott, his wife rushed into the corridor. She didn't call a nurse, she just kept going, past Gwyn, through the double doors and off the ward. Gwyn hurried to his room.

"Mr. Scott?"

He was watching the door, his face flushed, but with no more than his usual difficulty breathing. "You're back. Good days off?"

An apartment rental guide lay open on the floor. Gwyn picked it up and after smoothing the pages put it on the bedside table. "Very good. Yesterday Chris paddled a canoe for the first time. That was fun."

Mr. Scott kept glancing from Gwyn to the door. "How's he enjoying that camp? Meteorology for five-year-olds. I don't know. We used to learn knots."

Gwyn decided she wouldn't mention his wife's unexplained exit if he didn't. "I told you about the ice cores they're making, didn't I? Chris is getting inventive. This morning I left him using a coffee filter to drain water through garden dirt. You know what he told me? Around twenty thousand years ago Manitoba was under a mile of ice. Can you believe that?"

"A mile deep? That I can't imagine." Mr. Scott shook his head. "Have you seen that scientist fellow again? Ah, you have!"

"He runs the day camp. I can't help seeing him. Sometimes twice a day."

His smile had a little more sparkle this time. "That sounds as if it's not a hardship. They do say opposites attract."

"Do they say for how long?"

The smile widened. Mr. Scott looked at the door again. "I thought Rose would come back by now. Did you see her?"

"In the hall as I came in."

"She's upset." He made a sound that was part cough, part throat clearing and Gwyn heard an accompanying rattle in his chest. She put a new box of tissues within easy reach and rearranged his pillows to make sure he sat forward as much as he needed. "She was fussing over me. Pushing for decisions."

"You've had enough of all this, I guess."

He raised a wavering hand. "Up to here." His arm came back down in a jerking motion, as if it was heavy and hard to control. "You know what she's doing, don't you? She's got my brother and our neighbor helping her sell the house."

"Which in some ways is a good thing."

He gave a tired nod. "In some ways." After a minute he said in a flat voice, "I'm not going to come out of it this time."

That gave her a jolt. "You will, Mr. Scott. You're strong and you have a good doctor." She couldn't agree there was no hope—for one thing, she didn't believe it. His claim worried her, though, because she'd noticed patients sometimes had a feeling about how they were doing that tests and vital signs didn't support. Whether it meant they'd given up or sensed a change before it could be measured, she didn't know.

"You're as bad as Rose."

"Optimistic?"

"Not listening."

She blinked in surprise. She prided herself in taking time to listen. It was what made the job worthwhile. "I'm sorry."

"Ah, don't be. You make this place not altogether awful. Shouldn't grump at you."

They were letting him down. Leaving him alone with his fears. It wasn't necessarily the kind of thing an aide could say to the staff, to the doctors. "Does something feel different?"

A touch of his old humor enlivened his face. "I've lost all interest in rummy."

Gwyn's eyes dampened. "That won't do. The only thing I like better than playing rummy with you here is knowing you're home playing it with Mrs. Scott."

"That's exactly how I feel."

"When she comes back and I've finished my morning chores, maybe the three of us can have a game."

"Sure, sure."

It was nearly lunchtime before Gwyn saw the charge nurse at the desk, rather than rushing from room to room.

Dr. Li was there, too, writing orders. Hoping they wouldn't feel she was straying into their territory, she passed along what she'd noticed about Mr. Scott's frame of mind.

"He's doing fine," Dr. Li said. "His oxygen levels and vitals are improving. Discouragement goes hand in hand with the condition. The heart's not pumping well, oxygen isn't being transported efficiently. We need to keep his spirits up, Gwyn. Don't let a patient's depression drag you in."

Mrs. Byrd came out of the medication room. "I'll look in on Mr. Scott."

He must have put on a good show for her. She reported that he seemed optimistic about his future, then warned Gwyn to be careful about reading her own concerns into patients' communications.

GWYN ARRIVED HOME shortly after Molly and Chris. They both sprawled on the sofa near the air conditioner, limbs languid, faces glum. She had the feeling she'd interrupted a conversation.

"Did you have a good time with your friends today, Molly?"

"It was okay."

She touched Chris's forehead. "What about you? Did you have a good time at camp?"

"It was—"

"Okay," she finished with him. She added, "Why don't I believe either of you?"

Molly said, "His group researched polar bears today."

"That show was right, Mom." He sat up, more energized as he explained. His arms moved, rising, lowering, circling. "It's happening really fast. Warmer air, warmer water, less ice. The bears can't change fast enough. If the world changed really, really slowly then maybe they could, too. But they can't. So they're gonna die."

Gwyn didn't know what to say. She didn't believe anymore that everything was going to be all right. Maybe not as bad as David believed, but not as good as she'd always thought, either. When she was little and her cat died her mother had said, *He had a good long life and you took great care of him.* She couldn't say that for a whole species.

"That's horrible." She sat on the sofa between the children.

Chris's face was intent. "What are we going to do?"

Wasn't looking into the abyss a big enough first step? "What would you like to do?"

He stood so he could get his hand in his pocket and pulled out a piece of paper folded into a tiny square. "We need a hybrid car. Electric would be better or hydrogen fuel cell, but hybrids are what they're selling for now. I printed a picture of one for you."

She unfolded and unfolded and unfolded the paper. "Did your group research this?"

He nodded. "There's a better kind of lightbulb, too."

Molly got up. "Your mom needs dinner before she thinks about all this stuff, Chris. I'll stay and help." A note of pleading came into her voice when she made the offer.

"That's so nice of you," Gwyn said. "But you should join your own mom. She's on holiday, after all. She wants to spend time with you."

Molly looked as if she'd been betrayed to the enemy. She said a sad goodbye and left for home.

THAT NIGHT, the phone rang while Gwyn was cleaning the kitchen counters. She nearly leapt across the room to answer it before Chris woke up and began giving her more tips for an Earth-friendly life.

"Hello?" she said, almost whispering.

"Hi. I missed seeing you today."

David. She'd missed him, too. She didn't say it because she wasn't sure if he meant he was sorry not to have seen her or if he was only stating that he hadn't. "I was at work."

"You sound tired. Long day?"

She closed the kitchen door. "Long and…everyone seemed discouraged."

"Including Chris?"

"The polar bear project his group worked on today got to him. He wants me to buy a hybrid car. I told him in ten years we might find one secondhand. Our car stays in the garage most of the time, anyway. To help my budget, more than the environment."

"We're going to talk about transportation choices tomorrow. Walking, cycling, carpooling, public transit. He'll settle down about the hybrid."

"I hope he's not getting anxious again. He started a penny jar for polar bears."

"He's thinking of things he can do. That's better, isn't it?"

"I suppose so. I'm still wishing for some middle ground, something between reassurance and what you keep telling me is the reality of the situation."

"The penny jar may be the middle ground."

"I'm wishing for a better middle ground."

"What would it look like?"

She had to think about that. "Maybe it would start with what you say the reality is and go through my reassurance to a solution, a good solution. The world would be fine and we'd both be right."

"So your middle ground would say the climate is changing but that's okay because…?"

"Because all we need to do is—"

"Decrease greenhouse gas emissions."

"But only for five or ten years and then the climate goes back to normal, the way it's always been."

"That's an appealing middle ground. I want that one, too." He almost sounded sad.

"How close are we to it?"

He didn't answer right away. "I'm trying to be easier to get along with. I don't want you to hang up on me."

"I won't."

"All right." He went back over the ground they'd covered, replacing the answers she preferred with the ones he believed were true. "The climate is changing and we need to decrease greenhouse gas emissions, not for a few years, but forever. That will help us slow the change we've already put in motion. It'll increase our chances of coping with it successfully."

"That's not very close."

"Eventually the climate might return to what we think of as normal. Not in time for us. It would be our gift."

Gwyn went to the window so she could see the lights from the apartments. They blurred a little. Blinking didn't help. "I'm looking at your building."

"Hang on."

She heard a door close, then silence. While she waited for him to speak again she began counting windows up to the twenty-second floor.

"I'm back," he said, "and looking in your general direction."

She smiled. "You're at the picture window in the lobby?"

"Unfortunately without a telescope."

"I'm taking off my blouse."

There was a short, surprised spurt of laughter. Her cheeks felt hot. She couldn't believe she'd said it, either.

"Not really."

"But you've given me lots to think about until I see you again. Molly says you won't be picking Chris up for a few days."

"Thursday."

"Take care of yourself in the meantime, Gwyn. Go to sleep before two."

"I'll try. Good night, David."

MR. SCOTT, still wheezing with a touch of blue around his lips, had plans on Tuesday morning. He was determined to go home. His house, he told Mrs. Byrd and the doctors, could not be sold while he lay in the hospital. To them he stressed his responsibilities as a home owner, to Gwyn he explained his need to say goodbye to the place he'd spent his entire adult life. Finally the cardiologist agreed that with his meds and diet, with the Home Care hospital bed that had been set up in his living room and a window air conditioner working nearby he could go home long enough to do the job he was unwilling to give up to anyone else.

He had to wait all day for the arrangements to be made. Before he left near the end of her shift he thanked Gwyn for her company and made his usual jokes about rummy.

"I wish you'd wait until you're feeling better, Mr. Scott."

"And when will that be, my dear?"

She watched the orderly wheel him down the hall and through the double doors. She didn't think she'd see him again.

WHEN SHE GOT HOME that afternoon she found the table set for three and a number of pots simmering on the stove.

"I made dinner," Molly said.

"You did? That was above and beyond the call." Gwyn lifted the lids. Tinned beans, frozen vegetables, boiled potatoes. "Protein, minerals, vitamins. Good job. How did I get so lucky?"

Molly gave a self-conscious, one-sided shrug.

"Did you ask your mom if you could stay?"

"It's fine with her."

"Maybe we should ask her to join us."

"There's only enough food for three."

The conflict between Iris and Molly was getting increasingly uncomfortable for Gwyn. "Won't she feel left out?"

"She's got a headache."

Gwyn decided to leave it at that. Neither she nor Molly had much to say during dinner. Chris filled in the silences, telling them about his ice core, which now had seven layers, about the booklet he was making for his end-of-camp project, about the weather balloon they'd released that day and about how bright yellow the ultraviolet light-detecting bracelets had turned during the afternoon.

After dinner he went outside with his crayons and a pad of paper while Molly and Gwyn washed the dishes.

"He has so much energy," Molly said.

"Not you, though. You look very unhappy these days."

"I'm okay."

"Is that so?"

Tears filled the girl's eyes.

"Ah, sweetheart. Can I help?"

"No, I'm good, everything's good." Molly took a shuddering breath. Gwyn heard an unexpected sob, quickly silenced.

"I know you and your mom are having problems. I don't want to intrude but I'm concerned. Look at you, you're miserable."

"It's just…everything's messed up."

"What's messed up?"

"Everything." Molly rubbed the palm of her hand over her cheeks, wiping away tears. "Luke and everything."

Gwyn wasn't sure she should talk with Molly about Luke. Iris didn't seem to be able to think straight where he was concerned, though. Chris still looked happy drawing under the tree, so Gwyn took the tea towel from Molly and guided her to the kitchen table. She needed both hands to dry her face now. Gwyn went to find a box of tissues.

"Here you go."

Molly pulled tissues from the box, one, two, another. "I wish it wasn't summer. I wish I didn't live here."

"Because of Luke?"

She began to shake her head, then stopped and shrugged. "Have you heard about…never mind."

"About what?"

After a long silence Molly said, "There's these parties."

"What kind of parties?"

"I'm not supposed to tell anybody. It's kinda weird." She looked hard at the floor. "It's like, make-out parties, I guess. Have you heard of that?"

"Sure."

"Sort of like truth or dare."

"You mean it's a game?"

"Sort of. Sort of like a contest."

Gwyn absorbed that. "A make-out contest?"

"Yeah."

"That sounds awful."

"Yeah."

"But you still go?"

"Not always." She sounded defensive.

"Have you talked to your mom about it?"

"No! She'd kill me."

"She wouldn't, no matter what. She loves you so much. She gets mad when she's worried. You know that, right?" Gwyn waited, hoping Molly would agree to head home. "I can walk you to your door. She'll be glad you're thinking about this, and glad you want to talk to her."

"It's okay." Molly was trying to sound tougher. "I don't need anybody telling me what to do."

Right. That was why she was sniffling in Gwyn's kitchen. What if she really wouldn't talk to her mom? What if this was her one effort to get adult advice?

With the feeling of stepping into deep water, Gwyn said, "You don't seem to enjoy the parties. You say you don't go all the time, but you go sometimes. And that's bothering you."

Molly nodded.

"You go because…"

"Because they're my friends."

"And Luke. Does he go?"

She nodded again. In a low voice she said, "It's getting weird."

"Weird?"

Another nod.

"These don't sound like very good friends, Molly."

"They *are* good friends."

"I'm worried if something's so weird it's making you cry."

"It's just going kind of far."

Please, Iris, knock on the door. Right now.

"Luke, you know, wants—and then—well, there's these other girls—"

The picture was getting clearer. The parties were some combination of showing off sexually and daring others to follow. Did Iris know this stuff existed? She'd said it wasn't just spin the bottle anymore.

Gwyn went to the window to check on Chris and to give herself time to think. She turned back to the table. "Do you want to do what Luke wants?"

"Maybe, kind of." Her mouth twisted and she shook her head. "Not really. No."

"No? That's your answer, then. Isn't it?"

"But then he'll drop me."

"Maybe."

Up until now, Molly had been staring at the floor as if it was her only friend. She looked up, her face intent with the effort of getting her point across. "He's the hottest guy in the school. He's absolutely the best boyfriend I could have. Everybody wants him."

"That sounds as if you're shopping. He's not a car. He's not the latest fashion. Or maybe he is." She was almost sorry for the kid.

"You don't understand."

"I think I do. You're talking about trading sex, or some level of sexual activity, for status."

Molly stared, shocked enough at Gwyn's assessment not to hide it.

"Let's look at it from a practical standpoint. Supposing you're all right with the trade, even though you've told me you're not, are you ready to handle the consequences?"

"I know about that stuff. STDs, babies."

Two life-changing consequences, and she'd rattled them off in a bored tone. "So if you got pregnant, what would you do?"

"I'd figure it out."

"Figure it now, Molly. There aren't a lot of choices. If you have sex you can get pregnant. If you get pregnant, you can have an abortion or a baby. If you have a baby you can raise it or give it up for adoption. That's the whole menu. Choose."

"I'd use birth control."

Would. So this was still in the future. Gwyn relaxed a little. "Of course you would. This is if it failed. Which it does, sometimes."

After another long silence Molly said, in a near whisper, "I don't think I'd want an abortion."

"Okay. So you'd have a baby?"

She nodded reluctantly.

"Nine months of pregnancy, labor and delivery—that pretty much takes care of grade eight or grade nine—and then you either give your baby up or you raise it yourself. Which one would you do?"

Molly shrugged.

"And Luke. Where would he be? At your side?"

Molly sniffed, and swallowed hard. Gwyn wondered if she'd gone too far. Now Iris would kill *her*. "This isn't about right and wrong or bad and good. It's about being healthy. It's about doing what's best for you."

"I know." She sounded irritated. "They'd drop me, too, I'm pretty sure."

"They? Your friends?"

Molly nodded.

"Well...I've already said what I think about that."

"They *are* my friends."

She'd had no idea Molly was so unsure of herself. "Can you picture yourself alone somewhere? Away from your mom and all your friends, away from all the things that pull at you. Don't frown at me, Molly. Do it. Imagine yourself apart from everybody. Awake in the middle of the night, maybe. Alone with your thoughts. Who are you, then? What do you need? What are you hoping the future will bring?"

Molly was quiet. She had a faraway look and Gwyn hoped that meant she was managing to get a deep-down sense of herself.

Several minutes passed. "I just don't want to go to those parties."

"All right." Gwyn tried not to show her relief. "Do you need help arranging that?"

"I can call Jamie and tell her I'm not going anymore." She straightened, her face grim. "Then I'll be alone all summer."

"Maybe not."

"I know it."

"Then it was an extra-brave decision."

Molly blew her nose one more time. "I might as well sleep here tonight since I'm coming over so early to-morrow anyway."

"I think you need to go home."

"And tell *her* all this stuff about Luke? She'll go nuts."

"It's up to you what you tell your mom, and when."

Molly gave her a hug at the door. Gwyn hoped she deserved it. Maybe she'd dispensed the worst advice in the world. It couldn't be, though, because it was her father's advice. It was what he'd told her when she was ten and the most popular girl in her class had threatened that no one would come to her birthday party if she invited a new girl the others claimed had lice. She didn't have lice, they were just being mean. So Gwyn had gone off to think it through and found a core part of herself that was repulsed by the bullying. Scared that she'd end up without a party at all she'd invited everyone she'd planned to invite and almost everyone had come.

She hadn't done that sort of quiet thinking for a long time. Since high school? Oh, she knew exactly when she'd forgotten about it. The day she met Duncan. It was hard to think of much else with him standing there, funny, handsome, sweet. And that was in civilian clothes. Whenever she saw him in uniform a woozy, weakening feeling had spread through her. There was no time for reflection then. It was all about action.

Gwyn called Chris to get ready for bed. He washed and changed into his pajamas, put his stack of new drawings on his desk and climbed into bed hugging the polar bear. His drawings weren't of Earth this time. They were of an animal that looked like a big shaggy white dog. Over, underneath, or beside each picture, in different colors, he'd printed, SAVE THE POLAR BEAR.

"I'm going to put up posters, Mom."

Gwyn bent to give him a kiss good-night. "You went to such a lot of work. You know who you remind me of?"

He shook his head.

"You remind me of your dad. He always tried, too."

"Tried what?"

"To decide what he thought was right and then to do it."

Chris turned on his side, snuggling with the bear and looking pleased. She left his door ajar and went to sit on the sofa. The hum of the air conditioner made her think of Mr.

Scott resting in his living room, no doubt putting all the barriers he could think of in the way of selling the house.

She was exhausted. If only an airplane could appear in front of her and take her away to some cool spot, so cool she'd need tea and a blanket, and every thought in her mind would be erased, just for a while.

That was what sleep was for.

Gwyn got ready for bed, then opened her top drawer and took out the book hiding under her panty hose. The cover showed a healthy mammoth with its trunk in the air and its long curved tusks pointing at the viewer.

She arranged her pillows and her fan and began to read.

CHAPTER FIFTEEN

GWYN DIDN'T TALK to David on Thursday after all. In the morning children surrounded him, wanting him to mediate some dispute and in the afternoon his assistant said he was in a meeting with the rest of the camp staff.

The news gave her a pang. She hadn't noticed she'd been counting on seeing him. Literally counting the days. Three days of work, then David. There were things she wanted to tell him—that she'd read the mammoth book, that Chris had made a pile of polar bear posters. She wanted his opinion about that. Was it healthy coping or behavior that should worry her? Most of all, she wanted to hear the warmth of his voice and feel the way she did whenever he looked at her.

Her quietness didn't bother Chris. He chatted nonstop, telling her about every minute of his day. When they arrived at home he rushed to his room and returned with his blanket. He spread it over the kitchen table so it reached the floor on all sides.

"It's a little hot to make a tent, isn't it?"

Before she'd finished talking, he rushed away again. She heard him moving things around in the front closet. Then he was back with the space heater she sometimes plugged in near her feet when the furnace couldn't keep up with drafts in winter.

"Chris, be careful with that."

He disappeared under the blanket, then his head popped back out. "C'mon in, Mom."

"I don't think so." There was already sweat running down her back.

"Please? I want to show you something."

Gwyn got down on her hands and knees and crawled under the blanket. The air underneath was already hotter and stuffier than it was in the rest of the kitchen.

"So, Mom, this is how it works. We're people and this is Earth."

Her head banged against the underside of the table. "The planet's even more crowded than I thought."

She heard a click and the light that showed the heater was on glowed red. She felt around it to be sure the blanket wasn't touching.

"The heater is coal and gas burning," Chris said. "You know what that does."

It already felt like a sauna. "I'm going to lift one edge of the blanket."

"No, Mom. The blanket is the—" He paused, then said carefully, "The stratosphere."

Gwyn hadn't thought about the stratosphere since some long-ago science class. She vaguely remembered drawing circles around the Earth, layers of space.

"It's wrapped all around the planet," Chris went on. "It keeps the heat in. Too much heat, because of coal and gas. That's why the weather's changing." He turned off the heater and crawled out from under the blanket. Gwyn followed. "Neat experiment, eh?"

"Very neat." She wiped sweat from her forehead. "You've made me thirsty."

The doorbell rang. Chris ran to answer it and in a moment Gwyn heard him inviting Iris to take part in his experiment. Yesterday there'd been no sign from mother or daughter that they'd talked about Luke. Now Iris's eyes were red.

"Would you put away the heater, Chris?" Gwyn waited until he'd left the room. "Are you okay?"

"Molly and I had a very long talk. Actually, I'm relieved. I knew something was going on."

"I hope I didn't overstep."

"She's known you since she was Chris's age. Who else could she go to if I wasn't listening? I'm glad you didn't let her down."

"Did she call her friend?"

Iris nodded. "Then wept for an hour. I just talked to my aunt. She says she's recuperated from her last visitors, so I'm going to take Molly there for a few days. Remind her there's other things in life besides adolescent pecking orders. I don't want to leave you in the lurch for work, though. If we go Saturday would Chris be able to come?"

Day camp would be over. "You're sure there's room? Your aunt wouldn't mind?"

"She said she could use another egg collector."

Gwyn smiled. "Wouldn't he love that? Sit down, Iris, don't rush off. I'll get us a cold drink."

"Before or after you burst into tears?"

"Me? What are you talking about?"

"You look so tired and tense."

Gwyn opened the fridge door. "It's been quite a week, that's all, one thing after another."

"It's been quite a summer. And it's hardly started."

BY THE NEXT AFTERNOON Gwyn had begun to wonder if she'd misread David's interest. She understood that he was working and busy, but he'd made no effort to see her all week. Today he hadn't so much as crossed the room when she'd dropped Chris off or picked him up. He'd caught her eye and smiled, but that was all.

Of course it was all. A scientist who'd grown up in a big house on the river and lived in one of those riverview apartments would have a different set of women to choose from, women more like himself. Scientists or other riverview apartment dwellers. Skinny, weather-loving, diamond-wearing luxury apartment dwellers.

So maybe the dinner invitation had been because of Chris. David was sorry for the kid whose Dick and Jane–reading mother wouldn't let him go to day camp. He'd only been making sure mother and son both got some education.

That was all right. Anything more would be too complicated.

Chris had showed her his finished ice core sample, but he'd decided to leave it in the museum freezer until he could figure out how to store it. When they got home they sat at the kitchen table, the booklet he'd made during the week in front of them. On the cover he'd once again drawn Earth, round in a sea of blackness, with the familiar shapes of land and water.

Gwyn opened it and saw another picture, this one of a house much like theirs, with trees in front and a boy standing hand in hand with a woman. In a speech bubble coming from his mouth were the words, *WHAT WE CAN DO*. The remaining pages showed the boy walking, switching off a light, planting a tree, dangling a tin can over a recycling bin, hanging laundry on a clothesline and taking a very shallow bath. On the final page he stood beside a windmill. Chris commentated as she turned the pages, telling her all the details about how much less power would be used or gas and coal burned with each action taken.

"I love it, Chris. You've learned such a lot."

"A bunch of this stuff you and me already do."

"You and I," she said automatically. "We could probably recycle more."

He got off his chair and leaned close to her, flipping back to the cover. "Is that what Dad saw from the air?"

"He didn't go high enough. You'd have to be in a rocket ship."

"Or on the space station."

"He would have seen rooftops and streets with cars, playgrounds, rivers and fields, mountains and lakes, the ocean and the shore."

"What about now?"

"I don't understand, sweetie."

Chris tapped the cover. "Is this what he sees now?"

A small, hard pang twisted inside her. "Good question, Grasshopper." He looked at her uncomprehendingly. "Never mind." The name had popped into her head, a boy on a TV show questioning a kung-fu master. That made her the kung-fu master here, but she couldn't think of anything wise to say. "I don't know if Heaven is necessarily up, with people looking down at us. It might just be somewhere else."

"Another dimension?"

Thank goodness for *Star Trek*. When it came to philosophy she'd be nowhere without TV. Gwyn nodded and

Chris looked satisfied. She could see him thinking again and another question forming.

"But even if it's another dimension, he can see us?"

"Would you like him to see us?"

Chris started to nod, then stopped. "Well…not always."

"Bad enough to have a mom with eyes in the back of her head, eh?"

Chris grinned. Then he reached up, feeling through her hair.

"Ow!" she said. "Don't poke them!"

He giggled and she had to stop herself from hugging him breathless. His giggle was her favorite sound in the world.

IT WAS NEARLY MIDNIGHT when David left his parents' house. He'd tried calling Gwyn twice during the evening but didn't get an answer. Maybe she'd gone to the farm with Chris—he'd been full of that news at camp today. A real farm, he'd told them, with chickens and eggs.

Instead of continuing to his apartment he turned right when he reached Dafoe. She might be gone but if she wasn't, midnight was early for her.

He stopped on the sidewalk in front of Gwyn's little bungalow. All the lights were off. The spicy smell he'd noticed the last time he was here filled the air. It was a beautiful smell; he already thought of it as a Gwyn smell. He started up the path, then heard a sound on the porch.

"Hello?" Her voice came softly. "Is someone there?"

"Me. Sorry, didn't mean to scare you."

"David?" She stood up and moved closer to the screen. He could see her by the streetlight, a bit of outline, a bit of skin, a mix of pale light and shadow. "Come in."

He stayed where he was, thrown by the effect the sight

of her, the sound of her, was having on him. Intrigued, he'd told his mother. It was the wrong word. "I thought you might have gone to the farm with Chris."

"He's leaving tomorrow, but I've got work."

"That's good."

"Good I have to work?"

"Good you're not leaving town."

She moved to the door. "Why don't you come in?"

"Not if you're having an early morning. I'd hoped to see you this evening but my sister surprised us."

"What did she do?"

"My dad got an e-mail at noon that she was on the way from Vancouver. No flight number or arrival time. While he was on hold to the airport and Sam was checking flight arrivals online, in she walked. With a dog. Is it reasonable to adopt a dog from the Humane Society two days before you take a trip?"

"Maybe it really needed rescuing."

"That's what she said. She said their eyes locked and she had no choice."

Gwyn's voice warmed. "I think I like your sister."

"Anyway, I'm sorry how things turned out. I tried calling to let you know."

"We went out for a while. To the park and then for a cheeseburger. It was an end of camp, going to the farm celebration."

"You're big on celebrations. Maybe we should have one. Do you want to do something tomorrow? Dinner? No child, no canoe. No weather."

"You mean like grown-ups on a date?"

"Exactly like that."

"It sounds worth a celebration. Then we could come back here, play Monopoly or something."

"I love Monopoly."

LETTING CHRIS GO was harder than she'd thought it would be. They'd never spent one day and night apart, let alone four. An eight-hour shift gave her some distraction, from missing him and from getting butterflies about the date. The Date.

Sure enough, they went for sushi. She'd made a point all these years of avoiding seaweed and raw fish. David tried to tempt her. It was very fresh, he said, very tasty. Elemental, yet sophisticated, he teased

"And very raw." She hoped he didn't think she was narrow-minded on top of being unadventurous. "Fire was such a great discovery. Why ignore it?" She limited herself to vegetable choices and found she didn't mind seaweed. Before the meal ended she had a burst of courage and traded a cucumber roll for one of David's salmon rolls.

"Well?"

"Not bad."

"It'll grow on you."

"I don't think I'll let it." She took a gulp of green tea, then another.

Gwyn was sure Cinematheque would be next, but David suggested walking down the street to a dessert place that he said was at least as good as Johansson's. She lingered in front of the display cases, tempted by every one of the thirty or forty tortes, cakes and cheesecakes.

"Can't choose?"

"I'll have to come once a week for a year. There's no other way to handle this."

"That's okay with me."

It was small talk, not a promise. She told herself she didn't even want it to be a promise.

Finally she ordered a piece of cherry cheesecake because she'd never seen one so tall and creamy, with so much glaze and fruit. They made their way through the crowded room to a small corner table. The cheesecake was wonderful. She couldn't stop exclaiming over it.

David looked pleased. "This seems to be your preferred part of the meal."

"I'd give it a slight edge over the main course." She took another bite, then said, "I read that mammoth book you recommended for Chris."

His eyes got the focused expression they had when he talked about his work. "What did you think?"

"Some of the pictures were a bit icky, but not enough to be disturbing. Animals and plants seem to get preserved in ice or peat all the time. I've decided to let Chris read it. He'll love it."

"Did you notice I haven't talked about the climate?"

"I did, and it's made me happy."

"It's been quite an accomplishment. I could have talked about it now because there's a chapter in the mammoth book that gets into it. When we had dinner I could have talked about the effect of ocean temperatures on fish stocks."

"You're amazing."

"Imagine if you went hours without mentioning Chris."

Gwyn laughed. "The climate isn't your child."

"You could make an argument that it's a similar relationship."

"I don't think you could."

"I'm with it all the time. I lose sleep over it. I check it first thing after I wake up and last thing before I sleep."

"I was right, then."

"Probably. About what?"

"You're a zealot."

He put down his fork. "Let's call it something else."

"Your vocation, your passion?"

"That's better. Geeky, maybe, but not unbalanced."

"But, David." Before she noticed and could reconsider Gwyn reached across the table and hooked her finger through an opening in his shirt, around one of his buttons. "That's not healthy. Not for a man who's still…relatively young."

His hand covered hers and held it there. "Take back relatively."

She shook her head, but the urge to tease was gone. His heart beat against her knuckle, a strong, steady thud. She had a sudden, intense yearning to feel his palm on her breast, his skin against hers. She couldn't believe how much she wanted to feel that. She almost could feel it without it happening.

"Gwyn?"

She released a breath. "We're in a public place."

"Unfortunately."

"One of us is going to have to let go."

"Count to three and let go together?"

She nodded, but instead of counting and letting go, they kissed. It was a questioning sort of kiss, a light touch that sent waves of feeling along her nerve endings. Even though everything about it was unfamiliar it reminded her of the last man she'd kissed. The memory made David seem like a stranger again. She pulled away.

She couldn't believe what she'd said. She couldn't believe her ridiculous Mae West voice when she'd said it. *But, David, that's not healthy?* With her finger through his shirt? "I'm sorry."

He chuckled, a low, warm sound. "No problem. Want to head back to your house?"

The question was more complicated than it had been a few moments before. It wasn't just her house. It was Duncan's, too.

SOMETHING HAD CHANGED when they'd kissed.

The whole evening Gwyn had been relaxed, warm, happy. Until the kiss. Then, boom. Lights out, interest gone. Now she was using an unnecessary degree of concentration to find ice cubes and glasses. If she hadn't taken two out of the cupboard he might have wondered if she was pretending he wasn't there.

"You said something at the bakery, Gwyn. Relatively young."

"I was teasing."

"I'm older than you, though. It's not a May-December situation—"

She flashed him a smile. Quite a friendly smile. "More like June-July." She looked in the fridge. "Lemonade, orange juice, apple juice, grape juice…"

"Lemonade. Thanks. It doesn't bother you?"

"Our ages? No."

But something did. Too much, too soon? That could be fixed. "I like your kitchen. It's cozy." He went to the window over the sink. "You really can see the lights of my building."

She handed him a glass and stood where she could see them, too, but she kept her distance. "When Chris was really little he thought they were stars. Then he put it together. Apartment towers with neat rows of windows by day, neat rows of stars by night."

David laughed. "Poor kid, he can't see many real ones, can he? It'll be different at the farm."

He wandered from the window. A couple of Chris's Earth and polar bear drawings were stuck to the fridge with magnets. There was also a photo of a man he took to be Gwyn's husband. "Do you have family around to help you?"

"Duncan's family is in Nova Scotia."

"Bit far away for diaper changes."

"I wondered about moving there at first but—"

"This is home?"

She nodded. "It would have been too much change. You know? I didn't even want to see a different skyline. Duncan's parents send Chris gifts at Christmas and on his birthday, and we call back and forth."

"And your family?"

"I'm pretty much on my own. Except for Iris." She put her glass on the counter. "Were we going to play Monopoly? Or we could rent a video." Her cheeks colored. "Listen to those choices. I swear I have no idea anymore how to have fun."

"It'll come back to you." He waited while she pulled the box from under some others in the linen cupboard. "If we were at the lake we could sit on the dock with our feet in the water and cool off."

"Oh, that would be nice!"

Her voice had such longing in it. He wished he could take her to the cottage right now. "Come with me." He held out his hand.

"Where?" She hesitated, the Monopoly box under one arm, then slipped her free hand in his. He started down the hall. "What are you doing, David?"

He turned on the bathroom light.

"This isn't a very nice room. I was kind of hoping you wouldn't need to be in here at all—"

There was barely space for the two of them to stand. The tub was one of those deep old ones with a sloping back. He let go of her hand, pushed the plug in the drain, turned on the tap, which squeaked and sputtered, then took off his shoes and socks and rolled up his pant legs.

"David."

"One of the first things to remember about having fun is to put away all maternal devices, including the firm, reasonable tone of voice."

"That wasn't maternal—"

"In you get."

She laughed uncertainly. "There's nowhere to put the board."

"On my knees."

"It'll get wet." She used her toes to pull off her sandals and tucked her dress under her legs away from the water. "The houses will fall in."

"Oh, you think you'll get houses?"

"Hotels, even."

"We'll see about that."

HIS SMILE HAD a competitive edge. No hotels for her, it said. She rolled the dice.

He spoke before she'd finished counting the spaces. "Eight. Vermont Avenue. Do you want to buy it?"

"I'll pass."

"Someone told me it's a good strategy to buy everything you land on."

She didn't want to buy anything. She didn't even want

to play now, just to sit and talk, sit this close and listen to his voice. "I only buy dark blue."

"Then you'll lose."

She swished water at him with her foot. "It's your turn."

He rolled the dice but didn't move. "I can't see you being a nurse's aide. Isn't it kind of unpleasant? Difficult?"

"Sometimes."

"You seem like you'd enjoy a more challenging job. Intellectually, I mean. Or something with more authority."

"I'm just as glad not to have authority. I have more than enough responsibility at home." The Monopoly board tilted. She moved it to a more secure part of his knees. "Anyway, a hospital doesn't run on authority alone. Someone has to help people find their glasses."

"What happened, that you stayed with it instead of finishing your degree?"

"Duncan happened."

"I've known lots of married students."

"And Chris happened."

"I've known married students with children. Single parent students with part-time jobs and loans, too."

It had seemed like the right choice.

David smiled sheepishly. "How pushy am I?"

She laughed. "Pretty pushy."

"Sorry. I guess it can be hard to remember that not everyone shares the same goals."

"But you and I do. We both want to be useful and challenged. Between home and work I've got that covered."

"Anything missing?"

She hesitated. "Maybe. Recently."

The horse and rider dropped into the water. Gwyn reached for it, fumbling around David's foot to get it. He'd splashed as he stepped in. Drops of water clung to his legs, then ran in rivulets to his feet, plastering dark hair to his skin. It was a very masculine leg, with a muscled calf.

Gwyn rolled the dice, but she had trouble counting the dots.

He said, "Wasn't it my turn?"

"You used it talking."

They were alone in the house and she liked him. Was that enough? Should she take him by the hand and lead him to the bedroom, her and Duncan's bedroom?

David was on a different wavelength. "This might work in well with a presentation I'm doing in the fall."

"This?"

"Playing a board game in the tub to keep cool."

So, no to the bedroom, she concluded. How could he sit beside her and not sense what she was thinking?

"The museum's hosting a climate change conference," he went on. "Part of what I'll be talking about is the accommodations people will have to make to the new reality. Our effort to get comfortable here can be my anecdotal evidence and my joke in one—"

"Your joke."

He stared, caught. "Not you."

"While I was wondering about leading you into my bedroom, you were planning to make me part of a joke at a climate change conference?"

"You're wondering—"

"Past tense."

"I thought you wanted to slow things down."

"Come to think of it, I did."

He looked a bit chagrined. "Good thing I reminded you. I'm sorry, Gwyn. I was insensitive."

"No." He was sweet.

"Unromantic. My brain's like a weather office. Computers with radar and satellite images on every desk and hanging from the ceiling."

"That can't be all that's in there."

"My ex-wife thought it was." He must have noticed her surprise. "I was married for two years. We divorced three years ago. Not very impressive, is it?"

"What happened?"

He pointed at his head. "The weather office."

They couldn't have broken up because of that. "Anyone who knew you for five minutes would know that's a big part of your life, but you're much more than that. You're close to your family. You're wonderful with the children who go to the museum. You're wonderful to Chris."

"Thanks."

"And you're not unromantic, not exactly. There's all that passion we were talking about, for clouds and air masses—" She stopped because they were both laughing.

She folded the Monopoly board, letting the dice and cards and game pieces fall to the center. "We'll get wrinkled toes or athlete's foot or something if we're not careful." She stepped onto a towel and handed one to him. "Just so I understand where we are, you're not averse to—" She tilted her head, gesturing toward the bedroom.

"Not averse at all." He smiled, and her wish to take things slowly faded again. "But for now I should get going. You have work in the morning."

At the door he touched her cheek. "I had fun tonight."

"Me, too."

"See? It's like riding a bicycle. You never forget how to

have fun." He kissed her, light and quick, warm lips on hers. "Good night."

She closed the door and locked it, then began turning off the lights. The rooms had never felt so empty. Even when Duncan had left for Bosnia, she'd been expecting Chris. Tonight, she would sleep alone, all alone in the house, for the first time.

CHAPTER SIXTEEN

THE QUIET THINKING GWYN had recommended to Molly wasn't easy. When she tried to set thoughts of Chris, Duncan, the hospital and greenhouse gases aside so she could locate her deep-down feelings about David, they all popped right back into her mind moments later. She stayed awake most of the night, had a horrible day at work and waited with growing uneasiness for night to return. When it was almost dark she followed an impulse and dialed David's number.

"You know that tendency of mine to stay up late? Last night it was almost until morning. My mind's too full and the house is too empty. Could I come over?"

"Of course you can."

"I mean, could I stay over? Kick the Sabre out of the spare room?"

After the briefest of pauses he repeated, "Of course. I'll come get you."

"There's no need for that. I walk by myself at night all the time."

GWYN MIGHT be used to walking alone at night, but David still didn't like it. He went to meet her and they walked back to the apartment together. She wasn't exaggerating about

being up all night. She looked worn out, enough that it
worried him.

"The computer's on," she said. "You were busy, I've interrupted."

"Just a nightly weather check."

"Go ahead, finish what you were doing."

"Is this a test? I can resist Doppler radar."

She smiled. It made her look even more pale and tired.
"But should you have to?" She went to the other side of
the desk to look at the monitor. "Explain it to me."

It had to be a test. It was really important now that he
turn off the computer and find a book of sonnets. He must
have one. Everyone had sonnets somewhere.

"If you're sure." He pointed at white curving wisps over
the North Atlantic. "Those are tropical depressions—thunderstorms that have begun to organize around a center of
low pressure. The bigger one has winds about thirty miles
per hour."

"That doesn't sound like much to worry about."

"Not so far." The swirling bands and the eye hadn't developed yet but a rounded center was visible with scattered
cloud arching off one side. It made David think of drawings
in children's stories of the North Wind like an old man's
head. "With the ocean as warm as it is they'll soon be
upgraded to tropical storms. Then if the other conditions
are right for it they'll become hurricanes."

He clicked a couple of times and the image changed.
"This is an archived satellite image from the day of our
June storm."

The spirals were huge. "Kind of scary. It's beautiful,
though."

"Now you're teasing."

"I'm not."

He decided not to be influenced by the ways he'd disappointed Jess. Either Gwyn liked him, or she didn't. "Because I think it is. Visually, the patterns on their own, certainly. When you put it all together and understand what's happening, the intricate balance of forces that make Earth livable—it's more than beautiful."

"And then we're like bored kids with rocks or paint cans or something."

"Very destructive kids. I don't get it. I really don't." He heard how intense his voice had become. He'd been losing his cool about this too often. He tried to smile. "My strategy is to scare you into a deep sleep."

"Whatever happened to bubble baths and soft sheets?"

Bubble baths and soft sheets sounded good to him. "Would you rather go with that method?"

"This one's fine."

He led the way to the balcony. "After I've checked all the computer readings and images I come out here to sniff the air. There's some illogical feeling that I'll see something the machines don't pick up."

"Do you ever?"

"Nope."

"You sniff every night?"

"Every night. I look at the sky and the horizon, get my feelers out."

"Like those old sailors in books, waiting for a ship to come into harbor. A particular ship, the one carrying the treasure they've been expecting all their lives."

"It isn't a ship I'm waiting for, though."

"No," she agreed in a joking tone. "It's an ice age."

"It's a storm. A particular storm."

"How can there be a particular storm? Prairie storms don't have names, not like hurricanes."

"One of these days there's going to be a big one."

"Now you're getting mixed up. The Big One's an earthquake. You're being such a boy. Shaking the swinging bridge under me. Shoving a frog in my face."

"Is that what I'm doing?"

"Is it what you did with your wife?"

At first the question felt like an accusation. There was no sharpness in her voice, though. "Jess and I didn't talk to each other very much."

"Duncan and I always talked." She smiled. "He did, anyway, and I listened. Whose idea was it to give up on the marriage?"

"It was hers."

"What a ninny."

Nice Gwyn. So willing to comfort. Tonight she needed comfort but he wasn't sure how to give it. The *Firefly* DVD again? Popcorn, maybe a bit of a snuggle.

"Do you love her still?"

"Nope."

"Did you?"

He was about to say that of course he had, but then realized he wasn't sure it was true. Was she jealous or wondering if he was capable of deep feelings? He hoped that wasn't what had kept her up last night. "The relationship is long over, Gwyn. It's been three years. Jess remarried last summer."

"So it really is finished. No loose ends or yearnings."

"None." He was one hundred percent available. Gwyn wasn't, though. Wherever she went, her husband was in the room with her. David didn't think she still grieved for him.

Duncan just wasn't gone. Maybe *that* was why she couldn't sleep. "I wish I knew what to do for you."

She smiled. "You're doing it. You let me impose on you."

"You know you're not imposing."

"It feels all alone up here. You don't see or hear anybody. There's no traffic noise." She leaned against the barrier and looked farther out over the city. "Last night you asked me if being a nurse's aide is difficult."

"Was it difficult today?"

"I heard that a patient died, a man I really liked."

"I'm sorry."

"The really bothersome thing is that it wasn't necessary. He was sick but his condition could have been managed for a long time yet."

"What happened?"

"He asked to go home for a while to help sell his house. He said he didn't want to leave it up to other people." Tears glimmered, but she blinked them away. "His wife told us he insisted on sleeping in their bedroom with her even though the air conditioner was in the living room and Home Care had set up a hospital bed there. The head of their bed couldn't go up to ease his breathing, the pillows weren't high enough, the room was too warm." She'd begun slowly and quietly but she was speeding up and getting louder. "He knew better, that's the thing. When I think of the way he said goodbye…he knew exactly what he was doing."

"He risked death to be in his home with his wife? I guess I can understand that impulse. Be together the way you always have for as long as possible."

"That wasn't the promise he made to her!" She sounded angry. "He didn't promise to love and cherish her for as long as they lived in their house."

She held herself so tightly. David moved behind her and pressed his thumb against her spine, starting between her shoulder blades and working up the back of her neck with a gently rotating motion. She had knots all over the place. No wonder she couldn't sleep.

He felt her begin to relax but then she turned sharply and put her arms around his neck, pulling him close. She kissed him tensely, as if she was trying to prove she could do it, but her body eased into it. The kiss deepened and she pressed against him, soft but insistent.

David kissed her cheek, then her ear and whispered, "I don't think this is what you want tonight."

"Don't tell me what I want." She tugged at his shirt then felt underneath it, so he got rid of it, then started on her buttons, touching revealed skin with hands and lips. He shivered when his skin brushed hers.

Without warning she jerked away from him.

"I'm sorry. It was your skin. It was skin on skin. It made me think of Duncan. I'm sorry," she repeated. "What an awful thing to say to a man."

"It isn't awful."

"I can't do this." An arm over her chest, she dived for her blouse. She kept missing the sleeves until he held the blouse so she could see them. Her fingers fumbled with the buttons.

He reached around her and undid, then refastened them, putting them in the right buttonholes.

"I'm so embarrassed."

"How about instead of being embarrassed we sit on the balcony and try to find the space station?"

She smiled shakily. "Can we see it with all the city lights?"

"How about if we look and look but don't care whether or not we see it?"

They sat quietly, every now and then reaching to give each other a reassuring touch. Eventually they went to bed, in different rooms, and slept. In the morning they took turns with the shower and the toaster. Before they left for work he asked if she wanted to stay again that night.

"I don't think I'd better. Before Chris gets home I should face that empty house."

FOR A SMALL HOUSE, it loomed very large at the back of Gwyn's mind all day. She couldn't understand it. She loved her house. It was a refuge, safe, quiet, without a creepy corner anywhere, even in the basement. Chris called soon after she got in from work—that helped. He was having a wonderful time collecting stones, bones and pieces of wood, feeding the hens and finding eggs.

Hours later, at dusk, the phone rang again. It was David, checking that she was all right.

"Much better than last night, thanks. I'm looking through my parents' photo albums."

"Contentedly?"

"Very contentedly. Have you sniffed the air yet tonight?"

He laughed. "I'm on my way to do it next. Gwyn, what do you think? When Chris gets back I'd like the two of you to come over to the house and meet my family. While Sam and Sarah are here," he added when his question was met with silence. "Who knows when we'll all be in one place again?"

"Would they misunderstand? We're still feeling our way."

"They know we're feeling our way."

"Oh!" He'd talked about her with them. She supposed if she could she'd talk to her mother about him, but it felt odd. "Chris will be back tomorrow. He and I'll need to catch up with each other before we get back to the social merry-go-round." She heard a slight chuckle. "Can I let you know?"

"Sure. Remember, if anything gets too ghostly tonight, give me a call."

She hung up the phone and got back to the albums. Her mom and her dad, her grandpa and herself, at all the ordinary and special times that people snapped pictures.

There was even a shot of that ethics-laden birthday party. She studied the smiling child's face. "In nine years, little girl, your mom and dad are going to crash their car and you're going to get married."

It struck her like a brand-new idea that she hadn't always been Chris's mother. Where were all the threads she'd dropped? Old friends. Old plans. She'd wanted to be a history teacher. She should find her textbooks and see if she remembered anything she'd learned. They were somewhere in the basement, in boxes full of things that belonged to her or Duncan or her parents. That was the trouble. All her dropped threads included them.

Maybe meeting David's family wasn't such a bad idea. New threads, new friends.

A FEW DAYS LATER Gwyn and Chris waited for David outside the house, Chris on his knees on the sidewalk examining a bug Gwyn couldn't identify without crouching down and possibly wrinkling her dress. She watched David walk from the corner of the street, his stride quick but relaxed, his smile growing as he got closer. He stopped, separated from her by Chris's kneeling figure.

"You look beautiful," he said. "Doesn't she, Chris?"

"Yep," Chris said, still watching the bug.

David pulled at the knees of his khakis and squatted beside him. "What have you got here?"

"Dunno." He pointed, his finger a safe distance from the bug. "Is that a stinger?"

"It's sort of a feeler."

"It's got a feeler on its—"

"Chris," Gwyn said warningly.

"—rear end?"

Gwyn didn't know if Mrs. Bretton was the kind of woman who didn't mind people being late for dinner because of a need to crawl on the sidewalk looking at ordinary, everyday insects, so she started walking, confident that sooner or later they would follow. She was halfway to the main road when they finally sprinted to catch up with her. They stayed in the shade of boulevard trees most of the way, so they arrived barely flushed and hardly sweating.

As soon as she saw the house her dress and shoes felt wrong. It had an air of gentle decay, high-priced decay, as if it cost the Brettons a lot to wait for it to sink into the ground. A cupola, looking like a tiny version of the house itself, sat at the center of the roof and on the south front corner a turret ran from the ground to the third story. "There's a turret," she said.

"It's small, though, just one room on each floor." David pointed at the ground floor window, edged by shutters and a flower box. "That one holds nothing but a piano, the second floor is my parents' bedroom and the third was for our toys. Sarah used to act out Romeo and Juliet and Rapunzel up there."

"It's huge."

"Much too big," he agreed apologetically. "Even for a

noisy family of five that needs elbow room and hoards books and giant jigsaw puzzles."

An image of his childhood sprang to her mind, of David and his brother and sister behaving like the children she used to read about in British adventure books, trouble-free, confident children who drank ginger beer at midnight and solved mysteries during their holidays.

"Are there secret rooms?"

"Plural? Would you be satisfied with one?"

"There is one?"

David looked evasive. "If there were, it would be a *secret* room."

"What's a secret room?" Chris asked.

"You're kidding." David looked at Gwyn. "The two of you haven't been reading the right books. You mentioned that a few weeks ago and I didn't listen. We have the required material if you want to address the problem."

"Famous Five? Secret Seven?"

"What do you have?" Chris asked.

"I'll show you after dinner." He opened the gate in the hedge and they started up the path.

The front door opened and a tall, gray-haired man came out. He had a vibrant way of carrying himself and a bright gaze that instantly made her smile. "Gwyn, it's a delight to meet you. And this is Chris? How do you do, Christopher?"

A dark-haired woman had followed him out. "He never says who he is. He must think everyone knows."

"Everyone here knows. Who else would I be?"

The woman reached out to shake hands with Gwyn. "He's Richard, David's father, and I'm Miranda, his mother."

Gwyn had been murmuring how glad she was to meet them, but both of them kept talking and she wasn't sure they'd heard. She felt both welcome and invisible.

"Christopher," Richard said. "You don't meet many Christophers these days."

Chris stared at him, mute.

"He isn't always happy about it," Gwyn said. "He was named for Christopher Robin."

"You're not happy about that?" Richard looked at Chris with exaggerated surprise. "You should be. She could have called you Piglet. Or Pooh."

Chris turned red and giggled.

They went inside, Chris saying "Wow" every few seconds as he looked around at the size of the rooms, the paneling, even a stained glass window at the top of the stairs. Gwyn tried, with mixed success, not to do it, too.

David's brother and sister waited in the living room. Sam looked just like David. Same height, same hair, same brown eyes. Maybe not quite the same. Sam's were more reserved. The main thing she noticed about their sister was her clothes. They were expensive, *Vogue* magazine expensive. Gwyn felt like the wrong side of those you-can-look-like-more-for-less comparisons: here is the designer outfit, here is the cheap rip-off. David introduced her as Sarah Bretton-Kingsley-Bennett-Carr.

"David, you know I haven't kept all those names. It's just Carr, Gwyn. Sarah Carr. It will be back to Bretton soon, though. My current husband and I are wrapping things up."

"I'm sorry."

"Husband number three," Sam said. "I'm not sure of his name. Marriages come, they go. It's a seasonal thing."

David kissed Sarah's cheek. "You're an optimist, that's all."

"A somewhat impatient optimist," Sam said.

"How can you know what it will be like to be married to someone until you try it?" Sarah protested. "And if you find you don't like it are you supposed to spend the rest of your life wishing you hadn't done it?"

"So each marriage is an experiment," David said. "Periodically you analyze the results and start again."

"They're impossible," Sarah told Gwyn. "Do you have brothers?"

"No—"

"You're very lucky."

Sam caught his sister's eye. "Time to go, or we'll miss the kickoff." He explained to Gwyn, "We're off to a Bombers game."

There was a flurry of activity while Sarah found her purse, kissed a dog who'd been hiding behind the sofa and then her parents. At first it seemed too quiet after they left, but David crossed the void by giving an account of the day he met Gwyn and Chris beside the mammoth painting.

Richard said, "You're a man after my own heart, Christopher. We don't shrink from a problem when we find it, do we? See trouble, take action! Right?"

Chris nodded uncertainly.

"There's time before dinner, isn't there, Miranda?"

"It's chili and it's in the slow cooker. There's all the time you want."

"Right, then. Come with me, young man."

"Come where?"

"A skeptic! Excellent. I have a workshop in the garage. Let's see what trouble we can get into."

Chris started to follow, looking over his shoulder at his mother. She smiled and nodded, and saw the remaining doubt flow out of his body.

Miranda said, "There's nothing that can hurt him, Gwyn, so you needn't worry at all. Isn't that right, David?"

"That workshop is why I went into science. There was nothing I liked better than mucking around out there with Dad."

"Or without him."

"Well—"

"He nearly burned the place down, Gwyn, trying to accomplish nuclear fission with some coal and a wooden box. He didn't have a very firm grasp on the principles involved, I'm afraid."

"Still don't."

"But at least you've stopped burning down laboratories. That's great progress."

AN HOUR LATER Richard and Chris came in beaming.

"We're going to march," Chris told Gwyn.

"To the legislature," Richard added.

Miranda set a tureen of chili on the table. "What a good idea. Is there a purpose, beyond the obvious benefits of striding and swinging one's arms?"

"We're going to have signs."

"Signs are always good. As is the lifting of arms above the head in order to brandish them. Much more cardiovascular benefit than simply marching. Will any sort of message be written on the signs?"

"They'll say Save Our Planet."

"A worthwhile sentiment. They can hardly disagree, can they, no matter what party they represent."

"We're drawing up a list of demands," Richard added. "When we get there Chris will stand on a soapbox with a bullhorn and read them off."

Chris nodded and began reciting. "Walk, don't drive. Turn off the lights...."

Gwyn's mind jumped from hippies singing about peace to a single figure staring down a tank to gas masks and rubber bullets and charging horses. Five-year-olds didn't go to marches.

She looked at David to see how he was taking it. As far as she could tell, he was ignoring his parents and her son, and just helping himself to chili. She leaned close so only he would hear. "David? It's a game, right?"

"It sounds more like a plan to me."

"But your father isn't really going to take Chris on a march to the legislature?"

"Not without your permission, of course."

She wouldn't give it. She'd already let Chris go to the day camp and out on the river. She'd begun reading the mammoth book with him. That was enough. He was five, and her son. At this stage of his life political agitation seemed like a good place to draw the line.

After dinner David took Chris and Gwyn to explore the house. They went from room to room, climbing the stairs to the second floor and then to the third, where thick dust lay undisturbed.

The playroom was round like the tower and high enough off the ground that it was in the canopies of surrounding trees. There were child-size chairs and tables. Shelves full of books and toys ringed the room, tucked under sloping eaves so low Chris had to bend over in places. There was a dollhouse, a rocking horse and a puppet theater, all standing waiting for children.

Chris had climbed onto the rocking horse, a disbelieving look on his face. She thought she understood what he was feeling—amazement that there were really children who lived like this, with two parents, a rocking horse and all the room in the world they could ever wish for to play.

David came to her with a dusty hardcover book and a faint nostalgic smile. "Did you read this one?"

Famous Five and the Ring O'Bells Mystery. "Oh! In the big old mansion, the secret passage! This was one of my favorites."

"Take it, then."

"No—"

"It'll be nice bedtime reading for Chris."

"No." They had books of their own and they had library cards. She handed the book back. "Thank you."

"Has something upset you, Gwyn?"

She could see him thinking, reviewing the evening.

"Is it the march? You can say no."

"But it's always me saying no, isn't it?"

"Do you want me to tell my dad no?"

"No!"

Chris stopped rocking.

"No," she repeated quietly. "I don't want to be the only one who sees problems, the mean one, the narrow one, the oh, we all know how Gwyn is about these things one."

"You're not the only one who sees problems."

"For Chris."

"You're not the only one who sees problems for Chris."

David looked at the book in his hand. "You've lost me, starting with this."

"Chris, it's time to go."

"Gwyn."

"Hon, would you start downstairs and say your good-byes and thank-yous? I'll be right there."

She waited until he reached the second floor. "This was a bad idea, David. We shouldn't have come. It's pretty clear we don't fit in here with you, with your family, with the way you think, the way you look at things."

"I think you and I fit very well."

"Not in the important ways." She should never have let herself drift closer and closer to this man, let Chris drift closer, too.

"What do you mean, the important ways?"

My dress is wrong, she thought. *I couldn't afford your banister—even if my great-great-grandfather did make it—let alone all three stories of this picture-perfect house.*

He touched her hand. "Hey. Things aren't so bad. No-body thinks you're mean or narrow. And for good or ill, you're the one who's in charge of your son. You've got the thankless job of saying no."

She nodded. "Sorry about that."

"I'm sorry you were uncomfortable. Next time your place?"

She nodded again, even though she wasn't sure how many more next times there would be.

CHAPTER SEVENTEEN

GWYN WORKED a four-hour shift the next morning. She arrived home after lunch and puttered around the house, putting in a load of laundry and cleaning the kitchen shelves. Chris was happy in the yard, jumping into and out of his wading pool. There wasn't much water in it, but she kept one eye on the window just in case.

Between one glance and another, a huge cloud appeared. It was the darkest cloud she'd ever seen, looming in the west, steadily coming closer. At the first rumble of thunder she called Chris to come inside.

Until then he'd been ignoring the cloud. When he heard the distant, drawn-out sound, he stopped playing and looked at the sky. His body, so relaxed a moment before, stiffened. Gwyn could see the tension rolling in, changing him.

He hurried to the door. If she hadn't stopped him he would have gone dripping into the living room. "Don't check the weather station now, hon. If we're having thunder and lightning we should leave the television off. Get some dry clothes on, and we'll play a game till the storm's over."

There was a louder crash of thunder then, and Chris jumped.

"It's coming fast," Gwyn said. "That means it'll be over fast, too."

He dripped his way to his room and was back in minutes, the shoulders of his T-shirt already dampened by his hair. He looked out the kitchen window, then leaned into the living room to check the front yard.

"It's getting dark out back," he said, "but it's still light in front."

That didn't last long. Minutes later the whole house was as dark as dusk. Hard tapping sounds began—rain, and small lumps of hail. Chris moved closer to Gwyn. She breathed slowly, trying to keep her own uneasiness from communicating itself to him. Soon the air was white with hail. It bounced up from the road and sidewalk, it hammered the roof. Glass broke somewhere, leaves tore and hung in shreds.

And then it stopped. The dark cloud moved off and sunlight began to filter through the thinner clouds that followed it.

Chris went to the window for a better look at the hailstones covering the ground. "I can't even see the grass. Can I go collect some of those?"

"You can use your sand pail." Gwyn followed him to the front door. She stood on the step while he waded into the stones.

"They're like marbles, Mom." He lifted one to the sky, peering at it the way an appraiser would look at a diamond. Then his gaze lengthened and went higher.

Gwyn turned. It was a moment before she realized what she was seeing. Drifting along, turning, turning, lighter-colored wisps trailing down from a dark cone, drifting almost gently. Urgently, she called Chris into the house.

"It's a tornado, Mom!"

"It's a funnel cloud." Every summer the weatherman

reminded people that severe storms could bring funnel clouds and even tornadoes but she'd never seen one. "Go to the basement, Chris. Under the stairs."

He hovered. "Are you coming?"

"In a minute." She couldn't take her eyes off the cloud. She couldn't wait and wonder whether it would come right at them. It floated along the main street looking near enough to touch, sometimes shrinking up toward the sky, sometimes reaching down, wicked-witch-of-the-west fingers stretching. It sailed past Dafoe toward the Brettons' block, farther away and farther, until she couldn't see it anymore.

She went inside and called down the basement stairs. "It's okay, Chris, it's gone."

David would be at work. She dialed the direct number he'd given her. He answered after two rings, his voice calm. The hail must not have reached the museum.

"It's me. David, we had a funnel cloud."

"You did? I thought I saw some cyclonic activity on the satellite—you and Chris all right? I hope you went down to the basement."

"Chris did. I wanted—" She wanted him. Couldn't say that. "I wanted to talk to you."

SOON AFTER FIVE he came striding up the sidewalk, as if he belonged there. Chris met him with the bucket of hailstones. David looked up from the pail long enough to smile at Gwyn. That was all, but she felt a connection, as if they'd exchanged a message with the shorthand of one glance. *Are you all right?* it asked. *I know you were scared.*

They wanted her cutting board and a saw so they could look inside one of the larger hailstones. Heads bent close together, they pointed and murmured about onion layers and updrafts. When they were done they put the hailstones in the fridge freezer in case they wanted to study them further. Of course that reminded Chris of his ice core, still at the museum, too far from home to admire each day.

"My parents have a big freezer in their basement," David began.

Gwyn interrupted. "Chris, put your pail away, would you?"

He left the room, swinging the pail, and David turned to her, smiling.

"Why don't we all go out for dinner?" he suggested. "Make an evening of it."

"I don't think so." She didn't mean to sound cold, but she did. She looked into the hall to make sure Chris wasn't coming back to the kitchen yet. "We're acting as if—"

"As if?"

"Doesn't something seem wrong here? You're acting like his father."

"Cutting a hailstone in half?"

"On my kitchen table. With your heads together—" That sounded silly. There had been intimacy in their posture, though. Shared interest made an aura around them.

He looked hurt, puzzled, a little annoyed. "I don't want to make you uncomfortable. It seems to happen a lot."

"So we should draw back, I think."

"I don't agree. I think we should draw closer."

"With a view to what?"

He gave a shrug, a shake of the head. "Learning more about each other, I suppose."

"Learning more." The way his sister learned more about the men in her life, one after another?

"Is there a problem with that?"

"Not if you don't have a child who's learning, too."

"This is about Chris?"

"I don't know, is it? Sometimes I think he's what you like most about me."

David looked out the window, into the backyard. "Think you'll be done pushing me away anytime soon?"

For some reason the question hurt. Gwyn blinked and swallowed. "Let's just agree it isn't working. I don't know why we thought it would. Could you go before Chris comes back? I'll explain to him. He'll want to see you. Maybe we can have coffee a few times, spread it out? Lose touch gradually."

"If that's what you want."

It wasn't, not at all. But it was necessary.

CHRIS DIDN'T UNDERSTAND. "But I'm supposed to go back to plan the march with Richard."

"Mr. Bretton."

"He said to call him Richard."

Did anyone listen to her? Ever?

Chris went on, "Richard said in the old days, the really old days, like kings and peasants, people went to the palace gates with pitchforks and stones when they were mad about stuff. That's called the Mob."

"I remember."

"You can't remember that!"

"I remember learning it at school."

He looked at her with a little more respect. "We won't have pitchforks and we won't throw stones."

"I'm relieved to hear it."

"So can I go?"

"May you. No, Chris, I've already explained. Camp is

over and we won't be spending so much time with Dr. Bretton. That means we won't be going to his family's house, either."

Chris looked bereft.

"We can't visit people just because we like their houses or their toys."

"I like David. And Richard."

"I want you to find something useful to do. You can help me make dinner, weed the garden, dust under your bed—"

"What about the march?"

"There won't be a march. It was just an idea. People talk that way at parties. I'm sorry."

"I DON'T GET IT," Iris said later, sitting on the porch steps with Gwyn.

"They're too welcoming. I know that sounds ungrateful and unreasonable—"

"And nuts."

"Sure, but, Iris, they're overwhelming. Then there's his sister, Sarah. Beside her, I'm a moth."

"What's she, then? A spider?"

Gwyn laughed. "Nothing that sinister. A tiger swallowtail. Bright and flitting. Sam, I liked. I felt as if I understood him."

"Is he married?"

"Iris!"

She shrugged. "I think you've made a mistake."

Gwyn nodded. She knew she had. Lots of mistakes. She couldn't keep making them, not in front of her son. "You seem happy, though."

"I am. Molly was her old self at the farm, sweet with the kittens, laughing like she meant it. And did she tell you?

Today she got a thank-you letter from the Red Cross. She went to show it to the girls who helped with the fund-raising and one of them, Jamie, called her afterward. They've gone bowling. Regular summer stuff."

"I'm so glad."

"What are we going to do about you? Cart you off to the farm?"

"Can I tell you a secret?"

"Sure."

"It might sound illogical under the circumstances."

"Spit it out."

"I think I love him."

"Well, I knew that."

She thought she'd kept her feelings under wraps. "The problem is I just can't get to him. I can't get from here to there."

"Take a leap, Gwyn. Don't try to figure out all the steps along the way. Go from you love him to you're in his arms, whoosh."

"I tried that."

"Try it again."

SARAH AND SAM listened to the whole story and then told David he was handling it all wrong.

"Clearly she likes you," Sarah said. "She's stuck. She has the child on one hand and the husband on the other and outdated ideas about appropriate behavior for mothers."

"I've seen it before," Sam added. "It's hard to say goodbye to someone who didn't want to leave you."

"You've got to sweep her off her feet." Sarah made an energetic sweeping motion. "Sweep, David. Not pardon me and do you mind."

"I thought patience was a good idea. I thought she needed that."

"There's patience and then there's immobility. There's lost ground, too. You've taken several giant steps back. This girl's not going to budge on her own."

"All right. Tomorrow I'll start over."

GWYN WAS CLEANING up from breakfast when the doorbell rang. A florist's truck was parked in front of the house and a young man stood in the porch with a paper-wrapped package.

"Delivery for Gwyn Sinclair," he mumbled, as if he couldn't care less.

She supported the bottom of the box, decided recipients of deliveries shouldn't have to tip, murmured her thanks and closed the door. Something in the container rocked to one side while she walked to the table. She set the package down and began to unwind the paper. Before she was done she smelled roses.

A dozen, already in a vase. Ivory deepening to a pale pink. She opened the card.

When I first saw you a few years ago, carrying your son into the galleries, a blush of color in your cheeks, I thought of roses. And when I first saw these I thought of you.

Moments later the doorbell rang again. She hoped it was David, and it was.

"David, they're beautiful. And the message is beautiful. And thank you for not listening to me before. I'm so happy to see you." She would have taken the leap Iris had recommended, right into his arms, but he seemed to have something to say.

"The other night you said we don't fit in the important ways. That's not true, Gwyn. Here's what's important to me about you, some of the things, anyway." He looked so serious. "Your smile, your courage—"

"Courage?" she murmured, pleased but doubtful. "I don't have courage."

"Your softness, your sense of humor, your loyalty. How hard you work, how afraid you are to have fun, how delighted you are when you let yourself have it. Chris is the neatest kid I've ever met but he's not what I like about you."

She was having to work at not crying. She should give him a list, too. She had one, a long one, starting with his coffee eyes and warm voice, the way he made a canoe glide through the water, how clearly he looked at the world around him and how much he cared about all that was happening. Her throat was too tight for any of that. She could only manage, "I was jealous."

"Of Jess?"

It was complicated. "Of your family." His storybook home.

"I thought you didn't like them."

"Oh, I like them."

"Good, because they all want you to come to the cottage with us. They say they'll plan to go when you're off work for a few days."

"But it's your holiday."

"We've had lots of time just the five of us. Seven would be fun."

CHAPTER EIGHTEEN

GWYN FOLDED all the clothes she'd brought into one drawer and all of Chris's into another. She felt as if she'd arrived at summer camp. The Bretton cottage was more rustic than she'd expected, down to the braided rag rug beside the bed. Sarah's bed. Richard had set up a rollaway cot for Chris and Sarah had insisted she didn't mind sleeping on the porch. It was her favorite part of the cabin, she'd said. She often slept there.

"Can I go swimming, Mom?"

"Not yet."

"Sam's swimming."

"Mr. Bretton. Not yet." She had to find out how deep the water was and whether there were any currents. David had told her not to worry about the leeches…which she hadn't been doing until that moment.

Chris stood on one foot, watching her tuck their pajamas under the pillows. "Can I go to the beach?"

"As soon as I'm ready." She realized she was stalling. They didn't belong here. Invitation or not, she felt like a stowaway. A leech.

Miranda appeared in the doorway. "Here you are." She made it sound as if she'd been searching for hours. "When you're settled in we'll go down to the beach."

Chris gave a little hop.

Miranda looked at him more closely. "Goodness, you don't even have your suit on! Were you planning to swim like that, shoes and all?"

His eyes slid to his mother. The uncertainty she saw should have shamed her into action. Instead, it glued her to the floor. She wasn't up to this. A weekend at the cottage. A Weekend At The Cottage. It was like a short story, Noel Coward, she thought, remembering first-year English Lit. The sociableness of it was beyond her. Was she supposed to sit languidly in the shade with one eye on her gamboling offspring and the other on the martini pitcher?

"We won't be much longer, Mrs. Bretton. Sorry to keep you waiting."

"Miranda, really, dear. You'll make me feel like an old, old lady. You won't have any trouble finding it. It's right in front of the cottage. Richard and I will go down. Take your time."

Next, David came to their room in a bathing suit, flip-flops and nothing else. For a tall and slender academic he was surprisingly muscled and tanned. The canoeing, she supposed.

He looked from Chris to Gwyn. "Aren't we going to hit the beach?"

All she wanted to do was go home to her porch, her kitchen, her comfortable old tub. Where was that courage he'd claimed she had?

"I'll sit out the first swim. But you get ready, Chris. We'll wait for you outside." Her feet unglued and she squeezed past David and through the doorway. He followed, talking about warm water and how great it felt to jump right in.

In all of two minutes Chris joined them, tugging at his

suit. It was a little big, with the legs almost to his knees and the waistband falling under his belly button. His skin was so pale next to David's, his arms and legs spindly. She slathered sunscreen over him while he pranced like a race-horse at the gates. Then he took off over the grass, jumping rocks to reach the sand.

"Well, he's happy," David said, his voice warm with amusement. "What about you?"

"I'm happy."

"Feeling a little shy?"

"A little."

Richard and Miranda, wearing loose T-shirts over bathing suits, waded on the shore kicking water at each other. Way beyond them Gwyn saw a head, and arms curving out of the water one at a time.

"Is that Sam? He's so far out."

"He's been pushing himself."

"I hope Chris won't think he can—"

David picked her up, right off the ground.

"David!" She heard Chris laughing. "Not in the water, don't you dare drop me in the water!"

He carried her to a shady spot and put her down, but didn't let go. "I wouldn't drop you, not in the water or anywhere else. That would be rude."

"It would get you in serious trouble."

"Everything gets me in serious trouble with you. How do I please you?"

"You please me."

"Tell me which things so I can be sure to keep doing them."

Holding me like this, she nearly said. *This pleases me.* She moved a little so they were still close, but no longer touching.

A shout from Richard startled them both. "Christopher wants to swim. I'll go out with him."

Gwyn took one step, ready to intervene, and David's arm tightened around her. "My dad taught all three of us to swim here. Trust him, Gwyn."

"I don't want Chris to go over his head."

"He won't."

"And there's the leeches."

"Leeches come off."

THAT WAS A GOOD THING, too, because Chris had a footful of them when he left the water. Tiny black threads wiggled between his toes and no matter how hard he jumped up and down, they didn't let go.

"Looks like you stepped into a leech nursery," Richard said.

Glancing at Gwyn, who couldn't do anything but repeat "Oh" and "Eew," Miranda said, "Someone does, every summer," and pulled a saltshaker from her beach bag. As soon as she sprinkled the leeches they fell off, twisting on the sand.

Once they were no longer attached to him Chris thought they were fascinating, so he went back into the lake with a pail hoping to catch some big ones. Gwyn had to force herself not to remind him to be careful. He hadn't gone farther than waist deep yet, and Richard stayed close enough to grab him if he needed grabbing.

David waded in to help with the search. "If you don't move you'll see them come to you. Great big ones, like snakes."

Chris's shoulders bunched up. "Really? Snakes?"

"More like earthworms," Richard said.

"Great big earthworms."

No one seemed to mind that Gwyn didn't go in the water or carry on a conversation. Gradually she felt less uncomfortable, but still like a kid on the edge of the playground. The Brettons weren't putting her there—they had already welcomed and included her.

Birch and spruce trees growing all around the cottage made it feel private, but lots of others had been built in sight of the lake, following the narrow beach, a mix of sand and rock. Past a clump of sharp, scattered stones on the Brettons' section, there was a large, flat rock shaded by three birch trees. It looked good for sitting on, good for reading, good as a diving platform for anyone who didn't mind entering the murky, leechy lake headfirst.

She climbed onto one of the smaller stones. One ear tuned to Chris's high-pitched voice, she found her way across the rocky pile avoiding points and puddles and slippery-looking lichens.

"There's one!" Chris called. He finished with an excited squeak and repeatedly dug the pail into the water like a shovel, reaching deeper each time he tried.

David said, "You've scared him clear across the lake, Chris."

Gwyn saw a flash of blue near the cottage. It was Sarah in a sapphire-colored T-shirt and white shorts, walking with an unselfconscious rhythm as if she didn't know that everyone, man or woman, paid attention when she came by. Looking gorgeous when she was dressed up to go out for dinner was understandable, but at the lake?

She headed straight for the flat rock, jumping lightly from stone to stone and arriving with a smile, either unaware that Gwyn was wrestling with jealousy or unconcerned about it.

"You've found my favorite place in all the world!"

Gwyn nearly apologized, but Sarah put an arm around her and drew her to the edge.

"Let's sit with our feet in the water. Sometimes fish bite your toes and it tickles."

"Oh, no."

"Oh, yes."

So Gwyn took off her shoes and sat where she was told without mentioning leeches or asking how big these toe-biting fish might be. The rock was hot to touch, full of stored energy from the sun and the water was as warm as a bath, the temperature she'd choose for a late summer evening.

"Your son is loving it here. I knew he would." Sarah rocked to one side, nudging Gwyn. "Which brings me to the point uppermost in my mind." Her voice was light but not quite teasing. "Do you love my brother?"

Gwyn's eyebrows went up and stayed up.

"All right then, one to ten, how much do you like him?" Her eyes, her whole face, sparkled. Maybe she didn't expect an answer. "You know about Jess, I suppose."

Gwyn nodded.

Sarah turned to look at David, now teaching Chris how to float on his back. "They were only married for a couple of years. That's more like going steady, isn't it?"

Gwyn didn't think she should discuss David with his sister. She was so friendly and confiding, though, and Gwyn was so curious. "Except for the vows."

"Exactly. I don't know how they could say them with a straight face. It was so obvious to everyone else it wouldn't work and here they were talking about cleaving only unto each other. She really wasn't right for him. Whereas you, my dear, are perfect."

"Why's that?"

"Because you're a damsel in distress. Jess was too contemporary and too shallow. She didn't get him, not at all. It was annoying to watch."

"I'm not a damsel in distress."

"In a good way!"

"There isn't a good way."

"Sarah!" David called. "Are you picking a fight with Gwyn?"

"Of course not! We're having the nicest chat." She smiled at Gwyn. "You see? He wants to save you from me. For all his charts and careful equations, I always knew there was a Galahad in the mix."

Gwyn looked at her toes, blurry through water, and wondered if the whole family saw her the way Sarah did. It would be awful if they were just being kind, giving the distressed single mother and her son a little summer holiday. David could have a long list of things he liked about her and still just be kind. Then he wouldn't give her roses, though, roses with a romantic message.

"Are you always so quiet?" Sarah asked.

"I suppose I am."

Sarah leaned in again, with another of those sisterly nudges. "Want to help me dunk Sam?" He'd swum closer to them but he was still farther out than Gwyn would ever go.

"I don't have a bathing suit on."

"Neither do I."

When she couldn't persuade Gwyn to join her, Sarah stood and dived headfirst from the rock, surfacing twenty feet away. She stayed low in the water, only the top of her head and her eyes visible and approached her brother stealthily. He heard though and whipped around to dunk her before she got to him. She came up with a yell and leapt on his head, carrying him underwater with her.

"Mom! Look!"

David had left the shallow swimming area with Chris riding on his back. "You're not wet," David said, with a speculative look.

"You promised," she said.

"Promised?"

Gwyn backed up, feet out of the water, legs out of his reach. "You'd better not let your sister influence you."

"Come and swim, Mom. It's so warm, it's so nice, you'll really, really like it."

Chris was beaming. Beaming. So she went to change into the one-piece navy blue suit that had been stuck at the back of her closet for so long she'd had trouble finding it when she'd packed. It was meant for her pre-Chris body. She pulled the stretchy, clingy fabric higher up over her chest and lower down over her rear, then away from her tummy. There wasn't a single part of her that was as firm as it used to be. Did she have a long T-shirt? She tried three, but none went far enough. All right. There was nothing to be done. She hurried outside to get in up to her chin before anyone had a chance to compare her to Sarah.

LATER THAT EVENING Sam and David built a huge fire on the beach. Richard took Chris to cut willow sticks and showed him how to roast wieners and marshmallows near the flames. As the fire burned down they played charades and, after that, rummy on the porch by candlelight with fireflies sparking outside. Chris sat on Gwyn's knee watching her play her hand, his head drooping lower and lower. When he fell asleep David carried him to bed.

The adults continued to play until the game eased to a stop and conversation took over. Gwyn found herself telling them about her great-great-grandfather coming to Canada as a boy and growing up to make curving staircases in the houses along the river. His son had become a carpenter, too, and his son, and finally her father. The Brettons were so interested she felt as if it was a wonderful story. They wanted to know all about her family. Their warmth beckoned. She had to remind herself to keep her family apart, her people, not theirs.

FIRST THING in the morning Sarah suggested a hike to some rapids the family visited every year. Three miles through forest and over rocky hills. Richard had to rest a number of times but he insisted he was fine and got annoyed with anyone who fussed.

When they arrived Gwyn looked appreciatively at the shallow, rushing water, bubbling, sparkling, apparently so clean. Richard explained it was because the water flowed over Precambrain Shield, not mud.

She thought that would be the extent of the expedition, but the three younger Brettons peeled off their clothes, revealing bathing suits underneath, and waded into the water. Chris followed without asking her, reaching for David's hand. Then all of them, the four of them, got right down, half lying in the water, and let it carry them, shrieking, over and down the rock. They continued for an hour or two, Gwyn couldn't tell, while she stayed in the shallows with Miranda and Richard. When Chris waded back to them and said he was hungry, Richard pulled sandwiches from a backpack. They all sat with their feet in the water to eat. It was the first time she could imagine David as a child, growing up with Sam and Sarah. Drenched and laughing, they resembled each other even more, the differences of adulthood gone.

It was a quieter group at the cottage that evening. Richard went to bed before sunset; David and Chris played checkers on the porch; Sarah and Miranda stretched out to read. Sam was nowhere to be seen.

Gwyn decided to go out to the rock again. She didn't know when she'd ever got so much sun. She was used to being on her feet all day, but not to walking through sand and over stone, up hill and down.

She heard a splash nearby and Sam appeared. He pulled himself out of the water to join her.

"So here you are at the legendary cottage. Is it all you thought it would be?"

"It's simpler."

"Plain old cottage."

"But all of you are what I thought you'd be. The way you are here, I mean." Minus the imagined pitcher of martinis.

"Marshmallow roasts? Charades?"

"You sound disillusioned."

"Nah." He was quiet for so long she thought he wasn't going to add to that short answer. Eventually he did. "It's hard to enjoy it now."

"After all you've seen in Afghanistan?"

There was another long silence. "And done."

She hadn't been sure if he'd want her to mention Afghanistan. She was even less sure what, if anything, to say now. Duncan's letters had changed after he'd been in Bosnia for a few months. A person couldn't go to some of the most troubled places in the world from a comfortable life in Canada and not be changed by what happened there.

"I don't know what to say, Sam. I can't imagine all the things a soldier must experience. I appreciate it, though, that people like you and Duncan try to keep the rest of us safe."

"If you could imagine it, you might not appreciate it."

She could believe some details would be hard to accept. "We tend to be a bit too naive here."

Sam nodded. "I don't usually find common ground with anyone outside the service. People don't understand what we're doing. They don't want to know. It's like there's a perpetual childhood summer state of mind. Why not? Nice if you can manage it."

"You're a good man, Sam. Anyone can see that."

"Now you're mixing me up with David. He's the good guy." He stood, already dry except for his trunks. He lightly messed the top of her hair. "I hope you keep him."

She watched him go, finding his way easily over the stones, even in low light. He would have been climbing over those when he was Chris's age. The three of them must have been tough, confident children. Twenty-four hours in their company and some of that attitude was rubbing off on Chris.

The past six years had been about him, about providing a home. There was nothing wrong with that. Why had the thought even come into her mind? Providing a home for Chris was the point.

It was just that she wasn't quite living.

Guilt shot through her, a sharp, physical feeling. She couldn't say that. Being Chris's mother was certainly living. She was lucky to be doing it. Ask Duncan.

The Brettons—being with them was like being in a play. Except she wasn't acting. It was like being the only member of the audience, sitting on stage with the actors. A soldier, a scientist and a serial wife, and parents who made their own rules. If the Brettons thought of something to do, next thing anyone knew, they did it. That was what she meant about living. She'd only been keeping her balance.

"Goodness, that's a bleak expression if I ever saw one."

It was Miranda. The rock had seemed like a quiet place, but each time Gwyn climbed on to it, company followed.

"It's a well-known danger of sitting on this rock as the sun goes down and the loons are making their noise. Beauty can be an emptying thing."

"I've never heard loons before."

"Imagine that."

"You have a wonderful family, Miranda."

"Thank you. As do you."

"I was just thinking that all I've done for the past six years is keep my balance."

"And quite an accomplishment that must have been at times. Getting light-headed, are you?"

Gwyn nodded.

"There's nothing wrong with a little vertigo now and then."

"I've had vertigo all summer."

Miranda smiled. "I'm sure that's a very good thing."

GWYN COULDN'T TELL what had woken her. She listened but heard nothing, not even frogs or crickets or loons. It was very late, then, the middle of the night. She tiptoed to Chris's cot.

He wasn't there. She looked into the hall. No crack of light under the bathroom door. No one in the kitchen. She felt her way to the living area and whispered his name, then jumped at the sound of another voice.

"They've gone out."

"Sam?"

"David and Chris went out. Don't worry. We always used to sneak out at night. Usually to the rock."

In the dark? She headed in the general direction of the door.

"I'll go with you. Protect you from the bears."

She thought he was probably joking about bears, but her heart thumped anyway. He took her hand and she was surprised how brotherly the gesture felt. The moon made it a little easier to see outside, but she was glad to have him with her. He seemed to know his way around without light.

Before they got to the beach she heard their voices, David's deep rumble, Chris's high-pitched attempt at quietness. Sam led her closer to the rock, until she could make out their shapes. The two of them were lying on their backs, each with one hand pointing to the sky.

"I'm going up to the space station one day," she heard Chris say, "if Mom lets me."

"Are you going to be an astronaut?"

"I don't know. Maybe an astronaut or maybe your job."

"My job!"

"*Like* your job, I mean. Do you know about space travel?"

Gwyn didn't want to disturb them. She pulled Sam's hand, and they started back to the cottage.

"The two of them sure get along well," he said. "Almost like father and son."

The idea still gave her a twinge. "They hit it off the minute they started talking about frozen mammoths."

"Peas in a pod."

They couldn't be peas in a pod.

Sam squeezed her hand. "Kindred spirits, anyway. Mind the stump."

She saw it at the last minute and stepped around it, then

tripped over a stone. Kindred spirits. That was what they were. Not father and son, and not peas in a pod. It sounded much better.

"I've been wanting to ask you something, Sam. It's silly—"

"That's okay. I grew up with Sarah, remember."

She smiled briefly. "When I heard you were in the military I wondered if you'd ever met my husband."

"As in 'You're from Manitoba? Do you know my friend, Bill?'"

"Silly," she said again.

"I didn't meet Duncan."

She was disappointed, but not surprised. Hesitantly, she broached a subject that had been at the back of her mind for years. "Maybe you can tell me...I've wondered if he was frightened. The day the helicopter went down and all the other days."

"Of course he was."

She'd hoped Sam would have some theory about a hormone that kicked in to erase soldiers' fear. "He always had such a big grin, devil-may-care. I've pictured him getting in the helicopter like that—and that's all I picture. My parents, too. I see them getting into the car and driving away, and the picture ends. Like in a movie. Fade out."

"I don't see any problem with that."

"Is that what happens for you? Fade out?"

There was a long silence. "The opposite. Too much detail. But that's the job. You learn to live with it. I haven't told them yet, but I'll be headed back soon."

"Back to Afghanistan?"

"Wherever I'm told to go. So you'll have to time the wedding right. I want to be there."

"No one's thinking about a wedding."

"Everyone is."

"No one is."

He put an arm around her shoulders. "Just check with me before you set a date."

IN THE MORNING David wanted to take another hike, just the two of them. "It's tough slogging but worth it. There's a view I want to show you, a cliff that looks out over a lake. If we're lucky we'll see blue herons."

Chris was digging in the sand, making castles and moats. Sam lay under a nearby tree, a hat over his eyes.

"Go ahead," Miranda said. "We'll watch Chris."

"We really will," Sarah said. "Eight eyes on him every minute. I promise."

They were so relaxed she felt like an idiot for worrying about water and bears.

Sarah went on, "They've told you what a spoilsport I am, haven't they?"

Gwyn began to nod, then flushed and tried to deny it. Sarah laughed.

"It's true." Sam hadn't budged. "She'll make sure Chris doesn't have any fun at all."

DAVID AND GWYN didn't make it as far as the cliff. An hour into the hike she stepped over a fallen log and accidentally brushed against him. Then she had to kiss him, it couldn't wait. A kiss became a touch and the next thing she knew they were falling to the ground behind some bushes as if there was no such thing as poison ivy or mice or other hikers. The moss was soft enough to be comfortable and she hardly worried at all if there were bugs underneath her. Nothing came between them, not regret or guilt or doubts. Every touch felt right, what they'd been waiting for, new and familiar at the same time.

Late at night after Chris and the Brettons were asleep Gwyn went outside. She stood on the beach away from the moonlight, away from the windows, and with her mind full of prayers and apologies she wept one last time for Duncan.

CHAPTER NINETEEN

RICHARD HAD BEEN SERIOUS about the march. When Chris heard that, he gave Gwyn an undeniable "I told you so" look. She felt too content to protest the idea, or even to worry about it. Participating would probably be good for him. A civics lesson.

The day after they returned from the cottage they all got to work on the preparations. Molly came, too. Richard was glad of the extra help. He wanted signs painted, and lots of strong, straight branches cut to hoist them.

Chris hurried past Gwyn carrying a small saw.

"Careful! Don't run with that."

Miranda looked up from her flowers. "He'll be fine, Gwyn. Goodness, David and Sam were building tree houses at his age."

Chris had already disappeared into the rain forest the Brettons called their backyard. Gwyn followed, going through a narrow break between some lilacs. It was like a maze on the other side, with curving paths and no line of sight. She heard sawing from one direction and Miranda talking from another, but she couldn't see anyone.

"Lost?"

"David."

"My mother loves these nooks and crannies." He led her

to the left, away from the sawing sound to a bench tucked within a semicircle of honeysuckle bushes. Tiny Johnny-jump-ups, dark purple and light violet, grew in the grass and under the trees.

"I'm never going to want to leave," she said.

"Maybe we can build a little house here."

"One room, just for us." He could chuckle all he liked; she thought it was a great idea. She leaned against him and right away her body warmed, as if it remembered all the lovely things that had happened the last time they got this close.

It was the night before they'd come back to the city. They'd walked along the shore, far past the flat table rock, to a small bay with a beach of fine sand. Birch leaves had rustled all around and overhead, water had lapped against their feet, and David had devoted his focused nature and detailed mind to finding and exploring every sensitive spot on her body. She'd taken off her ring that morning. Now it was wrapped in the something-old hanky Duncan's mother had given her and packed in a trunk with his letters and her wedding dress.

"Lost in thought?" David asked.

"Indulging in it." They hadn't mentioned love yet. Neither of them had actually said the word. She hoped it didn't matter.

There was a sound through the shrubs and Chris went tramping past their nook, dragging a branch behind him. Gwyn smiled at his purposeful posture. "I can't believe the difference in him."

"I suppose we should help."

"Not yet." Kissing away David's logical, reasoned expression was still a novelty. Much better that sawing branches.

THEY TOOK their time leaving the maze and when they came out the only person they saw was Sarah. She was trying to teach her puppy to sit, but when David arrived it only wanted to sniff his shoes. She picked it up and held its wriggling body tightly.

"Chris and his babysitter have gone up to the play-room."

David decided to check on them so he and Gwyn could relax with a clear conscience. He found them stretched out on the floor, Molly reading one of the Secret Seven adventure stories to Chris. She was almost done so he stood in the hall and only went into the room after she closed the covers.

"Good book?"

"Great!" Chris said.

Molly shrugged. "Okay."

"A little young for you. We have some others you might like better." He ran a finger along the shelves, pulling several volumes partway out. "*A Wrinkle in Time. The Moorchild. Five Children and It.* Help yourself anytime."

Chris came close and whispered, "Remember, you said there was a secret room? Where is it?"

David bit his lower lip and raised his eyebrows as if nothing would ever drag that information out of him.

"Where?" Chris whispered again.

"If I show you you'll promise not to tell?"

Both children nodded, Chris eagerly and Molly with a touch of skepticism. He made them hook little fingers together to seal their promise.

"Okay, this way." He took them into the closet, a narrow, low-ceilinged space, and got hold of the board that formed the back. There weren't any nails—it only rested in place. He set it aside, and kept going.

It wasn't a real secret room, just a crawl space left after all the walls had been put in. Maybe the builders had made a mistake with their calculations, maybe it was for ventilation, maybe there wasn't any other way to make the cupola fit on top of the house.

David hadn't been here in years. He felt for the string that should be hanging down and pulled it. A bare lightbulb turned on. The boxes he and Sam had brought in to sit on were still there. So was a stack of comic books.

"Cool!" Chris crawled over to the comics and sneezed when he disturbed the layer of dust over them.

"We don't tell anybody," David reminded the children.

"Don't your parents know it's here?" Molly asked.

"They've never said so."

"Can we bring our stuff?"

"Yeah," Chris chimed in. "Can we bring our stuff?"

"No candles or incense or matches."

They nodded vehemently.

"Take any food garbage out with you. No kettles, hotplates, gas barbecues…"

Molly smiled tentatively. "Just things like magazines, a CD player."

David nodded, touched by how earnest she was. There was a bit of a sparkle in her face. He hadn't seen that since she'd burst into the yard the day of the barbecue and had her camping plans doused so firmly.

He crawled back out of the hidden nook, leaving them to play. At the top of the stairs he stopped, his attention caught by the small square of sky visible through the window. Nothing looked different, no matter how long and hard he watched. It was official. He was obsessed.

IT DIDN'T SEEM RIGHT to have to go back to work in the morning. Molly arrived just as Chris rolled out of bed. He went straight to the television to turn on the weather channel.

"...a chance of severe thunderstorms this afternoon. Winnipeg and the Interlake can expect to get the worst of it. Stay tuned for updates and to find out what precautions you may need to take."

Chris sat on his heels. "Mom, did you hear that?"

"I heard. We'll keep our eyes open. It's a beautiful morning, though." She picked up her purse and gave him a kiss. "I'll be back for lunch around one. Molly, you and Chris should be home by then, too, okay? I don't want you outside if there's lightning this afternoon." Last night Richard and Sam had printed fliers advertising the march. The children planned to distribute some today.

On her way to the bus stop nothing about the conditions felt as if a storm was coming, but two hours later she stared out the window of a patient's room at fast-moving, dark gray clouds. She'd never seen anything like them. They were massive, boiling, arched over a strangely turquoise sky. It shimmered with lightning that flickered above the cloud layer.

"Makes the hair stand up on the back of your neck," the patient said. "I haven't seen ten minutes of my show. They interrupt with one warning and not a minute later they've got another one."

"What are they saying?"

"Long story short? Stay the hell home."

His earphones muted the TV's volume. She unplugged them and changed the channel to the weather station.

"...winds over 95 kilometers per hour and golf-ball-to-tennis-ball-size hail have been reported near Portage la Prairie. We have several unconfirmed reports of funnel clouds. Please stay inside and be alert for changing conditions."

"You're welcome," the patient called after her as she hurried from his room. She went to the telephone. No one answered at her house. She'd try the Brettons, then Iris at work.

THERE WERE LOGICAL REASONS for a phone to go unanswered, but all David could think was that something must have happened to Gwyn. She should have been home by now.

He called Winnipeg General and argued with the operator until she agreed to connect him to Gwyn's ward.

"Is Gwyn Sinclair there, please?"

"She's off for the day."

"I thought she might have stayed late because of the weather."

"Far from it. She ruffled a few feathers by leaving early. Have you tried calling her house?"

"Thanks, I'll try again."

The afternoon session of camp had been cancelled. David waited until all the children had been picked up, then he was out the door, soaked by the time he got it shut. The rain stung—the wind turned drops into pins.

A few other cars were out on the main roads, but the residential streets were nearly empty. Gusts of wind caught at the side of the car as if it was a kite, not a ton of steel. He drove over a network of branches, car tilting. It had to be the entire crown of a toppled tree.

When he got to Gwyn's, Iris's side door opened. It whipped out of her hands, nearly pulling her with it, and banged against the house. David saw her flinch, then cradle her arm. He hurried over.

"You all right?" He had to shout to be heard.

She flexed her arm and nodded distractedly. "I don't know where Molly and Chris are. Your mother said they stopped by to get another load of fliers, but that was a couple of hours ago. Gwyn's gone to look for them."

"Look where?"

Iris shrugged helplessly. "Around the neighborhood. We kept my phone free in case they called and Gwyn used hers to phone everyone they know. I think she called half the phone book. They're not anywhere."

"Stay here in case they manage to call. I'll find them." Getting the door to shut against the wind was like pushing a car mired in mud. He leaned against it, holding it until she fastened the lock.

GWYN LEANED into the wind. She'd put on a hooded raincoat but not boots, thinking they'd only slow her down. An umbrella would have blown inside out as soon as it was opened. She hadn't seen any children yet. Everyone else had made sure their kids were safe.

Sodden corners of fliers protruded from mail boxes here and there. Gwyn pulled one out. It came apart in her hands but not before she recognized enough words to know they were advertising the march.

The fliers led her eight blocks north and four blocks east, fighting a panicked feeling that Molly and Chris could be anywhere. Not anywhere. They would have stayed in their own neighborhood. She just didn't know where they thought the boundaries were. She looked down every street and back lane she passed, calling and listening.

A car slowed and the window rolled down. "Need help?"

Wiping rain from her face she peered at the man inside.

"I'm looking for two children. A boy and a girl, five and twelve." She held one hand at hip level and the other near her shoulder. "About so high."

"Sorry." The car moved on.

Gwyn turned south. Water was ankle deep, deeper where the roads sloped. She reached a corner store, got the door open and was nearly blown inside.

"I'm looking for two children, a boy and a girl—"

"There's no kids here."

"They're five and twelve, brown hair…"

"Haven't seen 'em. Sorry."

"If they come in tell them to stay put, okay? And to call home."

The community center was on the next block. The front door was locked. She made her way around the building, pulling and pushing each door, banging and shouting in case they were locked inside. She shrank against the wall at a cracking sound, loud as a gunshot and watched a tree crash across the road.

She tensed at a new, quieter sound. Hail. Small pieces at first, small as unpopped corn. They stung, though. She ran, hands shielding her face. The hail got bigger, much bigger, and the stinging turned to bruising blows.

She hurried down a back lane, her feel sliding in water and muck. Garbage cans! Relieved, she picked up a lid to hold over her head. Big as golf balls now, hail pounded against it. Lightning flickered again and she dropped the lid. It was metal. Would Chris know not to hold one? Please let him be safe inside.

A hailstone hit her face. Plastic, weren't there any plastic lids? She tore off her coat and balled it into a thick, soft pad to protect her head. She leaned against a fence, making herself as small as she could.

And then she saw the figure in a window. Across the lane, a woman, waving to her. Beckoning.

She slipped across the muddy lane to a back gate. Locked. Stretching, she reached over the top, a hot pain on her arm where a wood plank scratched, and found the hook. Lifted it and the gate blew inward. One eager step into the backyard and she lost her footing. She landed hard.

The back door opened and banged against the house with each gust. Gwyn went the rest of the way more carefully, slipping, but not falling, and finally reached the open door. Into the landing. She stood gasping her thanks.

"Oh dear, oh dear," her rescuer said. She was white-haired and bent—osteoporosis, Gwyn found herself thinking. "You're injured."

"I'm trying to find my son and his babysitter. They were out earlier delivering fliers."

The woman shook her head. "Come in. You're bleeding, dear. We'll fix you up." Her face softened. "They won't be outside in this. Someone's taken them in."

"Are the phones still working?"

The woman picked up the receiver and listened for a dial tone, then handed it to Gwyn.

"Thanks so much." She called Iris, who was past distraught, and learned that David was out looking for her and the children. Then she tried Miranda.

"Nothing, dear, not a word. I'm sorry. They'll have taken shelter. Imagine if you saw children out in this. You'd take them in."

No one had taken them in. If they were safe in someone's kitchen they would have called home.

SOME PEOPLE sheltering in a store had seen Gwyn, half an hour ago, they thought. Not a boy and a girl, though.

David kept going. Each driveway was a creek overflowing into the river of the main road, the wind whipping water into a fine spray above the asphalt. It was getting so he couldn't see. It wasn't just a storm of the century, it wasn't even a two-hundred-year storm.

He saw her then, struggling through water rushing over the sidewalk. He stopped the car. "Gwyn!"

She looked up and relief replaced most of the fear on her face. He left the car in the middle of the road and hurried to her side.

"Did you find them, David?" The fear flooded back when he shook his head.

"You're hurt."

She pushed his hand away. "David, we have to hurry. The kids."

He guided her around the car and helped her into the passenger seat. "We'll stop by my parents' place. I'll get Sam and we'll go house to house. We'll check garages, garden sheds, everything. They're smart, Gwyn, resourceful. They're not going to walk around in this."

She tried to smile. "Like we are."

"That's right. They've got more brains."

Branches covered the grass in front of his parents' house. A maple was split where the two main branches had forked, split right down the middle, half still standing, half on the ground.

Sarah opened the door. "Have you found them? Oh, Gwyn, your face!" She rushed away, her dog following.

Sam came up the cellar stairs. "The backup valve's

doing its job. The floor's dry enough—" He stopped when he saw David and Gwyn. "No sign of them?"

"Not yet."

"I'll go out with you. We've been trying to persuade Mom and Dad to go downstairs."

"We can't just hide," Miranda said coming from the kitchen. "Your father's taping windows, I'm listening for the telephone."

Sarah ran lightly down the stairs, holding a small brown bottle and some gauze. "There must be water on the top floor, Sam. It's dripping through to the bathroom." She stopped in front of Gwyn, undoing the lid of the bottle. "They'll sting."

"All right," David said. "They came for fliers around nine o'clock, then returned at—"

"Around eleven," Miranda said. "They went into the workshop and then I didn't see them again."

Gwyn said, "But it was already getting stormy at eleven and I told them I didn't want them out if there was lightning."

David exclaimed under his breath, got hold of the banister and went up the stairs three at a time.

GWYN WATCHED David race up the stairs. He was gone five minutes, not even that, and then he was back, a child by each hand. They looked frightened, but completely unhurt. Gwyn pulled them close and held them tight.

"Where were you? How could you?"

"It's a secret, Mom. A secret room. We can't tell any-body." Chris lightly touched the bruise on her face. "Ow. Does it hurt?"

"Not a bit." Her whole body ached; she didn't notice one particular spot. "Sarah, could you show Molly where the phone is? Her mother shouldn't be left in agony another minute."

Molly looked alarmed and hurried after Sarah.

Gwyn sank to her knees to look her son in the eyes. "What did I tell you?"

"When?"

She stared at him and he stared back, honestly puzzled as far as she could tell. Then his face cleared.

"It wasn't lightning. Just cloudy. So we went up to our secret room. And then the storm started and we thought we'd better stay there."

"Stay there? Not let the Brettons know where you were?"

"It's a *secret* room."

"Not call me, not call Iris?"

The enormity of the mistake seemed to be getting through to him. "I'm sorry."

Gwyn waved her finger at him. She didn't know what she was going to do, but she was going to do something. Ground him. Give him chores for the rest of his life.

She stood. "Thank you, David. For finding them. For going out in this to look for them." She smoothed wet hair from his eyes, then water from his face. He'd started to relax, but then his face changed. Gwyn turned, alarmed, trying to see what was wrong.

"In the basement, now. Sarah, get Molly off the phone." He shouted up the stairs. "Dad, leave the taping! We've got about a minute."

IT WAS A plow wind, he told them, not a tornado, just as powerful but blowing straight ahead. They waited, mostly in silence, until the cracking sounds and the roaring of the wind stopped. Finally, they headed upstairs to face the damage.

One by one they went through the basement door into the hall. Water stood on the floor. They could hear dripping rain and rustling leaves as clearly as if windows were open. A hand to her mouth, Miranda leaned against the wall.

"I don't want to look."

Richard put an arm around her shoulders. "Come on. I'll hold you up and you'll hold me up. How's that?"

"You have the better end of the deal." She wasn't crying, but from her voice she was close.

"That's the way it's always been. Shall we?"

"Kitchen first?"

A tree had come through the window. Glass glittered on the stove and counter, and across the floor. An elm that must have been two feet around had crashed through the roof of the back porch. Splintered two-by-fours jutted from the wall and ceiling. Another tree, half uprooted, leaned against the garage, upper branches piercing the part of the roof over the workshop.

"Tea," Sarah said. "I'll make tea."

"I doubt that, dear girl. I doubt we'll be making tea." Miranda took a deep breath, then gave Richard's arm a pat. "Living room."

"Yes. Living room."

They led the way and found another broken window, another rain-covered floor. The windows in their turret bedroom had escaped damage, but water trickled through the ceiling. Sarah hurried away and returned with a pail to catch the drips.

Miranda sat on the edge of the bed. "Would someone

check upstairs? Not you, Richard. I need some of that holding up."

"Of course." He sat beside her. "Very nice of you to give me a reclining job, don't think I didn't notice."

As SOON AS the rain let up, they went out to tour the yard. All along the street the neighbors were out, checking their own damage and each other's. The younger they were, the more they acted as if this was the best thing ever, climbing on the downed trees, exclaiming to each other. Surrounded by fallen elms, maples and oaks, Miranda began to cry. David waited for his father to go to her, but Richard seemed lost in his own misery.

"Mom." He couldn't think of anything else to say but the word was enough to pull her together. Mothers didn't cry in front of their children no matter how grown up they were.

"We've wondered about thinning the trees. More light will get through to the house now." She gave a shaky smile, sniffed and took a shuddering breath. Her hand left her mouth long enough to indicate the many deep holes where roots had been. "And you know…fish ponds."

She picked her way between puddles and trees. "Dreadful. Dreadful. How many bad things is this? Do we count both storms separately or as one? Something wrong with Sam, bad weather and another bad thing to come." She smiled again, her eyes glistening. "Let's do it the other way. Something's wrong with Sam, two storms and we're done."

David nodded. "That's the way to see it."

"It's fixable, isn't it, Richard?"

"Of course it is. Everything's fixable." Then he pointed to the top of the house. "There's our water problem." The entire cupola was gone.

GWYN KEPT HOLD of Chris's hand. He and Molly were both subdued. She supposed they should leave, get back to Iris, but she hated to turn her back on the Brettons.

"Oh, the canoe." Sarah hurried away, running lightly, jumping over branches. Sam's canoe was partly in the river, swaying, the current tugging at it.

"Sarah, don't," Sam said. He started after her.

David came out of the garage. Urgency in his voice, he called, "Leave it, Sarah."

She slowed down near the water, walking on the saturated ground with obvious distaste, then leaned over to reach the hull. Her feet slid in mud. She found a new place to stand and leaned again. Her fingers touched the canoe but she couldn't quite get hold of it. Gwyn saw her stretch her arm, her hand, her fingers. Then, without a struggle or a sound she went over, into the river.

"Sarah!"

They all called her name. She disappeared, then broke the surface gasping and slapping the water before going down again.

Everyone took off at once. Sam headed straight for the riverbank and dived in. He surfaced yards away, swimming strongly, carried by the current. David ran along the bank, trying to get ahead of them by land, Gwyn thought. Richard called to the neighbors and hurried to the front of the house.

Miranda and Gwyn stood watching the two heads, yards apart, appearing and disappearing. David emerged from the woods beside a loop farther downstream. He jumped in, feet first, stayed afloat and started swimming. Away from his brother and sister.

Gwyn held Miranda's arm. "What's he doing?"

"He knows the current."

He went diagonally toward the far bank. Parts of it had collapsed, sending mud and trees into the water. He got hold of a branch and stretched as far as he could into the narrower width of the loop. They heard him call to Sarah, then Sam. Both of them tried to change direction, but they couldn't, not enough. He caught Sarah's hair as she went by and held on, but the current pulling her began to pull him, too.

Sam lunged at him, grabbed his shirt, used him to push away from the current and reach the same branch. Inch by inch, using the downed trees, the brothers worked their way closer to the bank, dragging their sister with them.

"Oh." Miranda made a long, sighing sound. "Please, God, is that a motor I hear?"

"It's Richard, he's got a boat!"

THE WHOLE FAMILY WAS at the hospital. Sarah, David and Sam had scrapes and cuts from debris washed into the river by the storm. They needed showers with antibacterial soap and a course of antibiotics. Things were worse for Richard. Through his run to the neighbors', the launching of the boat, helping his children out of the river, he'd suffered steadily worsening chest pain.

Gwyn met David in a treatment room after a doctor had stitched a laceration on his leg. He was in scrubs they'd given him to replace his soaking clothes, but he hadn't showered yet.

He backed away from her. "Don't touch me. The river's filthy. You'll catch something."

"I don't care."

"I do."

"David." She pulled him to her. His body touched hers, tense, resisting. She was sure she could comfort him.

Closeness, softness, quietness. Those were all calming things. And they had more. They had the memory of urgent, unquiet closeness. "Shh. Your dad will be all right."

"That'll be on your tombstone."

"What?"

He raised his voice. "*Everything will be all right.* It'll be on your tombstone."

She'd heard him the first time.

"Everything's not all right, Gwyn."

"I know that."

He repeated, "Everything's not all right," and strode out of the room.

CHAPTER TWENTY

AT THE END of her shift Gwyn went up to the private ward to see how Richard was doing. His eyes were closed, his body still. Without the piercing gaze and energetic movement, without that aggravating will of his, he hardly seemed present at all. She didn't usually know patients before their illnesses or injuries struck.

His eyes opened. They weren't piercing now, they were worn right out. "Gwyn." A faint smile. "Love a woman in uniform." The longer his eyes were open the more lively they became. "How are they?"

"Your family? They're fine. Upset."

"They don't take kindly to this sort of thing. Death and destruction."

"Lucky for them they only have to contend with destruction this time. That's thanks to you."

"The boys would have got Sarah. Silly girl." He gave her a glimmer of his old grin. "Don't suppose you have any inside information for me?"

"I'm afraid my power is limited to the fourth floor."

The grin grew. "Miranda and I would like you to come by tomorrow, around six o'clock. Chris, too."

"That sounds mysterious."

Richard nodded and winked, then closed his eyes and seemed to sleep.

Gwyn left the hospital and rode the bus as far as the Brettons' block. She'd been by the house a few times since the storm, but still got a sick feeling in the pit of her stomach. It looked as if a giant chain saw had gone out of control, flying through tree trunks and walls and windows without any plan at all.

There was no one in the yard, and the front door stood open, so she went inside. Sam was in the kitchen putting broken dishes in one box and unbroken in another.

"David's upstairs."

She checked the bedrooms on the second floor, then went up to the third. It was the oddest thing, like a tree house, sunlight coming in and birds singing. There were smaller holes here and there and a huge one where the cupola had been. Right over Chris and Molly's heads if they'd stayed in that secret room half an hour longer.

DAVID PICKED UP the books one at a time, shaking each one and watching water drip from the pages. It wasn't as if they were valuable. There had to be thousands, tens of thousands, just like them on bookshelves around the world. They could be replaced. It wasn't worth the trouble to do it, but they could be.

"You look exhausted."

Gwyn stood in the doorway. He'd been so deep in thought he hadn't heard her arrive.

"Let me help you with those, David. We can take them to my place and spread them out to dry."

"Dry?"

"We can stand them on end, open, like fans, you know."

He tried to smile, but his face felt stiff. "They're papier-mâché, Gwyn. Anyway, it doesn't matter. They're only books." He wished she'd go away. If they kept talking he was going to cry. Imagine that. The last time he'd cried he was ten and their grandfather had died.

She came closer. He turned away, but he could still feel her softness nearby.

"Your dad seems better."

He nodded. "A warning, they said."

"Why are you shutting me out, David?"

"I'm not."

"Of course you are."

He only meant to point but his arm flew out from his side to indicate the mess all around them. "I'm on the top floor of my house—where we played when we were kids—and I'm looking at the sky through the roof." He hoped he wasn't yelling. He didn't seem to have control over the volume. "I'm not shutting you out. I'm thinking."

"Thinking?" She said it as if she didn't believe him. She was starting to make him mad. "What are you thinking?"

He took a deep breath. Lucky there was lots of air. Lots of air pouring through the roof. "I'm thinking how clueless, how completely clueless, humans can be." He was building up a head of steam. He could tell because he was breathing fast.

"Picture this. Early humans stand on the highest peak and look over the Earth. And it's a Garden of Eden, the whole bloody globe. One says, 'Let's see what happens if we cut down most of these forests, cover the fields with a hard, oily substance, send clouds of chemicals and vapors into the air and pour poisons into the rivers and lakes.' A few of them say, 'No, no, if we do that we won't be able to live here anymore,' but the first guy says, 'We don't know that. Let's try it and see.' It's like a crazed surgeon replacing ninety percent of a man's lungs with asphalt, then encouraging him to smoke to see what happens."

He had to take another deep breath. She looked scared. Tears in her eyes. Good. She was too damn calm, had been ever since the storm.

"You were waiting for this to happen," she said. "You knew it would. I thought it was…theoretical. Just dooms-day games."

"It might as well have been." A knot had lodged in his throat. He tried to clear it, then he tried to swallow it but it wouldn't go away.

"David." She walked toward him, comfort oozing from her. She was born to comfort. He shook his head and she stopped.

"I didn't see it coming. Not this! The house, the yard. Sarah, Dad—" His energy drained away. "So, yeah, it was theoretical. Theoretical nonsense. Sorry about that. Sorry if I disappointed you."

"You haven't disappointed me. You've annoyed me and scared me, but you've never disappointed me."

She still had little bruises and cuts from the hail. Part of him wanted to hold her, very, very tenderly, in case she had other bruises, too, and tell her it'd be all right, he'd take care of her, take care of Chris. Thing was, it would be a lie.

She had her mother-bear glare, too. He could step behind it if he wanted, behind the protection of it, like Chris. What a thing for a grown man to think.

He tried to be polite. "I don't want…to get into a long conversation about this, Gwyn. Do you mind leaving?"

There it was. Disappointment. And pain. A new phase of the relationship. He turned his back and tried to focus on the books instead of her retreating footsteps. They faded, but minutes later grew louder.

It was only Sam.

He walked into the room and picked up a book, *Biggles of the Camel Squadron*. The pages fell away from the spine, crumpling and spraying water when they hit the floor. He threw the pieces into a big green garbage bag that was filling fast.

"Alabaster and roses. Seemingly delicate, but as tough as a wrestler. Any of that sound familiar?"

"Shut up, Sam."

"I had the impression you cared about her. From the way she left the house I'd say you were a jerk."

"It's none of your business."

"No? I like Gwyn, so I think it is."

"Was she all right?"

"On top of the world."

"I thought you were her, coming back."

Sam tossed another book in the bag. "Would that have been a good thing?"

"I don't know."

IT WAS PAST SIX o'clock the next evening but Gwyn hesitated to go into Richard's room. She could hear all the Brettons talking. He couldn't have known her days as a family friend were numbered when he'd invited her. She hadn't brought Chris. His summer had been confusing enough.

"Gwyn! Come in, dear. We're having a little dinner."

Sam and Sarah said hello, but David was silent. He and Gwyn tried not to look at each other, difficult in a small group standing together.

A white tablecloth covered the over-bed table. Bone-china bread-and-butter plates and silver cutlery were arranged on top. The bedside table held a teapot and cups. Miranda pulled containers from a Johansson's bag.

"Do you want to tell them while I'm serving, Richard, or after we eat?"

Sarah said, "If someone doesn't tell me what's going on in the next thirty seconds *I'll* have a heart attack."

"He didn't have a heart attack," Sam said. "Just an ischemic episode."

"While you're serving," Richard said. His color wasn't good and sitting up seemed to be an effort, but he looked around at his family and Gwyn, and smiled. "We've decided we're going to rebuild."

"Dad—"

"You can't—"

"It's too much work, you don't need the space—"

"Does everyone like these little buttered carrots?" Miranda asked. "We have a lovely bean mix, as well, yellow and green, growing on the vine just yesterday, I'm told."

No one answered her. David said, "The place has been condemned."

"We'll tear it down and start over. The Castle was an ideal home in its time. We'll build the ideal home for this time. Energy efficient, solar powered, we'll reuse all the wood we can—including the banister, Gwyn. What's the matter, Sarah? Happy or sad tears?"

"Oh, sorry, Dad, both. I'm so glad, but then I thought about the tower. I'll miss the tower. Sorry. I'm a brat."

"Who says a solar-powered house can't have a tower?" He took Miranda's hand. "We loved all those trees, didn't we? People say you can't replace a two-hundred-year-old elm. Well, you can. It just takes awhile."

WAY AT THE END of the street the copper dome of the leg-islature rose, the *Golden Boy* gleaming at the top. When they'd first started talking about the march Gwyn had pictured the Brettons and a few friends strolling up the sidewalk then going for ice cream. But so many people had gathered, so many voices rumbled through the parking lot where they'd been asked to assemble that Gwyn was sure the premier must be able to hear them, wherever in that huge building his office was.

AFTER THE STORM David had given interviews about the march on television and in the newspapers. Strangers had started dropping by the ruins of The Castle to help with preparations. Nearly everyone from Gwyn's block on Dafoe had pitched in. Sarah and Sam had arranged a huge picnic to follow in Memorial Park, and Richard, discharged from the hospital with a long list of instructions he mostly ignored, had worked with Chris to make placards of the Earth and a red, angry sun. Through it all David kept his distance.

David wasn't with them today—he'd ignored his unit—but Dr. Gerrard had come, with giant cutouts of the man in swimming trunks and the person in a parka. Molly and her friend Jamie had made traffic sign placards with the slogan We're Going The Wrong Way and Sarah had turned up with a crowd of people from Three Creeks carrying cutouts of animal species under threat. Two of the women with her, both with waving reddish hair, were expecting. It couldn't be very comfortable for them to walk in this heat. One held a sign that said 2024 My Child Comes Of Age: Will She Fight For Water?

Chris stood with his hands over his ears.

Gwyn bent close to talk to him. "Too noisy?"

"Are all these people with us?"

"All of them. Is that good?"

He didn't look sure about that. Maybe it made his fears more real to see hundreds and hundreds of people who weren't telling him it would be all right.

As far as she knew no music had been planned but when they started walking up Memorial Boulevard a few people began to sing. Others joined in and soon the songs were all she could hear. Gospel and folk, camp songs, summer day songs. Not everyone in the crowd could carry a tune, but it didn't seem to matter. It was like a party, a celebration. Not bleak at all, but she soon had a lump in her throat. They went past statues and war memorials and all of a sudden she felt that they were marching for everyone who'd gone before, the builders and fighters remembered along this road. Her generation and the next weren't going to watch it fail, were they? They weren't going to let it go.

There were speeches and the premier came out to the steps to promise more effective action now and in the future. With every passing minute Gwyn felt more the way she did beside a deathbed. Everything ended. Holidays, empires, love affairs. Maybe Earth as a home for humanity would end, too. Maybe the children here, the child beside her, the unborn, maybe they would fight for water and look out Winnipeg windows onto treeless landscapes. Maybe the Earth was already killed and in a generation or two its heart would stop.

The thought haunted her through the afternoon. She met the people from Three Creeks—Sarah's author and all her family. She ran a three-legged race with Chris, laughing as she fell to the ground. She shared cotton candy with

Molly and noticed David talking with everyone but her. His ex-wife, Ms. Gibson, Dr. Gerrard, strangers.

"Well, Chris?"

He looked at her, trying to wipe watermelon juice from his chin but only managing to smear it to his cheeks.

"Shall we go home?"

He nodded. "It's been a good day, eh, Mom?"

"Very good. Well done, sweetie."

BY BEDTIME, Chris was tired right out, but still beaming. "Do you think Dad saw us?"

"I'm absolutely sure he did."

The blue eyes looked uncertain. "You always say you don't know."

"How could he not see something like that?"

"Richard knows a lot about dimensions."

Gwyn was silent. They'd been perfectly happy with their *Star Trek* version. How much truth could one little boy take?

"It's pretty complicated," he went on.

"I'll bet it is."

"Some people think there really could be other dimensions. Not just in science fiction, but really. We've got all our senses, our eyes and ears and nose and stuff, and we've got our brains—" He broke off and added with a chuckle, "Richard says we don't use enough of them to remember where we buried our acorns."

Gwyn smiled.

"Anyway, Richard says even with all that we can't know everything in the universe. There's stuff that's bigger than our brains can figure out except little piece by little piece. So he says who knows what else there is and who says Dad's not in another dimension, maybe with a TV set thing that he can turn on and off so he doesn't have to see everything I do."

Chris's voice was slowing down. Eventually he mumbled, "Night, Mom," and that was it. He was out.

Gwyn tiptoed from the room and went outside to sit on the step. The street was deserted. Had everyone else stayed at the picnic this long?

A familiar figure materialized from the dark edges of the sidewalk past her yard. She didn't wave or call out. She watched him come closer, up the path to the steps.

"You disappeared, Gwyn."

"Did I?" She hadn't tried to disappear. She had just come home. The march was over, and the speeches and the picnic, so she'd come home.

"How's Chris?"

"Happy as can be. Thank you, David. I already thanked your father. He's been so good to Chris."

"He cares about him. We all do."

Gwyn nodded. The Brettons were a generous family, generous with their time and affection.

He said, "I think you know I care about you, too."

The words gave her a pang. He cared about the environment and he cared about Chris and he cared about her. He cared about Iris, too. And canoeing. "Summer's nearly over. We'll all get back to normal soon. A more difficult normal in some ways, but thanks to everything that's happened a better one in others. You wanted more people to care about what's happening to the climate, David. More do."

"I don't want to go back. I want to go ahead. Are you willing, after the way I've behaved? I'm so sorry, Gwyn. I love you. I know I haven't been acting like it."

Surprise and relief made it hard to answer. "As it happens, I love you, too."

"That's one problem taken care of, then."

She gave a small laugh. "We can strike it off the list."

"Next problem—I'm not sure how we go ahead."

"There's the one foot in front of the other way and the flying leap way."

He smiled. "I'm for strolling. So we can savor it. Trouble is, we wouldn't so much be walking into the sunset as into quicksand. I'm not sure that's a fair thing to ask you to do."

"It's a little early for a sunset."

"You sound so calm, Gwyn. How did that happen?"

"I'm done fighting it off. That took a lot of energy." She knew seeing his house destroyed, his family hurt, had taken a lot of his.

"Today felt good," he said. "Seeing so many people interested, ready to take action as a community…but not enough people want change. Not fast enough to affect what's happening." He shrugged. "So where does that leave us? Can you see us living happily ever after with tornadoes whizzing around our heads and cities flooding?"

"Won't the tornadoes whiz whether or not we love each other? No matter how complicated the science of all this is, one thing is simple—whatever's ahead of us, I know I'll be happier if I face it with you."

"So we do what we can, and we do it together?"

"How does that sound?"

"It sounds really good."

She had been sitting throughout the conversation, while he stood close by. Now he crouched in front of her, her knees between them. "Gwyn, I've been wondering—" He paused before continuing, "If you'd like to get married. I want to make all those beautiful old promises to you. I want everyone we know to hear it."

She smiled, blinking away tears. "Next time Sam's home."

He kissed her knee and rested his head there for a moment. "I thought you might say no. Think Chris can get used to having me around every day?"

"He'll love it. *I'll* love it. I'll love being a family of three."

"Of seven. At least."

David sat on the step next to her, an arm around her, the next best thing to forever. She leaned into him and let her eyes close. She'd missed him so much the past few weeks. He felt like that rock at the lake, solid and warm and secure. No matter what happened, ice, sun, wind or rain or continents shuffling their way around the globe, that rock wasn't going anywhere.

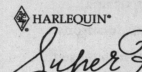

HARLEQUIN®

Super Romance

THE PRODIGAL'S RETURN

by *Anna DeStefano*

Prom night for Jenn Gardner and Neal Cain turned
into a tragedy that tore them apart. Eight years
later, Jenn has made a life for herself and her young
daughter. But when Neal comes home, Jenn sees that
he is still consumed with the past. Maybe she can
convince him that he's paid enough and deserves
happiness a second time around.

"Anna DeStefano's remarkable stories of the healing
power of love touch the heart with hope. One of the
genre's rising stars..."
—Gayle Wilson, two-time
RITA® Award-winning author

On sale July 2006!
*Available wherever books are sold, including most
bookstores, supermarkets, discount stores and drugstores.*

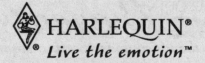

HARLEQUIN®
Live the emotion™

If you enjoyed what you just read,
then we've got an offer you can't resist!

Take 2 bestselling
love stories FREE!
Plus get a FREE surprise gift!

Clip this page and mail it to Harlequin Reader Service®

IN U.S.A.
3010 Walden Ave.
P.O. Box 1867
Buffalo, N.Y. 14240-1867

IN CANADA
P.O. Box 609
Fort Erie, Ontario
L2A 5X3

YES! Please send me 2 free Harlequin Superromance® novels and my free surprise gift. After receiving them, if I don't wish to receive anymore, I can return the shipping statement marked cancel. If I don't cancel, I will receive 6 brand-new novels every month, before they're available in stores. In the U.S.A., bill me at the bargain price of $4.69 plus 25¢ shipping and handling per book and applicable sales tax, if any*. In Canada, bill me at the bargain price of $5.24 plus 25¢ shipping and handling per book and applicable taxes**. That's the complete price, and a savings of at least 10% off the cover prices—what a great deal! I understand that accepting the 2 free books and gift places me under no obligation ever to buy any books. I can always return a shipment and cancel at any time. Even if I never buy another book from Harlequin, the 2 free books and gift are mine to keep forever.

135 HDN DZ7W
336 HDN DZ7X

Name	(PLEASE PRINT)	
Address	Apt.#	
City	State/Prov.	Zip/Postal Code

Not valid to current Harlequin Superromance® subscribers.

Want to try two free books from another series?
Call 1-800-873-8635 or visit www.morefreebooks.com.

* Terms and prices subject to change without notice. Sales tax applicable in N.Y.
** Canadian residents will be charged applicable provincial taxes and GST.
   All orders subject to approval. Offer limited to one per household.
   ® are registered trademarks owned and used by the trademark owner and or its licensee.

SUP04R   ©2004 Harlequin Enterprises Limited

Life.
It could happen to her!

Never Happened just about sums up
Alexis Jackson's life. Independent and
successful, Alexis has concentrated on
building her own business, leaving no
time for love. Now at forty, Alexis
discovers that she still has a few things
to learn about life—that the life unlived
is the one that "Never happened"
and it's her time to make a change....

Never Happened
by Debra Webb

HN49

Available July 2006
TheNextNovel.com

HARLEQUIN
Super Romance

COMING NEXT MONTH

#1356 A BABY BETWEEN THEM • C.J. Carmichael
Return to Summer Island
Aidan Wythe is too busy running Kincaid Communications and *not* thinking about Rae Cordell to take time off. Which is why his boss banishes him to Summer Island for a forced vacation. When a very pregnant Rae also shows up on the island, he knows he's not going to get any rest or relaxation.

#1357 A FAMILY RESEMBLANCE • Margot Early
Four years have passed since Victor Knoll's death, and his wife, Sabine, can't imagine another man who could compare with him as a husband or a father. Then Joe Knoll appears in her tiny mountain town, claiming to be Victor's brother—a brother she's never heard of. He says Victor wasn't the person she thought he was. And to complicate things even more, he says he's falling in love with her....

#1358 THE PRODIGAL'S RETURN • Anna DeStefano
Prom night for Jenn Gardner and Neal Cain turned into a tragedy that tore them apart. Eight years later, Jenn has made a life for herself and her young daughter. But when Neal comes home, Jenn sees that Neal is still consumed with the past. Maybe she can convince him that he's paid enough and deserves happiness a second time around.

#1359 TELL ME NO LIES • Kathryn Shay
Dan Logan is Citizen of the Year. He has an ideal marriage and two wonderful children. What he doesn't have is the truth about his wife. But can his ideals survive the truth when Tessa's past finally, inevitably, comes out?

#1360 A TIME TO FORGIVE • Darlene Gardner
Named for her deceased uncle, abandoned by her mother, nine-year-old Jaye Smith is in need of a little TLC. Good thing she has her uncle Connor on her side. But when sparks fly for Connor and Jaye's teacher Abby Reed, it sets them on a path toward uncovering a stinging truth, which they can only overcome together....

#1361 HUSBAND AND WIFE REUNION • Linda Style
Cold Cases: L.A.
If she finishes the magazine articles she's writing, she's a dead woman. But when her ex-husband, L.A.P.D. Detective Luke Coltrane, finds out about the anonymous threats, Julianna gets more protection than she wants....

HSRCNM0606